"I'm not used to making women angry. So an apology is in order."

Kate blinked in surprise. This was the last thing she had expected. In fact, she had assumed that *he* would be angry with *her*, not the other way around.

"You're sorry, then?" she asked tentatively.

"Somewhat."

Her eyes narrowed. "What do you mean, 'somewhat'?"

"Well," he answered, spinning her around, "I suppose I shouldn't have teased you so much, but I'm not sorry. And," he said, his amber eyes wandering over her face, "I shouldn't have kissed you, but I'm definitely not sorry."

"Oh?" She felt as if she was melting beneath his gaze.

"But I am sorry that I told you to leave. That, sweetheart, was a real pity."

* * *

The Rake's Proposal
Harlequin® Historical #820—October 2006

PRAISE FOR
SARAH ELLIOTT
and her debut novel
REFORMING THE RAKE

SARAH ELLIOTT

The Rake's Proposal

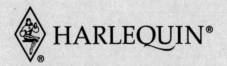

HARLEQUIN®

TORONTO • NEW YORK • LONDON
AMSTERDAM • PARIS • SYDNEY • HAMBURG
STOCKHOLM • ATHENS • TOKYO • MILAN • MADRID
PRAGUE • WARSAW • BUDAPEST • AUCKLAND

ISBN-13: 978-0-373-29420-6
ISBN-10:   0-373-29420-4

THE RAKE'S PROPOSAL

Copyright © 2006 by Sarah Lindsey

Available from Harlequin® Historical and
SARAH ELLIOTT

Reforming the Rake #774
The Rake's Proposal #820

DON'T MISS THESE OTHER
NOVELS AVAILABLE NOW:

Please address questions and book requests to:
Harlequin Reader Service
U.S.: 3010 Walden Ave., P.O. Box 1325, Buffalo, NY 14269
Canadian: P.O. Box 609, Fort Erie, Ont. L2A 5X3

I am very grateful to Jessica Alvarez and Laura Langlie
for reading my books so thoroughly and for being
so patient and encouraging. A huge thanks also to
Alex Duda and Brad Davis, who generously
gave their time to design my website.

Chapter One

March 1817

The world seemed to look favorably upon Katherine Sutcliff. Her face and figure were admired, at least by the residents of Little Brookings, her tiny Dorset village. Her mind and humor were considered quick and sharp. She had ample funds and a loving family who forgave her occasional lapses of memory, decorum and common sense.

Of course, her life was not as tranquil and carefree as it appeared: she had at least one—secret and very serious—problem.

Her most immediate dilemma, however, was her inability to fall asleep.

She lay in bed, sighed and stared at the ceiling. She'd been trying for at least two hours, and neither warm milk nor a large dose of Milton's *Samson Agonistes* had helped at all. Even conjugating irregular French verbs had failed.

Kate supposed she could blame her insomnia on simple nerves and an unfamiliar bed. It was only about twelve hours since she'd arrived—dusty from several days of travel—at her brother Robert's smart London doorstep. He would be getting married in the autumn, and she planned to stay with him in town until that time. That meant she'd be there for the entire season, and although she'd resigned herself to this fate, she wasn't too pleased about it. Oh, she got on with her brother tremendously well—it was the reason behind her visit that was causing her distress.

She needed to get married herself. She didn't want to, but there it was.

Kate sat up in bed, Milton sliding dejectedly to the floor as she did so. Marriage. It was a horrible but unignorable fact, and the only way to get that horrible thought from her mind, even temporarily, was…

A glass of brandy, preferably a large one. That would at least make her sleepy; it had better, since simple determination wasn't doing the trick.

She climbed out of bed, pulling on her robe as she did so, and slipped out her bedroom door. She padded lightly down the spacious hallway toward the study, feeling rather furtive beneath the disapproving glares of looming ancestral portraits. The house was completely silent, and even though she was doing nothing wrong, she crept along guiltily like a thief. Everything in her brother's house was large and dark, and she felt dwarfed inside it. She pulled open the heavy study door, lit a lamp, and in the dim light poured a generous glass of brandy. Robert's study smelled vaguely of smoke. She pulled out the heavy leather chair at his desk. Sitting down in this ultra-masculine seat and regarding the room in front of her somehow made her feel more in control.

So, too, did the brandy.

Marriage. Most girls did it. Some even had *to do it, and so what if she was joining their ranks? Surely worse things happened at sea.*

Surely?

Several long minutes of mentally debating this question had passed when she became aware of a knocking at the front door. She listened intently for a moment and it came again, louder this time and more insistent. Standing, heart racing, she crossed the room to peek from the window. It was well after midnight and the sky was pitch-black, so dark that the stars shone against it in sharp relief. Kate could see a carriage in the drive, a very elegant gilt-trimmed one at that, and she could just make out the shadowy figure of a man at the door. It was too dark to see his face or any details of his form.

Another knock.

"Robert, you're a bastard if you don't let me in…I know you're in there—your light's on…I need to borrow a bed for the evening." *Knock, knock.*

Kate made up her mind then and there. Her nervousness was ridiculous. She should really go rouse Robert's butler, as it wasn't entirely proper for her to open the door so late at night, particularly whilst wearing her dressing gown. But the butler would have gone to bed hours ago, and her dressing gown was so demure it was nunnish; her everyday dresses were more revealing, and that didn't say much considering she was determinedly

unfashionable. Besides, the man on the other side of the
door was clearly just some friend of her brother's, in
search of nothing more than a place to rest his probably
inebriated head for the rest of the night. Who but a
friend would speak about him so disparagingly?

Still slightly uneasy, but convinced that she was
being ridiculous, Kate walked into the hall. She squared
her shoulders, pulled her thick dressing gown tightly
around her body and opened the door.

Lord Benjamin Sinclair, eldest son of Viscount
Sinclair, was nine-and-twenty, wealthy and handsome
enough to make most women temporarily mute the first
time they laid eyes on him. It was a rather odd experience, then, to have the tables turned: for a moment, it
was he who forgot how to speak.

Hand upraised to pound on Robert's godforsaken
door one last time, he merely stared at the vision before
him—one of the most stunning girls he'd ever seen.
She was quite tall, reaching just past his shoulders, but
despite her height she appeared almost delicate—slim
frame, fair skin and full, slightly parted lips. Her eyes
were indigo, and so surprised…crowning all this was
glorious hair, cascading around her shoulders. Maybe
it was merely brown in the light of day, but by candlelight her hair was the richest auburn, highlighted with
strands of red and gold.

All this he digested slowly, indicating his interest
through nothing more than a slightly raised eyebrow.

"Hello."

Kate stared back. Shouldn't she be the one speaking? Right now she wasn't sure she knew what to say. The dark shadow she had seen from the window had done no justice to the man standing in front of her— tall, broad-shouldered…light brown hair streaked with gold, sun-burnished skin over chiseled jaw, accented by a snowy cravat and velvet coat…she realized she was gaping and closed her mouth. *Speak, you ninny, speak.*

"Hello." Well, that was pathetic, she thought scornfully. Pull yourself together. "Are you a friend of Robert's?"

Ben grinned, not missing a second of her reaction and frankly pleased that he had this effect on women. Who was this girl answering his friend's door so late at night? Robert was engaged to be married and Ben had yet to meet his bride-to-be…he supposed this girl *could* be she, but it seemed unlikely. The wedding was still a few months off, and the bride-to-be would hardly be spending the night. It was also improbable that Robert would keep a mistress in his own home, if indeed he'd keep one at all given his upcoming nuptials. This girl's innocent blush and cultured voice refuted such a possibility, anyway. Ben always liked a mystery, however, and as she didn't appear ready to speak, he stepped through the door, brushing past her lightly on his way in.

"Are you?" he countered with seeming nonchalance, although his amber eyes were piercing as he turned to face her.

"What?"

"Friend or foe. You must be one or the other."

Kate's head began to clear as she realized that her own question had been turned around on her. "I suppose

I'm a friend—when I'm not an enemy, that is. I'm Robert's sister. And you are…?"

Understanding slowly clicked in Ben's mind. "Friend. Benjamin Sinclair. Sorry to disturb you so late." He let his gaze wander over her body, not really sorry at all. When she blushed, he continued. "You see, I've been at sea for the past several months…arrived only this evening. I didn't want to spend another night aboard ship, and was going to go rouse my housekeeper…but then I saw the light on at ol' Robert's…has he retired for the evening?"

The man's familiar name should have put Kate at ease. Benjamin Sinclair was one of Robert's best friends, and she had actually met him many years ago when her brother had brought him home from school. Now that she knew his name, in fact, she couldn't believe that she hadn't recognized him right away….

Oh, no. She was suddenly and distinctly ill at ease— was, in fact, ready to groan aloud as she recalled the one and only time she'd met Benjamin Sinclair. She'd been eleven and she'd dumped a glass of water on his head for teasing her. He'd disparaged her looks, an easy enough feat when she was a scrawny girl. He was so handsome, and she'd been so ugly then, so clumsy and unfeminine…she'd quite hated him for it. Thank goodness he didn't seem to remember her.

Benjamin Sinclair was a scoundrel; his name was the stuff of legend. Stories of his misconduct had even made it as far as Little Brookings, and instead of relaxing, Kate was immediately on her guard. Perhaps it was the strange color of his eyes, neither a simple brown nor gold, but the way he looked at her made her exceedingly uncomfortable…uncomfortable and something else. A less familiar but equally disturbing sensation. She became suddenly and painfully aware of her inappropriate dress, her loose hair and her slippered feet peeking out from beneath her robe.

"He is asleep. I'm sorry. But please come in. I'll wake Mr. Perch and he can prepare a room for you. Do you have any baggage?"

"Nothing that can't remain in my carriage for the night. My driver can fetch it in the morning." He motioned to his driver from the doorway and then closed the door behind him. "And please don't bother about Perch. I'll settle myself in somewhere. I usually take the green room…" At her blush, he grinned again, "…or is that where you sleep…Katherine?"

She blinked in surprise. "I haven't given you leave to use my Christian name…I haven't even *told* you my name. How do you know it, sir?"

"We've met before. I'm wounded that you don't remember."

"I do remember. I'd rather hoped you didn't." Kate practically squeaked this admission, thinking about how annoyed he'd been by the water…goodness, he'd even threatened retribution!

She had to ask. She just couldn't help herself. "You don't still plan to thrash me, do you?"

He looked utterly bewildered by her cheekiness. "Surely *I* didn't say that."

"You surely did," Kate retorted.

"Then, yes, I suppose I must keep my word," he rejoined, his lopsided smile belying his words.

Kate felt her face go up in flames and could have kicked herself for being so cheeky. Why could she never behave like the proper young lady she was? She was certainly no match for Robert's rakish friend, and he seemed to know it. He didn't bother to wait for her to respond, guessing—correctly—that she was speechless. Instead, he turned and entered the study. She heard the sound of a drawer being opened and the thud of a glass being placed on the table. He was pouring himself a drink.

What bloody nerve.

Kate closed her eyes and counted to ten.

"So, why are you up so late, Miss Sutcliff?" he called from within, forcing her to follow him to the study in order to answer his question. She didn't fully enter the room, however, not wanting to commit to any more of his banter. She merely hovered by the door, mouth open, ready to tell him that she had only come down for a book and was now returning to bed.

But before she could formulate these words, he noted the half-empty glass of brandy perched on the desk. He raised an eyebrow. "Been drinking by yourself, have you?"

She cringed. "I was having trouble sleeping."

"It's a rather unhealthy habit, you know. Care for some company?"

Kate didn't want *his* company, but he refilled her glass to match his, not giving her an opportunity to decline his invitation. He settled into the capacious leather chair—the one *she'd* occupied before his arrival—and nodded at the smaller chair across from it, indicating that she should sit as well.

She still hesitated in the doorway, sensing that the

situation was beginning to get out of hand. "I really should go to bed. I have a lot to do tomorrow, but thank you...."

Even as she turned down his offer, he rose from his chair, walked to the doorway where she stood and lightly grabbed her by the hand, placing her glass of brandy in it. His touch was hot, and his unsettling eyes never left her face—"no," apparently, was not an acceptable answer. He returned to his seat, and Kate had no choice but to sit down as well. She gulped, her nervousness threatening to overwhelm her. He gazed at her with a mixture of amusement and curiosity, and she raised her chin in annoyed defiance. Damn him. She didn't know why he was forcing her to stay. She didn't really know him, didn't know what to say to him...the last thing she wanted to do was have a drink with this strange man in the middle of the night, and she suspected he knew it.

"Strange."

"What?" Kate asked in alarm, afraid he'd somehow read her unkind thoughts.

"You're not at all as I remembered you. I'd say you've definitely improved."

"I'm not exactly sure if that qualifies as a compliment or not, as you give it at the expense of how I used to look."

"Will you toss your brandy at me, perhaps?"

Kate blushed furiously, damning her fair complexion as she did so. She knew he was just toying with her, but something in his eyes—their darkness and the way his gaze moved over her body—made her feel like she was being seriously seduced.

She had to get out of there. It was getting far too dangerous. She'd have her drink as quickly as possible, and then make haste for her bedroom without wishing him a good night.

Resolved, Kate put her glass to her lips and drank: a big, hearty gulp. And therein lay her mistake. Somewhere on the way down the brandy made a wrong turn, and she ended up choking, spilling her drink down the front of her robe. Spluttering, she scraped back her chair and rose abruptly. This brought him even closer, hand-kerchief in hand.

"Steady, now. It's not a race. One would almost think you were trying to get foxed, *Miss* Sutcliff."

Kate could hear the amusement in his voice—he was hardly trying to conceal it—and despised him all over again. She'd never been so embarrassed, and her face was just as red from shame as it was from coughing. How had she allowed herself to get in this position? What respectable young lady in her right mind answered the door in her dressing gown so late at night? Perhaps she wasn't in her right mind at all—she'd long suspected it, anyway. At the very least she was foolish.

As she continued to cough, he moved behind her to pat her on the back. After a minute passed and her coughing subsided, his pats slowed, his hand rubbing her gently and finally going still, its motionless weight practically burning her despite the thickness of her robe. Kate went motionless as well, almost violently aware of his large presence, so close to her body. He touched her with only his hand, never straying from the top of her back, and yet her whole body felt his caress. Her skin seemed to tighten, and she felt hot from the tips of

her toes to every strand of hair. The feeling was so unfamiliar, she swayed under its intensity, unsure whether
she was ill or well.

He wrapped his arm around her waist to quiet her
unsteady form and slowly, deliberately, turned her
around in his arms. Kate looked up, her body separated
from his massive chest by mere inches, and made yet
another great mistake. She looked into his eyes and
became mesmerized by their color. Gold had smoldered
into deepest, velvet brown, and she turned to liquid
beneath his dark gaze.

Any air separating them vanished. Body touched
body, and lips touched lips. She couldn't think, didn't
want to think, didn't want his kiss to end. He tasted of
brandy, his mouth at once soft and hard. Slowly, her lips
parted, surrendering without a fight, without the realization that she was surrendering.

And then it was over.

He released her and moved away to create a wall of
space between them.

"I think you need to go to bed."

Kate desperately tried to regain her composure. She
couldn't quite understand what had happened, or how,
or what was happening now. So close just moments
ago, he had resumed his seat at the desk and was in the
process of refilling his glass. She shook her head, trying
to clear it and make sense of his words.

"I think you need to go upstairs," he repeated, his
voice level, even cool.

She simply stared back, the shock of what had
happened setting in. Here she was, making a conscious

effort simply to remember to breathe, and he looked calm enough to pick up a newspaper and read. Shame crept over her yet again that evening.

And she was angry. Furious, in fact.

Kate grabbed the nearest object at hand, a massive copy of Boswell's *Life of Samuel Johnson.* Anger willed that book to fly, and as it traversed the air, heading toward the desk, she fled from the room without a backward glance.

Chapter Two

Early the next morning, Kate was seated at her dressing table, her brow furrowed in concentration. An impossible tangle of threads was spread out in her lap, the result of her clumsy efforts at embroidering a handkerchief for her brother—not something to be attempted again. Her sewing skills, along with her skills in just about every other feminine art, were minimal.

"Is everything all right, Miss Kate?"

She pricked her finger as she looked up from her work. Her lady's maid, Mary, had just entered the room, a large basket of clothes in her arms. *No,* she answered Mary silently, *everything is quite wrong.* Even after she'd dashed out of the study last night, she'd been kept awake by images of dark, golden skin and warm, amber eyes. She hadn't fallen asleep until dawn had begun to break.

"I'm fine, Mary—just woolgathering."

Mary lowered the basket onto the bed, where she proceeded to fold the clothes with efficiency. She was not, apparently, particularly interested in what Kate was woolgathering about, and opened her favorite topic instead. "So. Tonight's your brother's engagement party...*and* your first real excursion into society. It could hardly come too soon."

Kate rolled her eyes. Since her mother had died when she was just a baby, in many ways Mary had taken her place. Bossy, she was, and far too familiar. "Oh, Mary, please let's not broach this subject quite yet. I've only just arrived here."

"I can't help it, Miss Kate. I'm just pleased that *one* of you will finally marry, even though I never suspected Lord Robert would be the first. Lady Charlotte Bannister must be a rather forceful young woman to have encouraged such honorable behavior in your brother."

Kate had met Charlotte for the first time yesterday, and thought *forceful* was an apt, if understated, description. "I suppose."

"*And* his wedding couldn't have come at a more convenient time. Now you'll be able to enjoy the full season, dear, and have the proper coming out that you deserve."

"I'm twenty-four, Mary—an age hardly conducive to a proper coming out."

"Well, you weren't much to look at when you were eighteen—"

Since *that* particular wound had been reopened by Benjamin Sinclair only the night before, Kate answered with unusual heat. "Thank you, Mary, for putting my nerves at ease."

Mary looked heavenwards for patience. "What I was going to say, *m'lady,* is that it wasn't until the past few years that you've really come into your own anyway. It's most unfortunate that your father's illness prevented you from coming out sooner, but sometimes waiting can work to one's advantage."

Kate grumbled inaudibly and rose from the dressing table. She couldn't argue. Robert's wedding really did come at a convenient time. The fact was, she'd been contemplating spending the season in London even before her brother had announced his plans—she hadn't really much choice about it. She, too, needed to get married, and the sooner the better.

Kate abandoned that worrying stream of thought and sat back down, this time on her bed. She changed the subject slightly. "I suspect Robbie thinks I've been a bit depressed since our father's death last year. I *have* been reclusive, and I haven't made any attempt to visit him in town."

Matter-of-fact as always, Mary nodded vigorously. "He'd be right if that's what he thinks. You've been in mourning for over a year now, Miss Kate. It's time to get on with your own life. Get married yourself." She opened an overstuffed suitcase, still unpacked, and grimaced. "Goodness, we probably shouldn't have brought all this. Most of it is unsuitable to wear in town anyway. You'll need to go shopping first thing."

Kate sighed elaborately as Mary began to move purposefully about the room. "I'm not a complete simpleton, you know. I realize I'll have to buy a few new things."

It was a long-standing argument. She spent little time or money on her appearance, and most of the clothes she bought were serviceable rather than fashionable. Little

Brookings society was provincial at the best of times, and she'd always seen little point in worrying about her looks when there were so few to notice.

But try and convince someone who'd spent nearly her whole life as a lady's maid. Mary believed in the importance of keeping up appearances. "Your clothes are fine at home, Miss Kate, but you know as well as I that London requires greater sophistication than, well..." she paused for delicacy, "that *thing* you're wearing now, for instance."

Kate looked down at her dress and tried to hide her grin. *Thing* was an accurate description. *Thing* was actually rather generous. Truth was, she only wore it for Mary's benefit.

"What's wrong, Mary? Do you not care for brown?"

Mary harrumphed. "What I care for is getting you married, like you ought to be. *Brown,* if you can even call it that, certainly won't help—" Her lecture was interrupted by Kate's powder puff landing squarely in her face.

"Take that, sweet maid. I hereby declare thee the most beautiful in all the land." She giggled at the comical mixture of surprise and grudging good humor on her maid's powder-covered face and gave a mock swoon, falling backward onto her bed. "Oh, Mary, I fear my constitution is too delicate even to consider a husband."

"Delicate, my foot," Mary snorted while Kate blinked her eyes in feigned shock at her maid's not-so-unusual breach of maid-to-mistress decorum. "I'm just thankful that something will finally motivate you to get out of your rut...and if it takes a kick in the...you know what...to get you to do something about it, well, that's fine by me."

"A kick in the…? Is that what you call it?"

Mary ignored her question and continued. "I know we've had this discussion before, but you should have been married ages ago."

"Mary, I know. You know I know. I was planning to go to London even before I heard from Robert."

"Yesss…only you have yet to seem happy about it."

"Well, I am. Happy. About it."

"I see."

Mary continued to unpack and fold clothes, and Kate walked over to the window. The morning was gray, and it suitably reflected her mood. People in dark clothes moved their way slowly up the damp street. After a minute she heard Mary leave, closing the door quietly behind her.

Kate returned to her bed, enjoying for the moment the restored tranquility that always followed in Mary's wake. They'd had this discussion *many* times before, and although Kate hated to admit it, Mary was right. As each year passed, it would only become harder for her to wed, and she was fast realizing that a husband was a necessity. Not that she didn't cherish her independence, for she valued it more than anything. The fact was, however, that marrying was the only way for her to maintain that independence.

Oh, was she ever in a pickle. Her life would definitely be simpler if she'd been born a man.

It was all her grandfather's fault. When, many years ago, he'd turned his gentlemanly interest in boats into a lucrative shipbuilding company, he never could have dreamed of the trouble this decision would cause his then-unborn granddaughter.

She lay back into the deep cushion of her down quilt and sighed, letting her mind wander back through her family history.

Her grandfather had called his business Alfred and Sons. He'd always chuckled about this name—there wasn't a soul in their family named Alfred. He'd actually named the company after his late Pekinese, figuring that although he might have to sully his hands in trade, he didn't have to sully the family name by advertising that fact.

Luckily, he proved an able businessman and reinvigorated the Sutcliffs' old and ill-managed money. He'd even earned the title of first Baron Gordon for supplying the Crown with ships during the Seven Years' War, thus elevating their family to the peerage for the first time. Indeed, a knack for business seemed to be a family trait, and with her grandfather's death, Kate's father not only inherited his title, but the company as well. In turn, he'd shared his knowledge with his two children…or at least, he'd tried. The fact was, though, only one of them really took to it: his skinny, freckled daughter. And that would have been perfectly fine if only she'd been a skinny, freckled son.

Kate's father had indulged her anyway. He let her tag along to the boatyard to inspect the account books with him, and she'd paid attention, absorbing everything she could. As she grew older, she'd frequently been her father's sole companion—by the age of ten, Robert had left for Eton, followed by Oxford. He'd learned Latin and ancient Greek and how to be a member of the ruling class…but never, alas, how to tie a decent knot.

But Kate was different. From a very young age, hardly a day had passed in which she didn't visit her father's boatyard. Over the years, this habit raised quite a few eyebrows around the village, and it was rumored that the new baron was terribly eccentric, if not completely mad, for allowing his daughter such free rein. Eventually, however, her cheerful smile, bony elbows and abundant freckles endeared her to even the oldest of the old salts. Although she had since grown into her elbows and lessened her freckles with Dr. Calloway's Lemon Complexion Balm, her presence was still grudgingly accepted—and secretly enjoyed.

Of course, this acceptance hinged on the fact that very few people really knew the true extent of her involvement in the company. Kate's father sensibly feared that even the most loyal employee would balk at the idea of taking orders from a young, pretty female. But the truth was that once he became too ill to head the company himself, Kate had stepped fully into his shoes. Out of necessity, Alfred and Sons' longtime clerk, Andrew Hilton, was named the company's director—after all, what self-respecting businessman would agree to deal with a mere slip of a twenty-odd-year-old girl? But Kate knew every detail of every meeting, and not a single decision was made without her approval.

She wasn't quite sure how it had come about, really. Perhaps it was simply because her father knew that there was none other as qualified as she, and Robert had little desire to be called away from London to slave over company ledgers. The reason didn't really matter. Kate knew she had placed herself into a role that women weren't allowed to play, and that she would become a social pariah if it were ever discovered.

This arrangement had worked well enough throughout her father's illness but became a little tricky after his death. His title and nearly all of the family property—the house in St. James's, the house in Little Brookings, another in Surrey—had passed on to Robert. Kate was given a dowry of four thousand pounds a year.

And Alfred and Sons?

In the strangest turn of events, it passed from father to daughter.

When her father wrote his will, he intended for his family to carry on as they always had, with none the wiser. He left the company and all its holdings to Kate…with a clause: she would inherit the company fully *only* after she wed. It was a purely practical consideration—lacking a father, she'd need a husband to ensure her legitimacy. Until she married, Andrew Hilton would continue to serve as nominal director. It should have been very simple.

But shortly after her father died, Hilton made it clear that he wanted more than nominal control. Although he'd never shown any interest in Kate as anything but the daughter of his employer, he suddenly began waging a serious war for her hand.

At first, she'd shrugged off his advances as harmless, but lately they'd become impossible to ignore. Most recently, he'd begun resorting to coercion, threatening to expose her role in the company and thus destroy everything her father had worked for.

Kate couldn't allow that to happen, but as an unmarried woman she had little legal recourse, nor could she seek protection from the courts—to tell anyone would betray her role in the company. She couldn't confide in her brother, either. Normally, he was completely disinterested in Alfred and Sons, but if he knew she was in any sort of danger he'd force her to give up all involvement with the company. He might even make her sell it. As the head of the family, he could do that.

The only solution she could come up with was to get married, and that was what she was determined to do: quickly and conveniently, romance not required.

There was nothing unusual about Ben's impromptu overnight stay. He'd known Robert since they'd been at school together, and when the season was in full swing and the drinks flowed a little too freely, he frequently availed himself of his friend's hospitality. Since Ben had been at sea for the past six months, however, his presence now was unexpected.

The two men were seated in Robert's breakfast room. Robert was tucking in eagerly to a large plate of eggs and rashers while Ben pushed his helping more aimlessly around his plate. Occasionally, Robert looked up from his food and smiled, but gave up almost immediately upon seeing his friend's dark countenance.

"So…how's business?" Robert asked after several minutes, obviously trying to fill the silence. "You've been away for a while. Everything in order?"

A dull ache had invaded Ben's brain that morning and he'd have been just as happy if they didn't talk at all. "Speak quietly," he whispered, "business is fine."

"I thought this shipping business of yours was only a lark, Ben. It sounds suspiciously like work. You look exhausted."

Ben ignored that. Unlike most ship owners, he liked to oversee many of the day-to-day operations of his business and often accompanied his crew on their voyages. He'd discovered his love of the sea during his Grand Tour, and once he'd returned to England he'd found that life on solid ground no longer satisfied him. He'd become involved in shipping as a diversion, really, hoping to find some way to alleviate the deadening boredom of high society. Somehow, though, he'd become completely caught up in the business. He found that he thrived on hard work, liked having a reason to get up in the morning and loved the thrill of traveling somewhere new. He kept this part of his personality largely concealed from his jaded friends, however.

And anyway, the reason for his current exhaustion had nothing to do with work.

Robert was still watching him. "Had a rough night, eh?"

Ben just grunted. Robert hadn't any idea how rough, and Ben felt certain that he wouldn't actually like to know the details of how his best friend had nearly seduced his sister. He wasn't quite sure why he'd done it himself. Granted, he'd been slightly foxed when he'd arrived, having stopped at his club for a drink en route. Perhaps his judgment had been a bit flawed....

No. Best just to pretend it hadn't happened. "Tell me again when the wedding is to be?"

Robert smiled. "Fifteenth of September. Charlotte

had the devil of a time getting her mother to agree to it—not to her marrying me, of course, but to doing it so quickly. Told me it was scandalous, the old bag. Horse Face must have ceremony. But I held firm. A man can only wait so long. Six months it shall be. But it is a squeeze, I know. Reckon there's a lot to do…dresses and flowers and such nonsense. I've elected to leave that business to the women, not that they'd want my help anyway. Charlotte has already begun to send out invitations like mad…on top of that, I have a host of bloody decorators to contend with because Horse Face says my home is entirely unsuitable." He shook his head ruefully. "I'm not looking forward to it, I tell you, but I suppose it's the price one pays. House has been full of bloody women, even now. My sister's here, you know."

Ben's expression must have betrayed something, because Robert narrowed his eyes slightly and asked, "Do you remember meeting her?"

Only too well, Ben thought to himself. His headache, which had begun to subdue, sharpened considerably. With undue heat he answered, "Not with much fondness, Robbie. She threw a glass of water at me, I remember that much quite clearly."

"I think you insulted her, Ben," Robert reminded him.

"I never insult women."

"Perhaps you called her scrawny. She was only eleven, you know. Always been a bit of a tomboy, though."

Ben snorted in distaste. "Age is no excuse. I'd rather hoped to continue avoiding her."

Robert nodded in agreement. "Can't say I'd mind if you avoided my sister either, old boy, but there's unlikely to be much choice unless you plan on leaving the country again. She'll be here for the entire season. It's her first, you know."

That piqued Ben's curiosity. "Not married, then? What, doesn't she believe in it either?"

"Keep your mind out of the gutter, Ben. She never had a proper coming out. Once our father became ill she remained home to tend to him. He died just last year, as you know, and she's been in mourning since. Anyway, for some reason she's become set on the idea of matrimony all of the sudden."

Ben merely grunted. "It happens to all women."

"You're being rather touchy this morning."

Ben supposed he was, and it was all the fault of his irrational behavior the night before. He'd known countless beautiful women in his life and had never lost control quite like that. Oh, not much had happened, but for God's sake, she was his best friend's sister. He should have gone straight to bed, yet he'd been so reluctant to bring their conversation to its hasty and logical end, with both of them heading off to their respective rooms for a good night's sleep. It was too much fun watching her blush, and he had simply poured himself another drink and all but forced her to join him.

Thinking of that blasted drink, Ben had to smile to himself. Served the chit right for choking on it. It softened the blow—literally—for that damn book she'd thrown at him. Lucky thing she kissed better than she threw or his head would be throbbing more than it already was.

But that kiss…

After she'd fled the room, he'd had another drink, trying to tame his rampant emotions. He was angry, but mainly with himself. Couldn't really blame her for trying to brain him. He'd treated her quite cavalierly after that kiss, but it was the only way he could think of to get her out of the room before his tenuous control slipped once more.

If it were any other female, he'd simply bed her—no better way to get a woman out of one's mind. But she was Robert's sister and seduction was not an option.

Robert was saying something about lunch and Ben realized he hadn't been listening. Robert was looking at him, clearly waiting for an answer.

Ben wasn't sure what the question had been, but took a stab at an answer anyway. "Oh, no. I have to return home. Mrs. Davis should be in today, cleaning or whatever it is she does to ready the house for the season. Have a few things to do myself. You on for White's tonight?"

"Tonight's the old engagement party, lad…as I've been telling you. 'Fraid I'm obliged to make an appearance. You should come, though—I know you weren't planning on being in town, but now that you're here…"

"I'll think about it. Right now I need to rest up and set my head to rights. Not quite myself yet this morning."

"Noted," Robert said dryly, "but I'll be expecting you tonight anyway—besides, I'd get great satisfaction out of unbalancing Horse Face's guest list."

Ben glanced at his pocket watch. It was nearly eleven. He'd better leave Robert's soon lest Kate make an appearance.

He nodded distractedly. "I'll try to make it, Rob. But

now I really must go. I have business of my own to attend to." He pushed his uneaten breakfast back and rose from his seat. "Enjoy your lunch…who'd you say you were dining with?"

Robert sighed. "Charlotte and Kate."

"Kate?"

"My sister, dunce. Did you hear anything I was saying?"

"Like I said, I'm not myself this early. But self shall return before this evening. You have my promise."

Chapter Three

When Charlotte Bannister opened the door to her bedroom that evening, she was preceded by an accusing face and followed by the strains of a waltz. Her engagement party was progressing beautifully downstairs; every room in her parents' elegant mansion was filled with the soft light of a dozen crystal chandeliers and buzzed with the latest *on dit*. *Everyone* invited had showed, and *everyone,* almost, was behaving.

The exception, Katherine Sutcliff, sat guiltily and unsociably in the center of Charlotte's bed. Such behavior could not be permitted.

Charlotte sat down on the yellow damask chaise longue with legs formed by black and gold caryatids at the foot of her bed. Kate tried not to meet her gaze and pretended to look around the room instead. The entire Orient converged there, owing to Charlotte's mother's exuberant taste for all things Egyptian, Chinese and Greek.

"You simply *must* come back downstairs," Charlotte

said after a moment of silence. Her pretty blue eyes brooked no argument.

"Well, you see, Char—"

"I do not." She tossed her dark hair impatiently. "I thought you were excited about this party! What can the problem possibly be? Surely you're not still worried about your gown? I will tell you again, you look lovely. You were the center of attention for the brief moment you deigned to remain downstairs. You *must* have noticed."

Indeed, Kate thought, looking down at her dress and blushing. Because she had arrived only the day before she hadn't had time to get fitted for anything new. Anticipating this problem, Charlotte had taken it upon herself to have something made up a few weeks ago without consulting Kate or even having met her first. The approximate measurements had come from Robert, who, in brotherly fashion, had badly underestimated her feminine attributes. In the tight bodice, her breasts had nowhere to go but up. She felt quite naked, and Robert's rakish friends staring openly at her chest did not help matters. Her unease, however, was spurred by the thought of only one of those friends. Benjamin Sinclair had already seen her half-exposed in her dressing gown, and look what happened then. She didn't know if he'd arrived at the party, or if he planned to attend at all, but not knowing was driving her mad.

"Bastard."

"I'm sorry, *what* did you just call me?"

"What?" Kate looked up in alarm. Oh, God. Had she spoken aloud?

"You muttered an inexcusable word under your breath just now—"

Kate cut Charlotte off lest she got any more offended. "I'm sorry. I didn't mean to say that—certainly I wasn't speaking about you. My mind isn't really where it ought to be tonight…I suppose I'm just nervous."

Charlotte smiled, satisfied by that response. Her eyes sparkled with mischief. "You've nothing to worry about. As I say, you've proved *very* popular so far."

"Charlotte—"

"Just come downstairs. I want to introduce you to my brother Philip. I promise he'll behave like a gentleman."

"I think I've met all of your brothers, thank you," said Kate, thinking of the solid line of dull, unsmiling manhood she'd met on arrival. Charlotte had five brothers—obnoxious oafs, the lot of them. Philip was simply King Obnoxious Oaf.

"He's not that bad. You'll grow to like him, I swear."

Kate wanted to snort at Charlotte's dogged self-assurance, but refrained. Considering how long they'd been acquainted, it was pretty presumptuous for Charlotte to assume anything about her feelings. But Kate could be just as strong-willed as her managerial future sister-in-law.

"Charlotte, you must promise me this—you will not play cupid tonight. Just because you're getting married does *not* mean that love is in the air."

"But you want to get married. Robert told me."

Kate nodded firmly. "I intend to."

"Um…do you have a particular gentleman in mind yet?"

"I've only been here a day, Charlotte."

"I know. It's just that you seem so…certain…about what you want."

Kate wasn't at all certain about what she wanted. *Want* didn't figure into the equation. "Well, it's about time, isn't it?"

"Your confidence is quite dizzying. I almost pity the male populace."

Kate sighed, feeling increasingly deflated. "It's not confidence, Charlotte, it's determination."

Charlotte smiled gently. "Mind if I offer my opinion?"

"I've learned to expect it in the short time I've known you."

"Well, Kate, it seems a rather haphazard method for getting married."

"My method is quite scientific, thank you very much."

"Since when is love scientific?"

Kate met her gaze. She knew Charlotte was right and only wished she could explain her true motivation. But if she told her, she'd tell Robert, and then…well, that'd be it.

"I'm not sure that I will fall in love, at least not right away. How did you know when you fell in love with my brother? Could you just tell?"

Charlotte blushed. "Well, it was just a feeling I had…maybe you haven't noticed, being his sister and all, but he's quite handsome—"

Kate snorted.

"—He was also rather bold, I suppose, in letting me know that he was…interested in me as well."

"Interested?"

Charlotte was blushing to her roots now. "You know…desired me."

"I know what you mean, Charlotte! You needn't spell it out! But what did it feel like?"

"I'm sorry?"

"Don't be embarrassed. We're friends now, and soon enough you'll be my sister. What does it feel like when two people desire each other very much?"

"You're awfully interested for someone who doesn't even have a chap in mind yet."

"Humor me." Kate didn't know why the answer had become so important. Presumably, one just knew when life-altering emotions like love and desire struck. Unlike most girls, however, she didn't have a mother to eluci-date the finer details of courtship, and she really wasn't sure that she would *just know.*

Charlotte continued. "Well, whenever he looks at me I feel rather warm. I blush a lot when I'm with him— rather like I'm blushing now, only it's much more pleasant…will that do, Kate? It's rather private."

"Uh-huh…" Kate wasn't certain if that delicate ex-planation helped at all, but could no longer bear to watch Charlotte squirm. She also wasn't sure she liked the answer. Only one man in her experience had ever made her feel like that and he was absolutely out of the question. She had a goal to reach, and, judging from his reputation, Benjamin Sinclair certainly would not help her along that path.

One more reason to dislike the scoundrel.

An hour had passed since Charlotte had led her un-willingly down the grand staircase. As the clock struck eleven, Kate finally let her guard drop. Perhaps he wasn't coming after all. Perhaps he, too, was embarrassed.

Not bloody likely.

Kate was standing to the side of the ballroom, watching the other guests sway to the music. She was enjoying a much-needed respite from dancing—her gown allowed for only the shallowest of breaths and she was feeling a bit faint as a result. She'd danced with several eligible young men already and had even taken Charlotte's advice and given Philip Bannister another chance. She'd forced herself to be less critical this time and found that, although he *was* still a bit dry, he wasn't really that bad either. Philip was a year older than her at twenty-five and was actually rather handsome with his dark brown hair and eyes. She hadn't minded dancing with him twice—even though, as she sadly noted, he fell just shy of her own slender height. No one could be perfect, she supposed. Kate mentally promoted him from the rank of King Obnoxious Oaf to the rank of somewhat dull, but generally good-natured, bore. In other words, he became a potential candidate.

No, everything seemed to be going to plan. A few more weeks of this, and hopefully she'd be well on the way to matrimony.

She scanned the sea of people, looking for a recognizable face. None registered, and she was about to go search out Charlotte when she heard a familiar voice behind her.

"There you are, goose. I've been trying to find you alone for ages."

She turned around, smiling broadly at Charlotte as

she did so. Her smile froze, however, when she saw who accompanied her.

"I'm sure you've met Lord Benjamin Sinclair, Kate—your brother's oldest friend?"

At her blank expression, Charlotte continued. "Well, this is Lord Benjamin Sinclair. Lord Sinclair, this is Miss Katherine Sutcliff."

"A pleasure, Miss Sutcliff," he said blandly for Charlotte's benefit.

"How do you do," she replied, curtsying as she did so and looking down to avoid his gaze. The feeling had returned in a flash…the nervous stomach, the heat…damn him again. She sucked in her breath as he lightly kissed her gloved hand.

"Well…" Charlotte went on, not at all blind to the sudden tension that surrounded her, "I think I see Lady Cheshire at the lemonade table, and I could use a glass myself, so…"

And with that, she smiled and flounced away. Kate couldn't help but catch the now familiar self-satisfied sparkle in her eyes. If only Charlotte knew that her matchmaking skills were wasted on this particular pair.

Kate could feel the heat from Ben's gaze returning to her face. *He's waiting for me to look at him,* she thought, aware that she'd have to give in to his gaze eventually. But too many other thoughts were still running through her head—had he been there all night? Had he just arrived? She couldn't very well ask. To do so would be to admit that she'd been watching for him.

She knew she had to look. She couldn't just stand there like a ninny, staring at the floor.

Resolved, Kate met his gaze, and immediately wished she hadn't. It was there again—the piercing, golden heat of his eyes as they wandered over her hair, her face and down…oh, God, that damned dress. Ben made no pretense of discretion, and she went red once again as he stared unabashedly at her breasts.

"I wondered if I would see you here tonight, but I certainly didn't expect to see so much of you," he said with a devilish grin.

Kate, of course, said nothing. What *could* she say to that? She settled for fixing him with a seething glare.

A waltz struck up and Ben moved a step closer.

"Do you have permission to waltz?" he asked as he placed his hand on the small of her back to guide her onto the dance floor.

"No," she lied baldly.

"Liar."

Before she knew what was happening, before she had a chance to refuse further, he was escorting her onto the ballroom floor, so thick with dancing couples that there was no room for escape.

She didn't know what to do but dance. To balk now would only make people stare—even more than they already were. Kate was keenly aware of the fact that people had begun to watch them from the very moment that Charlotte had left them alone together. She could feel every eye turned their way and knew that the gossip had started. She didn't know what they were saying, but she could count on the fact that it wasn't complimentary. Ben was simply too scandalous, and the way he was looking at her…

"Are you always this clumsy on the dance floor?" he asked as Kate, distracted, stepped squarely on his toe. "These are new shoes."

"If you'd given me the chance, I would have told you I didn't want to dance with you. And is it necessary to stand so close?" she retorted, annoyed into speech.

"Don't fuss, love," he said, holding her even tighter. "You'll only cause a scene."

Kate bit her tongue, at least for the time being. He clearly didn't care if she caused a scene or not. From what she could gather from the gossips and from what her brother casually let slip, he was used to scandal. Arguing with him would only lead to embarrassment, and protesting his proximity would just bring him closer.

"Are you enjoying yourself?" he asked, more amused at her discomfort than interested in her answer.

"I was," she answered curtly.

At this, Ben laughed outright, although he obligingly stifled his laughter as heads turned in their direction and Kate reddened.

He changed his approach. "You know, I was hoping to have a few words with you this evening. To make peace, in fact."

She raised a slender brow, and he continued. "You see, I suspect that you're angry with me—"

"Whatever gave you that idea?"

"—and I'm not used to making women angry. So an apology is in order."

Kate blinked in surprise. This was the last thing she had expected. In fact, she had assumed that *he* would be angry with *her,* not the other way around.

"You're sorry, then?" she asked tentatively.

"Somewhat."

Her eyes narrowed. "What do you mean, 'somewhat'?"

"Well," he answered, spinning her around, "I suppose I shouldn't have forced you to have a drink with me last night, but I'm not sorry. And I shouldn't have teased you so much, but I'm not sorry. And," he said, his amber eyes wandering over her face, "I shouldn't have kissed you, but I'm definitely not sorry."

"Oh?" She didn't know how she managed that. Her breath tripped in her throat, and she felt like she was melting beneath his gaze.

"But I am sorry that I told you to leave. That, sweetheart, was a real pity."

With this, he let her go, bowed, turned and walked away.

For a moment Kate just stood there, trying to recover her composure. She'd been so focused on Ben during the waltz that she'd lost track of what was happening around her. Slowly, she realized that the music had ended, that they were no longer dancing, that they had stopped dancing some time ago. Oh, God. How long had the waltz been over? How long had she been standing there?

She turned around, trying to gather her bearings and look as if she weren't completely flustered. Sometime in the course of their dance, he had maneuvered her back to Charlotte, who was standing along the wall with a small group of friends. They were all staring, although they tactfully averted their eyes once Kate became aware that she was the center of so much attention.

Chapter Four

"Could you pay attention, please, Ben?"

Ben glanced up at his friend Frederick Northing, who was seated across from him at the table. The two men, as well as several other refugees, were seated in something Charlotte's mother, the Countess of Tyndale, called the "Cerulean Room." For the evening's entertainment it had been given over to whist and brandy, much to her disgust.

Ben had hoped that the change of scenery would get his mind off Kate, but so far it wasn't helping. He'd seated himself with his back to the door so that he wouldn't have to see her as she twirled by in the arms of one suitor after another. His attempts were futile, however; he hadn't taken into consideration the large, gilt-framed mirror that hung on the wall opposite him. It reflected everything that happened in the ballroom behind him, and each time Kate danced by—so striking, so tall, and her dress so delightfully revealing—his eyes were drawn to her.

It was that dress that had brought him out of the gaming room in the first place. He'd actually been at the party for hours, had simply decided that his best tactic would be to make a brief appearance to pacify Robert and then hide out in the gaming room until he could politely duck out.

Only it hadn't happened that way. From the first moment that he'd noticed Kate, he couldn't keep his eyes off her. Even worse, he couldn't keep his mind off her. That was the most unusual part—he was accustomed to being attracted to a pretty face, but not to having that pretty face invade his thoughts. He definitely hadn't meant to seek her out....

But he had, and quite underhandedly at that. He'd known that he couldn't approach her outright, so he'd shamelessly besieged Charlotte and asked her in no uncertain terms to introduce him. He hadn't bothered to mention that he'd introduced himself just the night before.

"I know what you're looking at. Or should I say who?"

"You should mind your own business, Fred."

"Ah. But my friends are my business," Frederick replied with a smile. "You know, he'll kill you when he finds out."

"Who will kill me when he finds out what?"

"Sutcliff will, when he hears the latest *on dit* about how you have eyes on his sister."

"Are you blind, Fred? Every man here has his eyes on her."

"No, I'm not blind. I saw the way you were looking at her."

"And how was that?"

"Like she's dinner."

Ben burst out laughing and Fred grinned.

"Well, she is rather delectable."

"Ben, I wasn't the only one who noticed. Half the town will have your names linked by tomorrow."

"Fred, if you don't recall, half the town has talked about me plenty of times before."

"Yes," he said patiently, "and no one cares if they continue to do so. But Sutcliff is sure to care if his sister's name starts getting bandied around at the club. I figured you'd be wise enough to stay clear of things like this. You've been friends for years and I'd hate to see anything come between you."

Ben sighed and rose, stretching his arms and giving the impression of nonchalance. "Nothing will come between us. I don't have designs on his sister. She's just attractive, is all…habitual behavior is hard to change. Anyway, I'm about to leave, so never fear. I've reached my limit for dancing. Care to join me at White's?"

"Tempting, old chap, but I haven't suffered through this evening for naught. I've already made plans."

"Oh? And who is the lucky lady?" Ben asked as he made his way to the door.

"Oh, no. You see, I—unlike you—am discreet."

Ben snorted as he left the room. Fred had never valued public opinion highly enough to worry about discretion.

As he walked down the long hallway, he nodded to passing acquaintances. When he reached the antechamber, he retrieved his coat and shrugged it on as he stepped out into the cold spring air to find his carriage. To anyone watching, Ben appeared calm and collected.

But inside, he was completely on edge. His second meeting with Kate had left him feeling just as tense as the first had.

Damn. This would have to stop.

The situation was ridiculous, really, he thought as he climbed into his carriage and signaled for his driver to depart. Fred was right. He'd had more than enough experience with women to let any one woman turn him into a halfwit. Katherine Sutcliff was innocent and looking for a husband. He would be wise to stay away from her and she from him.

He sat back on the smooth leather seats, unsuccessfully trying to force himself to relax. The last thing he needed was to go to his club, where he'd only be surrounded by ornery old sots trying to drink and gamble themselves into oblivion. He still wouldn't be able to remove her from his mind.

What he needed was a substitution.

As his carriage turned out of the Bannisters' long drive, Ben called to his coachman. The carriage slowed to a stop.

"Yes, my lord?"

"I've changed my mind, Winters. Take me to Madame Dupont's instead of White's."

"Very good, my lord."

A quarter of an hour later, the carriage pulled up in front of a nondescript brownstone in a decent—but not too decent—part of town. Madame Dupont's was a place rather than a person. Surely once, Ben mused as he stepped from his carriage and walked to the door, she had been a real person. But the establishment had been around for so long that the original proprietress was certainly deceased, whatever her name had been.

Currently, the proprietress was a short, round woman from Liverpool. Because she was English, everyone referred to her as Mrs. rather than Madame, although Ben doubted she'd ever experienced the respectability of marriage.

He yanked the bellpull.

The door opened, for a moment spilling yellow light and gay, female laughter onto the dark street. Ben entered, and the heavy door closed behind him. The street returned to darkness once again, and Winters tucked a blanket around his legs and settled in for a lengthy wait.

Kate was standing in the Bannisters' antechamber, waiting for her carriage to pull up. It was almost two o'clock in the morning, not actually that late by society standards. She'd decided to go home early, although the party would last for another few hours. In fact, she'd been waiting to leave for quite a while because she had refused to depart until *he* had. To leave first would be to admit defeat. So she'd camped out in the ladies' retiring room, avoiding the gossips and occasionally peeking out to see if the coast was clear.

As her carriage began to make its way through the crowded drive, she pulled her fur-lined pelisse tightly around her shoulders. Too impatient to wait for her carriage to reach the front steps, Kate stepped into the night and began to weave her way through the traffic. The moon was a mere sliver, and the only light was the brash, artificial glow of the coachmen's oil lanterns. The driveway was cast in gloomy shadow, making her shiver as she maneuvered herself through the throng.

When she reached her carriage, the door was already open. Kate waited a moment for her driver to assist her entry, but by the time he finally made a move to alight, she was already halfway inside the cab. She waved him off, knowing she'd be faster on her own.

How strange. Owens was usually not so lax at his post.

She settled back into the deep seats as the carriage lurched into motion, reviewing the evening's events in her mind.

Kate couldn't believe her stupidity. She so wanted to make this whole process quick and easy but was afraid that particular goal might have been dashed that night, all in the span of a single dance.

She supposed that she was being a bit histrionic. It wasn't as if Ben had whisked her from the ballroom and kissed her behind the curtains. Surely a waltz and a few heated glances wouldn't ruin her completely.

Yet she'd already heard the gossip, little snippets here and there.

"The only girl he danced with all night…"

"He doesn't usually flock to young innocents, now does he?"

"Oh, but my dear, she's not *that* young…"

"Twenty-four, I hear. She's been on the shelf for ages.…"

"Ha! I heard she's nearly thirty…innocent my foot, that's what I say!"

Much as Kate *tried* to be optimistic, she was a realist

at heart. Gossip like that could be very damaging, and she knew that her search for a husband had just become much more difficult.

She looked out the window, trying to gauge by her surroundings how much longer the ride would last. She was surprised to realize that she was traveling through a completely unfamiliar neighborhood.

"Owens? Have we taken a detour for some reason?"

There was no answer other than the carriage picking up speed.

"Owens? Owens? Stop this instant. Where are we going?" In desperation, Kate began pounding on the window at her side, hoping to attract the attention of any passersby. But it was too late and the night too cold and cloudy. There was no one on the street to hear her. Even screaming would do no good....

She screamed anyway. Loudly. And then she screamed once more for good measure.

The driver—who, she was now certain, was not Owens—increased his pace.

Kate began to panic. She wasn't used to that emotion but didn't have a clue what else she could do. There wasn't a soul to help her, no one to notice anything amiss about the carriage. There wasn't even anyone at Rob's town house to notice that she was missing—Rob would be at the party for several more hours and none of the servants would be expecting her home this early. Most likely, no one would notice that she hadn't arrived safely until morning. By that time, no end of horrible things could happen....

Kate tried to change the direction of her thoughts. If

she started thinking about what *might* happen to her, she knew that panic would take over. She had to remain calm and focus on how she could escape.

Taking a deep breath, she squinted out the window, looking for any landmark that might tell her where the coach was headed. They were moving quickly—not conspicuously so, but as fast as possible without drawing attention. She barely had time to focus on anything long enough for it to become familiar, and since she didn't know London very well anyway, everything she passed managed to look much the same.

The coach slowed slightly, and Kate realized that they were turning a corner. She sat up straighter, peering out the window even harder. Through the steamy glass she could make out the solid form of a row of town houses, all with shadowy doorways and black, empty windows. Surely the area was inhabited, but at this hour no one stirred.

Then she saw it—just the soft glimmer of candlelight shining from the windows of one of the narrow buildings ahead, but a sign of hope nonetheless. As the coach neared the building she could make out the form of a man climbing the steps to knock on the front door. She saw the door open, spilling light out onto the street.

Help.

It was either one of the bravest or one of the most foolhardy things that Kate had ever done. Shoving aside the possibly dangerous consequences—the man on the street might just as soon hurt her as help her—she let out a scream shrill enough to curdle the blood of a saint. Every resource she possessed went into attracting the attention of the people in the building. She leaned back across her seat, and with both legs kicked at the window. Her slippers were designed for dancing and did no damage to the glass, but they did make a solid thud.

As the carriage came abreast with the building, she rose from her seat and screamed one final time, a scream so deep that the very power of it abraded her throat.

The door of the town house opened and a woman looked out apprehensively. A man came running out behind her.

That was the last thing Kate saw before the carriage stopped abruptly, throwing her into a heap on the floor. She quickly resumed her seat, wanting to be prepared for whatever might happen next. She heard the driver quickly alight, heard heavy footsteps approach the carriage door. It opened.

Kate closed her eyes, seeking the fortitude to protect herself. She raised her reticule over her head, and with all of her might swung it down, connecting solidly with…she wasn't sure what.

She opened her eyes. Standing in the doorway, framed by the light that filtered from the town house, stood Benjamin Sinclair, looking utterly bewildered. Without taking his eyes from her he reached up and rubbed his head.

What bloody luck.

Chapter Five

An hour and a half later, Kate was sipping hot tea in front of a fire, a heavy wool blanket tucked around her legs. Ben had brought her inside the town house and left her in the care of a slim, mousy-looking girl named Margaret. She was in a plush, although rather ostentatious, room outfitted with overstuffed armchairs and red damask wallcovering. There were several large windows, but all were covered in thick, velvet drapery.

She hadn't seen Ben since he'd brought her inside and was anxiously awaiting his return so she could find out where she was and what was going to happen. Kate had tried to get some answers out of Margaret, but the frail girl was not very forthcoming.

"Margaret, I am aware that I asked you this question before, but are you certain you haven't any idea where Lord Sinclair has gone?"

"Sorry, m'lady. I know no more than you do. He just

told me to make sure you stayed in this room and didn't cause a scene."

"Oh, he did, did he? Well, could you at least tell me where I am? So maybe I can take a guess as to where he has gone and when he might get back?"

"I'm afraid I can't—"

"You *can,* or I *will* cause a scene!"

"Thank you, Margaret. You can get back to work now," Ben said as he quietly entered the room. He held out a coin to Margaret, which she gladly accepted before picking up her skirts and racing from the room. As she did so, Kate noticed that the nondescript girl wore the most shocking pink stockings.

Ben gently closed the door behind Margaret, smiling as he caught the direction of Kate's scandalized gaze. "So, we meet again. You know, I was thinking as I left the party that my evening wouldn't be complete if Miss Sutcliff didn't hurl some object at my head at least once. You have made my night."

"I didn't know who you were. I'm sorry."

"You have nothing to apologize for."

Kate just smiled faintly. "Where are we? This isn't your house, is it?"

Ben burst out laughing for the second time that evening at something that Kate hadn't intended to be humorous. She waited patiently for him to stop. When he didn't, she became annoyed and began to glare.

"I'm glad I amuse you so much, Lord Sinclair, but would you mind answering my question? I've had a rotten night." She was trying to be as condescending as possible, but Ben seemed to be oblivious to her sarcasm.

"I'm sorry. I shouldn't be laughing at a time like this. But I must assure you that my house is decorated a little bit more tastefully."

"Yes, well this place looks like a harem. All this red!" As Kate said these words, she realized her mistake. She could see that Ben was all but biting his tongue trying not to laugh. She quickly began to explain. "Not that I know what a harem looks like, or anything. It's just that I've heard…" she trailed off as Ben raised his hand.

"Please, don't try to explain. I'm certain you have reliable sources. And I'll tell you where we are, but I think we should figure out exactly what happened first, while it's still fresh in your mind."

Kate nodded in assent. "How did you see my carriage?"

"Well, it wasn't so hard to see, really. Or rather to hear—you were making quite a racket in there. I had just entered the building when you went by. Mrs. Wilson…um, she owns this house…opened the door to see what was going on outside, and I recognized Robert's carriage. So I ran out to try to stop it."

"How *did* you stop it?"

Ben actually looked sheepish. "I wish I could tell you I did something heroic like throw myself in front of the horses, but I didn't actually have to do anything at all. The second the driver saw me coming, he pulled the carriage to a stop and jumped off—fear of recognition, I guess. Anyway, he ran off into the night before I could even catch a glimpse of him."

"And then you opened the door and I clobbered you?"

"Yes…and where does a young lady like you learn to clobber so effectively?"

Kate smiled cryptically. "Around."

"Around. Hmm. So d'you mind if I ask you a few questions?"

"Not at all."

"Well, can you tell me what happened when you left the party? Did you leave by yourself?"

"Yes…there's not much to it. I just left. There were a lot of carriages in the drive—it was dark. The only thing amiss was that when I reached the carriage Owens was very slow to help me in…I called to him not to bother and got in on my own. I never actually saw Owens."

"He wasn't there."

"No. He wasn't there. Oh, I do hope nothing awful has happened to him."

"My driver has gone back to the Bannisters' to look for him. There's a very good chance he's there still." They fell silent for a moment before Ben asked, "I assume you told your brother that you were leaving?"

"Well, no, not exactly. I told Charlotte to tell him…she said her coachman would take him home when the party ended so I could leave early. I hadn't seen Robert in a while—couldn't locate him, really." That was a lie. Kate had been patently avoiding her brother, too afraid that he would have heard of her embarrassment and would want to grill her on the particulars.

"Hmm." Ben mulled over her words for a moment, leaning back in his chair and stretching out his long legs.

Despite her nervousness, Kate couldn't help but notice how sinfully handsome he was, how perfectly formed. He wasn't paying attention for the moment and she let her gaze travel up his body, admiring the perfect fit of his evening attire and imagining what was beneath it….

She'd made it up to his chest when she felt the uncomfortable sensation of being watched. She quickly met Ben's eyes and blushed when she realized that he was the watcher.

He smiled but continued, not yet ready to drop the subject. "Did the driver say nothing to you out of the ordinary?"

"He said nothing at all, but the incident was so strange itself…would you tell me, please, what you were doing while I waited here?"

Ben smiled. "Of course. I went for a walk in the surrounding area to see if I saw anyone who looked suspicious…can't say I got a very good look at our man before he dashed off, though."

"You didn't find him."

"I hardly expected to. These things happen all the time and the culprits rarely get apprehended. I notified the authorities while I was out, however, and they're also looking for Owens. I'm certain he'll turn up soon."

Kate hoped so. It would be entirely her fault if Owens were injured. She was quiet for a moment, thinking of the potential consequences of her unwillingness to tell her brother her concerns about Andrew Hilton. "Do you reckon he was a highwayman? Perhaps he was just waiting to get me out of town so he could rob me in peace."

"I suppose it's possible, although he was taking you in the wrong direction to do that. It also seems like an awfully big risk to take for a simple robbery, abducting you right in front of the Bannisters'. Any number of people could have witnessed it."

Kate nodded, unable to speak as her worst fear began to crystallize in her mind. Perhaps it wasn't just a robbery…

She rose to pour herself a drink from the side table, anxious to occupy her shaking hands.

"So, it makes me wonder, Miss Sutcliff."

"Yes?"

"Do you have any enemies?"

Kate never felt herself hit the floor. All she knew was that she suddenly found herself lying on the sofa, her head propped up on a pile of soft pillows. She felt something warm by her side and lifted her head to look, only to find Ben, seated next to her, watching her revive.

"How are you feeling, Sleeping Beauty?"

Kate was feeling like she was no longer safe in London, and she was realizing for the first time that Andrew Hilton might be a real threat rather than just an annoyance. Although he could be unpleasant, she'd always considered him to be a bit of a coward. She never would have expected he'd try to hurt her. But what if he did?

"Kate? How do you feel?"

"Pretty dreadful. What happened?"

"You fainted."

"Rubbish."

Ben smiled, giving the impression of infinite patience, although he was feeling anything but. Every muscle in his body was tense, and had been since the moment he'd pulled her from the carriage.

"Of course you didn't faint. How silly of me. I'm sorry if I frightened you…I was only jesting about the enemy bit. I was actually trying to lighten the mood. I'm sure it was just a highwayman—probably not a very clever one, but…"

"Yes, I'm sure you're right."

He could sense that she didn't want to revisit the subject, so he changed it. "Are you ready to go home now?"

"I think so." She sat up a bit too quickly, and a wave of dizziness washed over her again.

"Easy now. Take your time." He put a steadying arm around her shoulders as he said these words, and she found that it actually helped. She took a deep, calming breath and carefully placed her feet on the floor.

"I think I can make it on my own from here. Thank you." She glanced up at his face to reassure him that she was fine, and for the second time that evening wished she hadn't. His eyes had darkened once again, becoming that deep, smoldering brown that ignited every one of her senses and left a trail of heat as they roamed over her body.

Kate knew that she'd already lost. As Ben leaned down to kiss her, she raised her hands to his chest, intending to push him away. But the second her hands reached him, all thoughts of protest vanished. She was powerless to say yes or no, and instead of pushing him away, she found herself pulling him closer, relishing the feel of his hardness, his heat. Her eyes closed, and as his lips settled over hers, she felt drunk with sensation.

This second kiss differed from the first, which had been so fleeting, so abrupt. This kiss was softer, slower—painfully slow, and yet so pleasurable. Kate gasped for breath as Ben gently tugged at her lower lip with his teeth, urging her without words to open her mouth. She was more than happy to oblige, eager, in fact, to taste him more fully. When his tongue entered her mouth, she met it with her own, her inexperience overcome by passion and instinct. When Ben's hands moved down her body, stopping at the firm, round peaks of her breasts, she didn't even notice. He laid her down on the sofa, sliding between her legs and grabbing her buttocks to press her against his hardness. Kate didn't think to object, and wouldn't have had the will to do so anyway. All she knew was the burning need she felt, deep down inside, a sweet throbbing that she couldn't begin to comprehend. She moaned.

That moan was Ben's undoing. He dragged himself off her, cursing as he looked down into her desire-clouded eyes and swollen lips. Damn. Where the bloody hell was his control? Here he was, seconds from making love to his best friend's sister on a sofa in a gaming house, for God's sake. After the girl had nearly been abducted, no less. Ben knew he was no saint, but it wasn't like him to take such advantage of an innocent. She had been distraught, and he had enough experience to tamp down his desire, no matter how powerful it was.

"Kate. We have to stop. I have to take you home." He didn't add that stopping was one of the hardest things that he'd ever had to do. He just waited, watching her violet eyes slowly focus and reason reenter her body.

Kate only nodded, too embarrassed to speak. She sat up slowly, putting enough space between them so she could think. She knew that if Ben hadn't pulled away, she wouldn't have been the one to stop. When he held her in his arms, her common sense vanished, and her actions were ruled by pure sensation. What must he think of her, to have lost such control? She could only guess: a provincial miss, swooning every time he looked in her direction.

"Kate?"

"Yes?"

"I'm sorry, you know. That wasn't very well done of me. I usually demonstrate a bit more restraint." His eyes smiled as he said this, but for once his smile was not at her expense. He seemed truly apologetic, and his admission helped put her at ease. So he lost control, too, eh?

"I am usually more restrained myself," she replied with mock solemnity.

"Usually? My, my, I had no idea you found yourself in this position so often," he retorted, enjoying the color that returned to her cheeks. "Come. It's time to go. My driver should be back by now."

Ben helped Kate rise from the sofa, and waited in silence as she donned her pelisse. He pulled his watch from his pocket and swore silently. It was nearly five o'clock in the morning, and Rob's servants were bound to be stirring by the time they reached the town house.

"You know, Lord Sinclair, you never answered my question."

"I think it's all right if you call me by my Christian name, Kate."

She blushed, feeling foolish once more. "Benjamin."

"Ben will do. Now what was your question?"

"Where are we?"

"Where are we?" he repeated, looking her over distractedly. "Here—draw your hood a bit tighter."

"Why? And why won't you answer my question?"

"I'll answer both questions, m'dear. First, we're in a gaming house, and second, I reckon you'd rather not be recognized on our way out." He didn't add that the upper floors of the house occasionally served as a brothel as well.

"We're in a…a house of ill repute?" Kate was completely shocked and, she had to admit, more than a little bit delighted. This *was* an evening of firsts. She began scanning the room avidly, trying to absorb as many details as possible.

"You needn't look so pleased about it," Ben said wryly, glancing over his shoulder as he opened the door and perused the hallway for passersby.

"There can't be anyone here who'd recognize me," she protested.

"You'd be surprised. Let's go," he said, grabbing her hand and pulling her into the hall.

Either the night was too late or the morning was too early—Kate wasn't quite sure how to make the distinction—but there didn't seem to be a soul about. Her mischievous side began to surface.

"My, that's quite a painting," she said, pausing to point at a large-scale portrait of a reclining nude. "The artist has captured her…red hair…most effectively."

"Time *is* of the essence, Kate."

"Of course." She kept walking, but wasn't about to

let her one and only visit to such a place end so quickly. Curiosity also got the best of her.

"Um…so what were you doing in a house of ill repute?"

"Certainly not what I came here to do."

"Oh." She didn't ask for clarification. She could only imagine what sorts of nefarious activities her presence had interrupted, and wasn't quite sure how she felt about it.

Ben smiled to himself, hoping to have shut her up with that remark. Fine time for her to start getting chatty. If they wasted any more time leaving, it would be daylight before they reached Rob's.

After descending a wide staircase, they approached the door. A butler opened it, and Kate paused to give him a thorough once-over, noting that he looked more like a pugilist than a butler. Ben prompted her with a yank, and they were out in the cold once more, the dark sky just beginning to give way to the first pink traces of dawn. Thankfully, his carriage was waiting. His coachman alighted and opened the door, but before Kate could thank him, Ben unceremoniously hoisted her off the ground and tossed her into the carriage.

"Take us to Lord Gordon's, Winters, and hurry, please."

"Yes, my lord."

Ben climbed into the carriage and settled into his seat. Winters shut the door, enveloping his passengers in total darkness. Not dark enough, unfortunately, for Ben to miss the sullen glare Kate turned on him. He chose to ignore it, however, and closed his eyes, hoping to fall asleep in the twenty minutes it would take to reach Robert's house.

Kate watched him, too wide-awake herself even to think about sleep. She was annoyed with his treatment of her, but was not above admitting that perhaps she deserved it. There was a time for cheekiness, and now, apparently, was not it.

Nevertheless, she huffed loudly, hoping that he would open at least one eye. But as that elicited no response, she decided to change tactics.

"Ben?" she asked softly.

He cracked open an eye, pleased at the way his name sounded when she said it. He hadn't really been sleeping; like Kate, he was far too tense to contemplate rest seriously. But he knew that his composure would bother her, assumed though it may have been. And for some reason, he felt like bothering her.

"Ben, what happened to my carriage?"

"While he was waiting for us, Winters brought it round to Robert's. It should be tucked neatly into his carriage house by now…there's a slim chance that it will have arrived before your brother returned home, and in that case nothing will have appeared amiss."

Kate nodded uncertainly. "I told my maid not to wait up for me, and none of the other servants were to wait up either…I suppose there *is* a chance that no one will have missed me."

Ben hoped to God that this was the case. He had visions of Robert running his hands through his hair, pacing, and polishing his pistols as he frantically waited for his sister to return. He could only imagine what Robert would think when she finally showed up with *him*.

The carriage rattled along for another ten minutes,

then slowed to a stop in front of the town house. Kate peered out of the window, noting that there seemed to be an unusual number of lights burning in the windows. Her hopes began to sink.

"Will you tell him?" she asked, turning around and pleading with her eyes.

"He'll certainly need to be apprised."

"I understand. But will you tell him *everything?*"

Ben shook his head, finally understanding the true nature of her question. "I'm sure he'd rather not know *everything,* nor do I care to inform him. We'll tell him only what we must, all right?"

She nodded, wondering how she'd get out of this fix. Truth be told, she'd be happier if Robert didn't know anything about the evening at all. He'd only start asking the same questions that Ben had, wondering why anyone would go to such lengths for a simple robbery. But at the same time, she wanted to stay safe…oh, there was no easy answer.

Winters opened the carriage door, and Kate steeled herself for a very long walk to her brother's front door.

Kate had resigned herself to meeting her brother at the front door. She was not prepared, however, to have the door opened by Robert, his friend Frederick Northing and Charlotte. Just beyond them, sprawled out in a chair, was Charlotte's father, the Earl of Tyndale. Charlotte's chaperone, Kate supposed. Apparently her brother felt he might need reinforcements.

"Where the hell have you been?" Robert barked.

Kate had never heard her jovial brother speak in such

a tone—not even when, at the tender age of eight, she'd glued the soles of his riding boots to his bedroom floor. She felt immediately guilty. It wasn't her fault that she'd nearly been abducted, but she had taken her sweet time getting back home. She opened her mouth to reassure him of her safety, but it was at this moment that he spotted Ben standing beside her.

"You bloody bastard!"

Before Kate knew what was happening, Robert leaped out the door to tackle Ben, and the two of them ended up rolling round in the front lawn, fists flying.

"Robert! Robbie! Stop—you don't understand!" Her pleas had no effect as Robert took another swing at Ben, who retaliated by planting his fist in her brother's stomach.

She turned to Frederick to plead, "Can you make them stop?"

"Why would I want to do that? Seems justified if you ask me."

"Charlotte?" Kate's face was desperate as she turned to her brother's fiancée, not fathoming how the petite girl could possibly stop the two large men from maiming each other. "Charlotte, please make them stop, if you can. Ben did nothing wrong—he saved my life."

Charlotte considered this for a moment, and then nodded and turned to Robert. Without raising her voice, she said, "Robert…Robert…you have to stop. Kate needs you to listen."

He looked up at her, giving Ben enough time to shove him off and pin him down to the ground.

"Oh, no! Don't you start being unreasonable, Benjamin Sinclair! Get off him!" Charlotte was truly angry now and added emphasis to her words by grabbing the nearest object, a book, and hurling it at Ben's head with all her might. Luckily for his already tender head, she missed, but the noise of the book hitting the ground was deafening.

Kate was the first to break the stunned silence. "Well, Charlotte, I didn't suppose that you really would be able to stop them. Appears I underestimated you."

Charlotte smoothed her gown and tucked a strand of dark hair behind her ear, serenity, dignity and composure restored. "Yes, you did. Now first things first—are you all right, Kate? Tell us what happened. And you," she said, fixing Ben with an imperious glare as he rose from the ground, "don't interrupt."

Ben nodded curtly, although he and Robert continued to glower at each other, and Kate began to answer questions.

Chapter Six

It was about two o'clock in the afternoon when Kate finally awoke and made her way downstairs. Only Robert was in the breakfast room, drinking a cup of tea and perusing the paper. Upon seeing his sister, he put the paper down, smiling gently. Clearly he'd been waiting for her.

"How are you doing this morning…er, afternoon?"

"Well as can be expected," she replied briefly, feeling deeply uncomfortable. She didn't want to discuss her late-night activities again, so rather than answering Robert's question in detail, she walked to the side table and began heaping her plate with more food than she could possibly eat. She stretched this activity out for over a minute, hoping the topic of conversation would have passed into more pleasant territory by the time she sat down.

But when she finally turned around, her brother was still looking at her. He was simply too perceptive. "Do you want to tell me what happened between you two?

And don't try to tell me that nothing happened—I know Ben too well to believe that. Only a fool would miss the way you two were looking at each other."

"Nothing happened, really," she mumbled, coloring intensely as she took her seat.

"Listen, Katie, you have nothing to feel ashamed about. You hardly *asked* to be carried off. It wasn't your fault that you ended up…where you ended up. Sinclair should never have brought you in there. He should have taken you home right away."

"Well, he did, all right? I…I fainted and had to recover."

Kate was being evasive, and she knew that Robert was well aware of that fact. She didn't care. She was *not* going to go into any details with her brother. She had some pride left.

He just shrugged, knowing he wouldn't be able to get any more out of her than that. "Would you like to know what I've been doing this morning?"

She nodded eagerly, hoping he had good news to report.

"I found Owens…well, one of the grooms found him anyway. Poor chap was trussed up and locked in a closet in the carriage house. Don't worry," he held up his hand to still her questions, "he's fine. Just a little bit bruised."

"Why, that's brilliant news! I've been so worried!"

"It's good news for Owens, but it complicates things. You see, if he'd been found at the Bannisters', or in their vicinity, then we could safely assume that this was a random crime. Thieves have been known to prey on the carriages at *ton* parties, so this wouldn't be that unusual. The thief would have given Owens a good rap on the head, hid him in the bushes and got on with it."

"But because Owens was found in our carriage house, that means that whoever did this was near our house, and might know where we live. He must have driven me to the party, too…is it possible I wouldn't have noticed?"

"Well, it would seem so. Your mind was probably on other things. But I don't want to alarm you, Katie. I don't think anyone is trying to hurt you, or us, specifically. He probably saw our carriages getting ready for an evening out and assumed that we had well-lined pockets."

"Surely he would have robbed me en route rather than waiting around all night?"

"Well…there weren't many people around to witness the abduction so early in the morning, were there? That wouldn't have been the case if he'd tried to rob you on the way to the ball."

"I suppose."

"Still, though, it's a bit chilling to think of someone lurking about my carriage house like that. Unfortunately, Owens didn't get a look at his face."

Kate nodded, her own flesh crawling at the thought. She'd definitely been distracted when she'd left for the party, fretting about whether she would see Ben and how to react if she did. It was perfectly conceivable that she simply hadn't noticed who was driving the carriage. "We should notify the authorities, I suppose."

He nodded his head. "Yes, I will…but I think I should do it alone. I want your name to stay out of this ordeal. The damage it could do to your reputation, especially if your…um, late-night excursion became known, would be irreparable. I'm certain it was no more than a misconceived robbery. We'll tell them only what we must and be very careful with ourselves for the next few days."

She nodded slowly, wondering if she should confess her suspicions about Andrew Hilton. In the end, she held back, hoping that Robert was right. His explanation seemed reasonable enough, and if she weren't already suspicious, she'd assume no more herself. Mentally laying the subject to rest, she said, "Well, I suppose there's little else we can do. No sense in dwelling on it."

"Said like a true Sutcliff."

"What are your plans for the day?"

"Thought I'd try out my new curricle…I've been meaning to take Charlotte for a drive in the park, but the weather's been so abysmal lately. Did you notice the sun?"

Kate looked out the window. The sky was blue and cloudless, and sunlight streamed into the breakfast room. It looked glorious, and frankly, no, she hadn't even noticed.

"It does look beautiful," she said wistfully.

"I'd invite you along, sister dear, but…well, you understand. It's bad enough that her lady's maid has to come along." He paused and grinned unabashedly when Kate sniffed in distaste. She had no problem understanding her brother. "Perhaps you can dredge up a suitor to take you out," he suggested mischievously.

"I have correspondence to attend to, thank you, and I don't have any suitors," she gritted out through her teeth. Her brother was being altogether too cheerful.

"I suppose, then, that you wouldn't be interested in the roses you received just this morning—"

"No."

"Don't you even want to see who they're from?"

"Hang him, whoever he is." They could only be from Philip Bannister, and she just couldn't get excited about that prospect.

"I see. Mind if I give them to Charlotte? Hate to see them go to waste."

"Go right ahead," Kate said, "although it's not so romantic, you know, giving your lady fair someone else's flowers."

"Charlotte is a practical girl. She'll understand. That's why we get on so well."

"You? Practical?" Kate asked with a smile as she rose from the table. "I'm not so sure if I agree, but if you prefer to think so, then go right ahead."

She turned to make her exit, satisfied with her patronizing tone. When she reached the door she turned again, hoping to get in one last jab at Robert. But it was too late—his spoon was at the ready, loaded with half a buttered crumpet. He cocked it back and fired, sending her running from the room with a squeal. The crumpet hit the door just as she closed it behind her.

Robert grinned smugly. He rose from his seat, picked up his gloves and headed for the front door. On his way out, he grabbed the large bouquet of white roses and plucked the note from them. Without reading it, he placed it on the table by the door and left.

Two minutes later, Mary entered. She had planned on bringing the flowers to Kate's room and frowned at their absence. All that remained on the table was a small envelope. She picked it up.

Mary knew she shouldn't. She really did. But she slipped her finger under the seal, opened the note, and read it anyway. Her eyes grew wide and a pleased smile touched her lips.

She put the note into her pocket and left the hall with a renewed spring to her step.

The drive through Hyde Park was largely silent. Charlotte was too tired from the previous night's escapade to speak much, and Robert was brooding. At least he'd managed to convince her maid to sit outside, next to his driver, leaving him alone inside the carriage with Charlotte. That should have made things all right.

But then she began to giggle.

He raised one supercilious brow.

Charlotte stifled her laughter to explain, but continued to smile. "I'm sorry—I was just thinking about Kate…the look on your face when she told you that she'd spent the better part of the evening in a gaming house!"

And she began to giggle again.

Robert did not so much as smile. In fact, he had been thinking about the same subject and it didn't amuse him at all. "I hardly see any humor in this situation, Charlotte, and please refrain from mentioning it again. I just hope to God that all of London doesn't know about last night's stunt. That would devastate her chances of making a suitable match."

Charlotte turned more serious. "I don't think anyone will know. Ben said they saw no one as they left."

He sighed. "Gossip has a way of getting out. I suppose I'll find out sure enough when I visit my club tonight."

"Pessimist," she said, nestling herself into his shoulder. "Everything will be fine, Kate will get married, and it will all end happily ever after. And, well, if it doesn't exactly happen that way, everything will still be fine. She's a pretty capable person, you know. For such a protective brother, I'm surprised you allow her all the freedom that you do. Although truth be told," Charlotte added, turning her eyes up toward Robert's face, "that's one of the reasons I love you most. Any brother who allows his little sister to run the family business must be first-rate. It makes me hope we have many daughters."

He rolled his eyes, but there was true affection in his expression. "I hate to shatter your illusions, Charlotte, but you overestimate my tolerance. Believe me, it's simply a much easier task to let her do as she pleases than to try and stop her." He put his arm around her and pulled her tight. He'd told her his entire family history, as she would soon be a part of the family as well. The company itself was no secret, but it certainly wasn't something that the family advertised; although it wasn't altogether unusual for aristocrats to dabble in commerce, it was downright unseemly for them to take it as seriously as his family did. The fact that Kate had actually *run* the business—and eventually might do so again—was so scandalous it went beyond thinking.

"Besides," he went on, "I've never been all that interested in boats. If it were up to me, I'd sell the company altogether."

"Kate would hate you if you did that."

"Probably, but there's no reason to worry. Her sole

ownership of the company is a well-protected secret, so why not indulge her?"

"What on earth will she do when she marries? Her husband will have to know, and most husbands wouldn't be as tolerant about her…er, hobby, as you are."

"She'll probably grow out of it."

Charlotte raised an eyebrow, not believing it for a minute. "Will she? I wonder if she doesn't care about it so much that she's getting married just so she can be in control once more."

"No…even if that were partially the case, that wouldn't explain her hurry. I think she's just being sensible for once…probably realizing that she wants to be a wife and mother. It's my good example, getting married, you know. She's always looked up to me."

Charlotte interrupted him with a snort.

Rob suppressed a smile at her obvious irritation. "As I say, she's already growing out of it. When she does marry, I'm sure she'll give up the company for good and let her husband run things."

"You're fatuous. I take back all the nice things I said about you earlier."

Rob's grin broke through. "I'm trying to annoy you."

"You're succeeding. I think you underestimate your sister. She cares very much about her company. I admire her, as should you, you…you dilettante."

"Now stop. I'm teasing. And it's *you* who underestimate her. As you've guessed, my father's will said nothing about preventing her husband from gaining control of the company by marrying her. So she had our solicitor draw up a very explicit contract, full of stipulations and big words, for said husband to sign. When that's taken care of, I suppose her husband will be a figurehead, of sorts…the poor, unsuspecting sot. And to think she had the nerve to call *me* unromantic."

"Why ever did she say that?"

Robert looked guiltily at the flowers in Charlotte's lap. In that instant, he vowed he'd buy her flowers every day for the rest of her life.

"Just because she's my sister," he grumbled.

Charlotte smiled. "I hope there isn't any bad blood between you and Ben because of last night. He was really just an innocent bystander."

"I somehow doubt that."

"Does that mean you noticed the attraction between them, too?"

"Charlotte? I'm sorry—*what* did you say?"

"You heard me, Robert."

He turned to look at her with very clear, very serious eyes. "I'm wishing I hadn't. Charlotte, you may not play matchmaker here. You have no idea how unsuitable he is. In the first place, he has no intention of marrying, and in the second place…well, blast it all, he's my best friend. I know *everything* that he's done."

"Pretty dastardly, huh?"

"You cannot even begin to fathom. He's too attached to his life the way it is, without anyone to tie him down to one spot. He spends half the year traveling, for God's sake, and I can't see him changing that for anyone. Even if he *could* be convinced to marry, he'd make a bloody rotten husband."

"Well, I believe in reformation. I think she should set

her cap for him. You said yourself that you hope the man she marries likes boats. Doesn't Ben have some sort of shipping company?"

"That hardly signifies in this instance. I think I should thrash him, after all."

"You will not," Charlotte said, looking up into his face and waiting for a kiss. Kissing was a surefire way to cheer him up. "You know, maybe Kate won't find marriage so distasteful."

Rob leaned down and kissed her hard on the lips, damning the fact that they had just arrived at the Bannisters' front steps. "Personally, I can hardly wait."

When Ben had left Robert's house early that morning, his day had grown steadily worse. By ten o'clock that evening, he was quite drunk and in a foul mood. He had started drinking with supper, and had not yet stopped.

He was seated at a corner table at White's, not talking to anyone and not looking as if he would like to. He'd actually cringed when he'd seen his reflection in one of the many mirrors that hung from the walls of the club. He couldn't blame everyone for giving him such a wide berth—he really did look ominous, with circles beneath his eyes and his cravat askew. Damn that bastard Jones.

He usually got on with Simon Jones quite well, but tonight the chap's humor had rubbed him the wrong way. Indeed, it was only because they were friends that Simon had felt comfortable enough to take liberties.

"So, I hear you had quite a romp with Katherine Sutcliff. Can't say that I blame you, even if she *is* Robert's sister."

"Where'd you hear this nonsense?" Ben had asked.

"It's been making the rounds all day. Let's see...I guess it was Peter Weatherton who told me—said he saw her get out of your carriage in front of her brother's early this morning. Come, you can't deny it. You were definitely holding her rather tightly last night at the Bannisters'...just let me know when you're through, though. It'd be a shame to waste such a pretty thing on you alone."

Ben had hit him. Hard. A closed-fisted blow to the face, making blood spray from his nose. Simon staggered back, holding his hand to his nose.

"What the hell's the matter with you, Sinclair?"

Ben didn't know what was wrong with him, but he took another menacing step forward, ready to strike Simon again.

Simon stepped back, knocking over a chair as he did so. "No thanks, Sinclair. I'm not going to tangle with you when you're in this mood. See you when you're sober." He turned on his heel, wasting no time to exit.

Ben had sat back down, lost in his thoughts. Bloody hell. It couldn't get much worse. He'd been in this situation before, had had his name connected with countless other women. Usually he would just shrug off the scandal. Marriage was not for him, and he wasn't about to get tricked into it. He'd worked rather hard creating a life for himself in which he could climb aboard ship whenever he felt like it and travel to some new part of the world. That freedom meant almost everything to him, and every relationship he'd so far had with a woman had caused him, after only a short while, to want to escape.

So why couldn't he just shrug off this incident like all the others? Why the hell did he just now completely lose his temper? Sure, Simon was being a bastard, but Ben could admit that his own scruples were hardly much better. Hitting him was inexcusable, not to mention an admission of guilt.

But Simon had bloody well made him angry, and he knew that this situation was different. This time it was Robert's sister, and his problems were compounded because, blast it all, Ben realized that he actually liked the girl. She didn't make him want to run away and he wasn't exactly sure why. She was argumentative and far too sensitive, two qualities that manifested themselves every time she hurled object or insult at his head. But she was also intelligent, entertaining and, damn it, beautiful as hell.

It was almost laughable to think about, but he wasn't really *interested* in most of the women he slept with; *dis*interest was more like it. These women fulfilled a purely sexual need, and when he was done with them, he never looked back. Unfortunately, Kate Sutcliff just didn't fit that mold.

He still wasn't about to do the honorable. He'd done nothing wrong, had just kissed the girl, for God's sake. But even as he tried to justify his actions, Ben knew he was kidding himself. That had hardly been *just* a kiss, and if he had the chance to do the evening over, he probably would have made love to Kate on that sofa, damning the consequences. She'd be compromised one way or the other, as he now knew. He felt his body grow hard just thinking about her, her luscious curves, the way she'd responded to his touch…

"Looks like you're having some pretty heavy thoughts. Care if I join you?"

Ben flushed, his thoughts actually being rather lascivious, as Robert pulled out a chair to take a seat opposite from him.

"Came by to see what kind of damage was done last night," Robert went on, disinterestedly brushing a fleck of lint from his sleeve. "Is the gossip mill grinding away as usual?"

"If you haven't already heard the latest, you will soon enough."

"Hmm."

Ben looked hard at his friend. He was being far too nonchalant, and if last night was any indication, Robert didn't take his sister's reputation lightly. Even after she'd pointed out that Ben was essentially an innocent bystander, he'd continued to shoot him murderous looks, presumably for jeopardizing her reputation in the first place by dancing with her so closely—*that* much had nothing to do with circumstance; *that* was free will. Although Ben could now admit that dancing with Kate was a rather stupid risk to take, he couldn't seem to help himself at the time.

"You're taking this rather well," he offered.

Robert shrugged. "There's not much else to do. You don't have any ideas, do you?"

"No," Ben answered warily, suspicious of the direction things seemed to be taking.

"You know, she's here to get married."

"Aren't they all," Ben said wryly, and immediately wondered why this should bother him so much.

"You haven't exactly helped her goal, Ben."

"I won't marry her, if that's what you're getting at."

Robert had never looked so appalled. "Well, good God, you don't think I want you to marry her, do you? Perish the thought. I can't think of a worse choice."

"Thank you," Ben replied tightly. "So what do you want?"

He was all seriousness now. "What I want is for you to stay the hell away from her. You can't tell me that you're not attracted to her, or that nothing happened last night. I know you too well."

Ben knew it was futile to deny this accusation. "A blind man would be attracted to her, Robbie, but rest assured, I don't plan to complicate her life or yours."

Robert nodded deliberately. "See that you don't." Then he began pouring himself a glass of sherry, ready to move on and hoping to smooth over the acrimony that had developed between them. "It's settled, then. D'you want another drink?"

Ben nodded, watching the amber liquid sparkle as it filled his glass. "So, have the police learned anything about last night?"

"Not really. There's not a sign of the man anywhere. He pretty much vanished into the night. Seems it was just a simple robbery gone awry."

"Just a simple robbery?"

"Well, all right, not simple. It was rather elaborate. But just a robbery all the same, I'm sure."

Ben nodded, although he was not entirely convinced. He had a strange, niggling sense that there was something more complicated than robbery going on. He didn't know why he was suspicious—perhaps because Kate had seemed so scared. He'd expect that from another woman, but not from her…she'd even fainted, for God's sake.

He forced the problem to the back of his mind, however, letting the subject drop. It wasn't his concern, so there was no sense in worrying about it. No sense in thinking about Katherine Sutcliff at all, in fact. Thoughts of her irritated him in all the wrong ways.

But as the night wore on and Ben was visited again and again with visions of rich, copper hair and dark, violet eyes, he realized that forgetting Kate wouldn't be so easy.

Chapter Seven

The fat, striped ribbon on Kate's straw bonnet tickled her face terribly, but it would be unseemly to scratch whilst promenading in St. James's Park. It was unusually warm for springtime, and she was surrounded by similarly uncomfortable people. She didn't really want to be there—she'd hoped to spend the day at home, sitting in a comfortable chair with her feet tucked up, having her tea. Charlotte, however, had all but insisted that she come with her to the park for a picnic. Mary—who'd been enlisted as chaperone—had done her part by haranguing Kate mercilessly that morning when she'd clung to her quilt and refused to leave her bed. It was almost as if they were working in collusion. When Kate had tried to delay their excursion by an hour so they would miss the heat of high noon, neither woman would listen to her protests. They were definitely acting strangely.

Kate had no idea why they should be *so* adamant, but supposed it might be due to the fact that she'd been avoiding most social outings recently. Her eventful evening with Benjamin Sinclair had caused a minor scandal, and she'd simply been too embarrassed to leave the house until it subsided. But now, over two weeks later, the rumors had mostly dissipated—instead, everyone was talking about Samantha Bainbridge and her mysteriously expanding waistline. She hadn't even seen Ben since that night, a good thing since it meant she hadn't had to face the temptation of seeing him again either. Still, it also meant that she'd had to face the gossip alone, and she couldn't help resenting him slightly for that.

"Ah, Kate, it's glorious," Charlotte said, linking arms with her and inhaling deeply. "Aren't you pleased you came?"

"Certainly, Charlotte. And Mary seems to be enjoying herself, too. Are you not, Mary?" She looked over her shoulder as she asked this question. Mary, who'd formerly been so enthusiastic about the outing, straggled a few paces behind, discreetly wiping sweat from her brow. She made a face at Kate and didn't answer.

The plan was a picnic by the lake, and Charlotte had overseen everything. An impeccable white linen quilt lay folded in a wicker hamper, along with silver cutlery and a dainty lunch of cucumber sandwiches, chicken, fruit and cake. She'd even packed extra bread for the swans…although Kate had noticed Mary leave that bit of ballast by the side of the road. She was carrying the heavy thing, after all.

The park was crowded, and Charlotte frowned slightly as they approached the lake and scanned it for the perfect picnic spot. "We cannot stop here. There are simply too many people around."

"It isn't that bad, Charlotte. I don't think we'll find anything better today."

"No, Kate," she said firmly, "I do not like to be overlooked. Come along."

The perfect spot was finally located a long quarter of an hour later, on the far side of the lake. It was really quite secluded, a surprising treat for one of the royal parks in the spring. Mary spread out the blanket and began unpacking their basket. Charlotte perused the setting with satisfaction, her hand over her eyes to shield them from the sun.

"I say," she said after a moment, gazing across the lake. "Is that Lady Danbury?"

Kate looked, too. The woman's features were hard to make out at such a distance, but she did not look familiar. "Um…I'm not sure. I don't think so."

"But it is! Oh, Kate, I have something to tell her. Really, I *must* dash off for a minute. You won't mind, will you?" She phrased it as a question, but it wasn't, really.

"No…but I don't think that's Lady Danbury."

Charlotte ignored her. "I will only be a few minutes, darling. Do start your lunch without me." She took a step as if to leave but then hesitated for a moment, chewing her lip. "Kate, I'm afraid Mary must come with me. I cannot be seen walking alone. You will be all right here, will you not? No one is likely to come by."

Kate shrugged. Their picnic spot was protected by the lake on one side and by a dense crescent of trees on the other. "I'll be fine. Give Lady Danbury my best…if it is Lady—"

"It is, Kate. I'm certain. We'll return soon."

Kate sat down on the blanket and watched them walk purposefully off. It would take them at least twenty minutes to return. Very strange behavior indeed.

Alone at last, she took off her hat with a sigh of relief and lay back on the quilt. Everything considered, her life was progressing favorably…things could be worse, at any rate. Although her name hadn't survived unscathed, Philip Bannister hadn't been bothered by her slightly damaged reputation, largely because Charlotte had thoroughly explained to him the unusual circumstances of that evening. Although Kate had hoped to have a larger pool of suitors, he was the only one to emerge so far. Charlotte assured her that he was certain to propose by the end of the season.

There had also been no further incidents, making Kate think that her attempted abduction was just a random and isolated act after all. Perhaps a highwayman, as Robert had suggested. No more, no less.

For the moment, at least, she could do nothing but close her eyes and enjoy the sun.

But then a rustle in the bushes behind her caused her to open her eyes and sit up with a start. She turned, expecting to see Mary returning to retrieve some forgotten item.

Instead she saw a man. Medium height and graying, sandy hair…an acceptable if not truly fashionable suit. Something about him was vaguely familiar, but Kate simply could not place his face. He removed his hat and opened his mouth to speak, but another noise, this time coming from the opposite direction, drew her gaze away.

This time, it was a more familiar figure: Benjamin

Sinclair, looking just as surprised to see her as she was to see him.

"Hello."

Kate nodded, blushing. "Oh—" She turned quickly to acknowledge the other man, but by that time he'd vanished.

Ben moved forward somewhat reluctantly. "Odd chap. Turned and left the moment he saw me. Do you know him?"

"I'm not sure…he must have accidentally wandered this way."

"And delicately left the moment he realized he'd stumbled on a young lady alone?" Ben suggested, sitting on a rock to face her. Obviously he had no plans to be so tactful.

Kate rolled her eyes.

"Your secret admirer, then?"

She snorted this time. "That is highly doubtful. Most potential admirers seem to be avoiding me."

"That's my fault, is it?"

It wasn't, really. He hadn't been the one to abduct her and it wasn't fair to blame him for the consequences. She shook her head guiltily.

"You're not *really* alone here, are you?" he asked, looking at the capacious picnic hamper.

"I'm with Charlotte…only something rather urgent took her away for a—" She broke off, suddenly suspicious. "She didn't tell you to come here, did she?"

"Sorry?"

"Charlotte told you to come here!" Kate exclaimed in outrage. "She just cannot stop meddling. That's why she was so insistent that we should come here today…that we should sit in this spot in particular. She planned this!"

Ben looked a bit taken aback. "Charlotte doesn't tell me to do anything, Kate. And I hate to inform you, but I'm still pretty much anathema where your brother is concerned. He's yet to fully forgive me for that night…and I don't think Charlotte would dare go against his wishes."

Kate knew without a doubt that Charlotte would, but Ben seemed to be telling the truth. It was highly unlikely that he'd have wanted to seek her out, anyway, and she blushed at her naiveté for even suggesting such a thing. "You've just come for a stroll, then?"

He nodded. "I was returning home, actually… thought I'd stop at the lake first, though. It looked so peaceful. The water always has a way of restoring order to my mind."

She smiled and looked out at the lake—he was sitting much too close, and if she were to look at him she'd go all to pieces. He was speaking to her as if she was a friend…it was at once odd and extremely pleasurable. "I agree. I've missed the ocean terribly since moving to London. The lake in St. James's Park, fond as I am of it, is a poor substitute. I can never understand how my brother can live here year round, having grown up so close to the coast. I don't think I could do it. Perhaps you can better understand it, living in London as well."

"Then I should surprise you," he answered with a smile. "I only spend about four months of the year in town. I split the rest of the year between my father's home in Hampshire—not far, in fact, from the Bannisters' country seat. The rest of the year I spend on a boat."

"A boat?"

"A few years back, you see, I was foolish enough to think it would be a lark to try my hand at the shipping business, and now I'm obliged to make sure that my company doesn't go into debt. Actually," he lowered his voice and leaned in close, grinning conspiratorially, "it's just an excuse to travel."

Robert had mentioned this fact about Ben once, several years ago, but Kate had actually forgotten about it until that moment. In fact, she could remember resenting him at the time, assuming that his business was a typical diversion of some spoiled, dilettante lord—*she'd* have given anything to be in his place. But hearing him speak so candidly made her suddenly suspect that he really did care and that, just maybe, they might share some interests after all.

"Where on earth did you get the idea to begin a shipping company?" she asked, and then realized that her question sounded rather rude. "Not that there is anything wrong with it…it's just an unusual occupation for a lord, is all."

"Well, after I finished university, I traveled a bit…to Greece and Rome, mainly, like the rest of my contemporaries. But while the rest of them, your brother included, were seasick for most the way, I suddenly found that I felt better than I had in years. I felt like I had a purpose. So my love of the sea was born."

"And that was that?"

"That was that. You know, it always surprises me that Robert isn't more involved in your family's business. I've even offered to buy it from him."

"Oh, you have, have you?"

He blinked in surprise. "You needn't sound so defensive. He wouldn't sell it, and I wouldn't know what to do with it anyway. I hardly have the time for another commitment."

"I wasn't being defensive."

Ben sighed. "It was rather nice, fleeting moment though it was, not to argue with you, Kate. Peace—I beg of you. What's in the hamper, by the way?"

"This one next to me?"

"Yes. Is it lunch?"

He looked so hopeful that she had to smile. "A feast. Please, help yourself."

Ben rose from the rock to rummage through the basket, and Kate had to force herself not to stare at him as he walked toward it. Damn. She almost suspected that she picked arguments with him so that she could forget how appealing he was. But now that they had called a truce…

She wasn't even going to let her mind travel down that path. Benjamin Sinclair was an acquaintance. She would be polite to him. At times, she might even permit herself to enjoy his company. But she could *not* take his flirtation too seriously…he probably flirted with every woman he met.

"Kate?"

"Yes?"

"I asked you if you cared for anything from this

basket. Apple…chicken, biscuits…some rather offensive cheese…"

"Apple, please."

Ben took two apples from the basket and returned to his seat on the rock. "How has your season been going?"

She almost choked on her first bite. She'd hardly expected Ben to ask such a polite, bland question, and it put her immediately on her guard. "It is going well, thank you. I trust yours is, too?"

"You forget what the London season is really intended for, Kate. I haven't been having one."

She blushed again. Of course. The season was designed for debutantes and their prospective beaus— not for people like Benjamin Sinclair.

He continued, a touch of sarcasm lacing his voice. "You've actually surprised me, Kate. You confess to very few admirers and yet almost three whole weeks have passed. I'm amazed that you are not already betrothed after such a lengthy time."

From anyone else she might take these words as a compliment, but this statement sounded rather rude coming from him. She shook her head in answer, thinking of Philip's apparently impending proposal. "Almost, perhaps, but not quite."

"But that is still your objective, of course."

"I suppose. It's everyone's objective, isn't it?"

Ben smiled faintly, shaking his head and mimicking her words. "Almost, perhaps, but not quite."

"I see." She had no doubt who the exception was.

"There's really no incentive for me to bother with the season and its dull events. Unlike you, I suppose."

"What do you mean by that?"

"Perhaps there are things—people, maybe—that make these social events more tolerable for you."

Kate wasn't sure why, but she felt as if she were treading on the conversational equivalent of very thin ice. He had tossed his question off casually enough, but something in his eyes, some sudden and inscrutable intensity, made her wonder if his question didn't have an underlying purpose. He seemed to be looking for a specific answer and she wished she knew what he was thinking. "Well…" she replied tentatively, "There is my brother and Charlotte…I haven't been to that many events, really…" She trailed off in embarrassment, unsure of what else to say.

Ben finished his apple and threw the core into the lake. For a moment they were both silent.

"I should go before Charlotte returns," he said, looking at Kate once more and rising.

Kate nodded. "I think so." She couldn't help but feel that something strange had passed between them, something she didn't understand but was powerfully aware of nonetheless. There was a guarded quality to his eyes that she hadn't seen when he'd first arrived.

He said no more. He bowed slightly and left.

When Charlotte and Mary returned a few minutes later, Kate couldn't help but notice the questioning looks they both gave her.

"You've been all right here, have you not, Kate?" Charlotte asked expectantly.

"Yes." It was obvious she was hoping for more of an answer than that but Kate was unwilling to play along.

Damn Charlotte again for her meddling. Clearly she was up to something. She *must* have known that Ben would be there. But if he didn't tell her, then who did? Maybe Robert had inadvertently mentioned something…yet that just didn't make sense.

Charlotte still pressed her. "Nothing unusual has happened?"

"No."

"Oh…well, that's a relief. I was a bit…worried at leaving you here alone for so long. I mean, if someone came across you unchaperoned, why, then it would be a bit scandalous. It might look as if you were waiting for a tryst or something. But I guess if no one saw you…"

Kate merely shrugged and rose to get a cucumber sandwich. Dratted matchmaker. As if she didn't find Ben hard enough to resist without Charlotte's help. She was doomed.

Chapter Eight

September 1817

Kate was seated at her dressing table, looking intently at her reflection in the mirror without really seeing it. She sighed, telling herself again that she should be happy. All told, everything had been going pretty well. Lord Clifford, in fact, had already proposed—an offer that she had graciously declined due to his habits of trying to paw her in dark corners and snorting when he laughed. She also sensed that Philip would propose any day now. Kate wasn't quite sure how she felt about that. She got on with Philip well enough, but knew that under normal circumstances she wouldn't have even considered an offer from him; in an ideal world, she would love, rather than simply like, the man she married. But under her abnormal circumstances, all Kate required was someone she could exist with amicably. By that criterion, Philip's proposal would be a godsend. He was kind, attractive and a dutiful son and brother. She *should* be happy.

But Kate wasn't happy and knew the reason why. God, how she wished she'd never met Benjamin Sinclair. He'd put a definite kink into her well-laid plans. No matter how hard she tried, she couldn't help but compare Philip to Ben, and unfortunately the former came up dreadfully short in the comparison. She didn't know why it mattered—Ben wasn't exactly a candidate for the position of husband, wasn't even a factor in her day-to-day existence. It had been nearly five months since that day in the park, and she hadn't so much as seen him. He'd stayed far away from Robert's town house, and it hurt her more than she cared to admit. She was dying to ask her brother where he'd been, but resisted out of pride and because she knew that he'd only lecture her on Ben's many flaws.

Of course, Kate wasn't quite sure what she would do if she *did* see him again. Probably run and hide. Despite her curiosity about his whereabouts, she was in no hurry to encounter him again and had actually done her part to avoid him, too. She'd steered clear of any events that he might have attended, an easy enough task since he himself confessed to shun most balls.

"Are you ready, m'dear?"

Kate turned around to smile at Mary. They were preparing to leave for the Bannisters' country estate, Peshley, where the wedding would be held. Every guest had been invited to spend the week there with promises of beautiful autumn weather and prime hunting.

Kate was dressed. She was packed. And still she didn't feel quite ready to depart.

"I suppose."

"Well, you couldn't look lovelier. Your brother, on the other hand, is a sorry case this morning. Humph. He was out all hours last night."

"Yes—it was his last night out on the town as a bachelor. Apparently his friends wanted to toast him on the way out."

"It was disgraceful, whatever it was. You should have seen him, stumbling home. Drunk as a loon, he was, and smelling like a distillery. Don't think he would have made it home at all if it weren't for his friend helping him…oh, what's his name—you know, dear, that terribly handsome one with the golden hair?"

"Be—" Kate began to answer, but caught herself in time. She fixed her maid with a fulminating glare. "Mary! Are you trying to trick me?"

"Trick you? Heavens, no," she avowed as she began to whisk about the room, tidying up as she moved. "I only asked a simple question."

Kate sighed. Mary was *never* simple. Sharp as a tack was more like it. "His name, as if you've really forgotten, is Benjamin Sinclair. But he may not be the man you refer to because he isn't necessarily all that handsome. Only slightly."

"Only slightly? I see. And here I thought he was the gentleman you've been sighing about all season. It must be I who is mistaken."

"Sighing? Ladies do not sigh, Mary, especially this lady. And even if I did, I wouldn't do it over *him*."

"Oh, of course. D'you suppose Lord Sinclair will be at Peshley this week?"

Kate had been dwelling on that thought almost obsessively, but lied through her teeth. "I haven't been supposing anything at all about the matter. But, yes, now that you mention it, he probably will be there. He's one of Robert's best friends, after all, even though he's been pretty scarce lately."

"Maybe he's avoiding you."

"I don't think so. He'd actually have to think about me in order to avoid me. It's not avoidance—it's total disregard."

"And you haven't been thinking about him, either?"

"On occasion, yes, but in the main, no."

Mary, of course, could see right through her. "It might make you feel a little better to know that he hasn't even been in town for the past few months. He's been in Hampshire to visit his father."

Kate could only stare dumbfounded for a moment. "Mary, how on earth do you know all these things?"

"Oh, I heard it from Mr. Perch, who heard it from Dolly, the upstairs maid. She heard it from Lord Sinclair's driver, one Mr. Winters. He's sweet on her."

Kate nearly burst out laughing. "Mary, if the British government only knew what a gem they had in you, our problems with Napoleon would never have started. You're a fount of information."

"Yes, well, if I had known that this information would have cheered you up so much, I would have told you when I first heard it—I had only thought, perhaps, that you were trying not to think about Lord Sinclair."

"You mean I *wasn't* thinking about him."

"Yes, of course that's what I meant."

Kate sighed and turned around in her seat at the dressing table. She wasn't quite sure how to take the news about Ben. On one hand, she was relieved to learn that he had been out of town—that meant that he hadn't necessarily been avoiding her. But it also hurt a bit to learn this news from someone else, and to learn it so long after the fact. Her response was illogical. She should be pleased that he'd forgotten her. Yet she felt disappointment and, yes, embarrassment, at the fact that she had to be told by her maid. He'd occupied her every thought, but she clearly hadn't had the same effect on him.

Kate took a deep breath, straightened her shoulders and looked hard at her reflection in the mirror one more time. She normally paid little heed to her appearance, but had to admit that she was looking well. She was wearing a pale green riding habit, and her auburn hair had lightened over the course of the summer, becoming streaked with blond. Tiny amethyst earrings matched her eyes to perfection. Simple, but very becoming.

A new resolve began to set in, and she smiled for the first time that day.

Benjamin Sinclair can rot, she thought. *I'll make him remember me.*

"Well, Mary, I think I finally am ready. Shall we proceed?"

The ride to Peshley took about a day and a half and was fairly uneventful. Both Kate and Robert rode outside most of the way—she enjoying the fresh air and feeling optimistic for the first time in weeks, and he simply too hungover to sit inside the bouncy carriage.

They spent the evening at an inn along the way, and Kate was back to her sunny self, teasing her brother unmercifully for his overindulgence the previous night, and entertaining the small party with stories and jokes.

The next day began with a slight drizzle. They left the inn early and arrived at the Bannisters' estate around ten. Kate was awestruck by the loveliness of their home. Peshley was an ancient manse built of crumbling silver stone—quite picturesque, really. As they made their way up the drive, they passed acres upon acres of rolling lawns, dense woods and misty lakes. She trotted up to Owens—her fast friend ever since that fateful evening—and promised to catch him a large trout in appreciation for his faithful service. He chuckled in surprise.

"Will wonders never cease! So you're a fisherman as well, Miss Sutcliff? Or would that be a fisherlady?"

"Don't you make fun, now, Owens. We take our fishing very seriously in this family. I'll catch you ten trout with one hand tied behind my back!" Kate grinned impishly as she halted her horse in front of the house and dismounted. She breathed deeply, loving the crispness of the country air. It felt wonderful to be away from London, and she began to muse on whether it was actually the city air, and not a certain gentleman, that was responsible for her recent ennui.

Before she could ponder this too long, however, Charlotte came bursting out the front door to welcome them, looking rather harried. She made a beeline toward Kate.

"Kate, darling, I'm so glad to see you! But I have to warn you, there's a lot to do before the rest of the guests show up later this afternoon and I'll need your help! I

hope that everyone arrives in time for a riding party—
do you think the weather will improve? Oh, I do hope
so—I wanted to have supper served outside."

Kate grinned at this barrage. "Slow down, Charlotte!
My goodness. Worry about one thing at a time, please.
Just tell me what I can do to help."

"Would you mind telling the head groom to plan to
have the horses ready at three? You passed the stables
on the way—it's just a brief walk—a lovely walk, really,
and it's hardly raining now."

Kate blinked. When she had offered to help, she'd
assumed that Charlotte would suggest she go calm down
her mother, or something along those lines. Not trudge
down to the stables to converse with the head groom.
Surely the Bannisters had servants to do that sort of thing.

All told, however, she didn't mind. The servants were
probably busy, and she'd prefer the stables to talking to
Lady Tyndale any day.

"All right. I think a walk would be nice."

Charlotte hugged her gratefully. "You're such a dear.
I'll show Mary where to direct your things."

And with that, both Charlotte and Mary were gone.
Kate thought their heads were bent a bit close, as if
some secret were being passed, but shrugged it off as
her imagination; she was a little tired from the ride, and
perhaps she was seeing things.

She began to walk briskly toward the stables, her
optimistic outlook unfazed. She still felt fairly invin-
cible. Her long legs and the spring in her step brought
her quickly to her destination.

Kate had always felt particularly comfortable

around horses. She loved the earthy smells and the sounds of a stable: the soft nickering, the crunching of hay. As she entered the barn, she paused so her eyes could adjust to the dark. A large bay stuck his head out of his door to greet her.

"Well hello, prince. I'm sorry I haven't any treats for you. I didn't have time to get any." She rubbed his slender nose, admiring the stallion's fine lines and glossy coat. "But I promise I'll bring you a carrot when I come back later."

"He'll love you forever for that."

Oh, God. Kate knew that voice as well as if she heard it every day, which she certainly did not. She turned slowly, skin tingling, heart racing, trying to locate that steely resolve of which she'd recently been so proud. She needed something witty to say, some smart retort…

"What?"

Well, that was certainly clever.

Ben stepped out from the shadows, reaching his hand out so the horse could sniff his palm. "Food's the way to this one's heart. But he's dreadfully disloyal…he'll follow just about anyone who's willing to feed him."

"He's yours?"

Ben nodded. "His name's Hubert."

She stared at him blankly, and then burst into laughter. Shocked at her rudeness, she quickly stifled it. "I'm sorry. I didn't mean to laugh. It's a rather unusual name for a horse, is all."

"It's a bloody awful name, is what it is. Laugh all you please."

"Then why don't you change it?"

"Can't. You see, I won Hubert in a wager I made with Fred Northing a few years back. One of the conditions to winning was that Fred got to pick out the name."

"What was the wager about?"

Ben didn't answer, just grinned wickedly, a teasing sparkle in his eyes. Clearly the answer to her question was not meant for a young lady's ears and must therefore be left up to her imagination. Unfortunately, Kate had a rather vivid imagination, and she blushed accordingly.

God, he was dangerous to her composure. His blond hair was windblown and his cravat loosened, and she supposed he'd just come from a bruising ride. Just looking at him made her short of breath—she'd thought he was devastating in formal wear, but he was even more so in his snug riding breeches and Hessian boots. Even his scent made her weak. He was standing too close, so close she fancied she could feel his heat…unless it was the heat of her own indecent thoughts. She stepped back to put more distance between them, fumbling for a way to direct the subject away from lovemaking and safely back to horses.

"I should like to ride him." Oh, you stupid, stupid girl.

"Should you?" Ben raised an elegant eyebrow as he deftly made innuendo out of her innocent words.

She wasn't *exactly* certain what he was talking about, but she'd spent enough time eavesdropping about her father's boatyard as a child to have a pretty good idea. She could have died on the spot and not cared, was actually rather praying that a stray bolt of lightning would strike her down. But having no such luck, Kate stared at the wall, suddenly fascinated by each crack, by every mote of dust. She watched a fly struggle in a spider's web and tried not to read any symbolism as the spider slowly moved in for the kill.

But then God intervened after all.

"Kate—my little lambkin! So wonderful to see you! Charlotte said I'd find you here. My, my, how well you're looking…quite the little woman, aren't you? A bit plumper than when I last saw you in town, hmm?" Charlotte's mother, the Countess of Tyndale, came bursting into the stable: red, round and never a more welcome sight.

"It's wonderful to see you as well, Lady Tyndale, and I'm fine. I trust you're acquainted with Lord Benjamin Sinclair?"

She squinted at Ben in the darkness, frowning as she did so. "Hmm. Yes. Although I do not know that this is where he ought to be. Lord Sinclair, do you belong here unescorted with this young lady?"

"Madam, I am innocent. I was minding my own business when Miss Sutcliff came traipsing along, and lingered with her only because I saw you ambling down the path. I figured I might as well put both my arms to good use and escort you two ladies to the house for lunch. Shall we?" He held out his arms, giving Lady Tyndale his most devastating smile. She quivered like a jelly.

"Why, aren't you a nice young man. You know," she said, turning to him with her most confidential whisper, "I never believed what they said about you."

"No?" It was Ben's turn to whisper. "You should believe them, madam. I'm quite wicked."

Lady Tyndale gasped, but Kate could swear she'd

never seen the woman look more delighted. He'd completely charmed her without even trying, and she had to admit she was more than a little charmed herself.

As the trio wended their way up the path toward the house, one woman on each of Ben's arms, Kate suddenly remembered that she had never spoken to the head groom. She momentarily considered returning to the stables to complete her errand, but it occurred to her that there was no point. Recalling that conspiratorial glance Charlotte had given Mary, Kate realized that the Bannisters' groom knew quite well when he was to prepare the horses. No, Charlotte had sent her to the stables knowing that Ben would be there already. She was at it again.

Chapter Nine

Dinner was served on the lawn, and the linen-draped tables, so heavily laden with food and drink, promised a decadent feast. Kate stood along the edge of the terrace, gazing across the lawn to the lake, golden in the setting sun. She hadn't seen Ben yet that evening. He'd gone along on the hunt that afternoon, but the pace had been such and the people so many that they hadn't had an opportunity to speak. She wasn't sure that he would have spoken to her anyway, given his pattern of flirting with her outrageously and then ignoring her completely.

"You look serene," Philip Bannister observed as he moved up behind her. "Admiring the view?"

Actually, Kate had been imagining a violent and inexplicable tidal wave sweeping up the lawn, scattering all the guests, save one; she smiled, envisioning Benjamin Sinclair riding the crest of a muddy wave all the way back to London.

"Tradition has it that the fish in that lake are magic."

Kate continued to smile and turned toward Philip. "Magic? Why is that?"

"Well, if you catch a fish from that lake and throw it back, whatever you wish for will come true."

"Do you believe it?" she asked, knowing what the answer would be. Philip was far too pragmatic to believe in such stories.

"No. Anyway, I've never so much as seen a fish in that lake—don't think there are any. Though I guess that means it would have to be magic for someone to catch one."

"I plan to try tomorrow."

"What will you wish for if you catch one?"

Kate felt suddenly uncomfortable under his intense gaze. "I never throw fish back. According to my tradition, *that's* bad luck."

He threw back his head and laughed loudly, causing several people to look their way, smiling at the happy couple. She inwardly cringed. She couldn't help but feel somewhat annoyed, knowing that her name was attached to Philip's. The *ton* expected them to announce their betrothal any day, and he, too, had been acting as if it were fait accompli. Because his intentions were so well-known, most other potential suitors had backed off, leaving him as her sole prospect.

Kate suppressed these thoughts with all her might, however, knowing that she must accept her fate. Philip would propose, maybe that night, maybe the next, and she would say yes.

"Come. Let's have a seat," he said, placing his hand on the small of her back and guiding her to a table where several of his acquaintances were seated. Kate knew them all: nice enough sorts, but boring. There were only two seats left, one at each end of the table—in an act of unprecedented and probably not to be repeated informality, Lady Tyndale had eschewed a seating arrangement. Kate sat at the end closest to the house, fancying that she'd be the first to safety if the blasted wave ever materialized. She didn't really care for the women seated around her—Melissa Cheswick was a simpering fool and the heavyset Myrna Peters was a society autocrat and notorious gossip. Kate looked longingly across the terrace to the table where her brother and Charlotte were seated, laughing and seemingly having a brilliant time. She knew that, much as she would have liked it, she couldn't sit there. In the first place, Robert merely tolerated Philip—they were hardly what one would call fast friends. In the second place, that was where Ben was most likely to sit.

"…scandalous, isn't it?"

Kate, who hadn't been minding the conversation around her one bit, asked Myrna to repeat herself.

"I said Sarah Thomas is being scandalous as usual. The way she carries on, just because her husband is so old he doesn't even notice her affairs. Just look at her," Myrna said, pointing indiscreetly over Kate's shoulder. Kate couldn't look without turning her head completely, so she just nodded, pretending that she knew exactly what Myrna was talking about and silently vowing that she would look as soon as she got the chance.

That chance came sooner rather than later.

"Here they come! Nobody look," Melissa squealed,

practically leaping from her seat and causing her long-suffering husband to roll his eyes heavenward and pat her condescendingly on the hand.

Kate, for one, looked straightaway, having no idea what could possibly cause such unconcealed excitement. And there was Sarah Thomas, all right, and Benjamin Sinclair, walking together down the path from the house.

"Do you think she's his mistress?" Melissa whispered.

"Don't be vulgar, Melissa. And anyway, I've heard that that one doesn't even keep mistresses, like a respectable chap. Prefers more variety than that."

Kate was listening intently now. She watched the way Sarah delicately rested her hand in the crook of Ben's arm, just as she had herself earlier that day, feeling like a queen because he'd paid attention to her. Sarah was quite pretty, she supposed, if one were attracted to the petite, blond sort of the fluffy female variety. Sarah was the kind of girl who tittered instead of laughed, and Kate disliked her in an instant. Ben, however, was smiling broadly, his head inclined to hear whatever nonsense she uttered. He seemed to be enjoying himself just fine.

Although Kate generally refrained from this sort of gossip, she couldn't help but ask, "So…if she's not his mistress, then does that mean…?"

Myrna snorted indelicately. "Is he sleeping with her? Don't be naive, girl. I'd put money on it. Care to wager?" She leaned forward as she asked this, a competitive glow in her eyes and a feral set to her jaw.

Kate tactfully declined, adding a mental postscript to place Myrna right next to Ben when the big wave struck. She glanced down the table to Philip, wondering if the conversation at his end had gotten half as lively. He was speaking passionately to Lord Sackville, emphasizing his words by pounding on the table. She had seen him thus animated on only a few select occasions, and knew for certain he was talking about his dogs.

She sighed, pushing her food around on her plate without eating. Supper was a boring affair. Although Myrna and Melissa talked almost unceasingly, they never managed to say anything new or interesting. Rather, they rehashed the same gossip that Kate had heard all season long, and she reckoned that they would discuss her as well once she left the table. She took perverse pleasure in making them bite their tongues by waiting the unpleasant meal out until the bitter end.

As luck would have it, however, the evening was washed out anyway, although not in the dramatic fashion that Kate had prayed for. The footmen were pushing aside the tables for dancing and the musicians were tuning their instruments when it began to rain. It started as a slow drizzle, but soon escalated to a heavy downpour. Bright flashes of lightning illuminated the way as the guests dashed back to the house for refuge.

Although Charlotte announced that there would be activities in the drawing room, Kate decided that she'd had enough socializing for one day and made her way back to her room. She hated to admit it, even to herself, but she was greatly troubled by the evening's gossip. She may have denied mooning over Ben, but there was some small part of her that sorely wished that *he* were mooning over her. Clearly that wasn't the case, and she was determined to conceal her feelings from him and from anyone else.

Exhausted, she readied herself for bed, not bothering to ring for Mary. She imagined her maid was in the kitchen, gambling and drinking a stiff one with the other servants. At least *she* was having a good time, Kate thought, as she climbed into bed and snuffed the light. She fell asleep almost the instant her head hit her pillow.

Kate woke up instantly at the loud crash, her heart racing, not knowing what time it was or how long she'd been asleep. Lightning flashed outside, creating eerie shadows in her room. She crept out of bed to peek out her window, and as she pulled back the heavy curtain, the thunder rumbled again, making her jump.

She'd loved storms ever since she was a child, especially watching the way they rolled in off the ocean. On a few occasions, she'd been caught in a storm while sailing alone in one of her father's small boats, and she'd delighted in the sensation of racing against nature, to see which made it home first. Kate usually won this race, albeit with a pounding heart and sodden clothes. Her father would rant, telling her how foolish it was to be on the water in a storm, swearing he wouldn't let her out alone in a boat again. But he'd always relented in the end.

The windowpane was streaked with rain, and she could see nothing but slick blackness. With an effort, she pulled the window open to get a better look at the storm outside, but even with it open, she could make out no definite objects in the rain, seeing only shadowy suggestions of shapes. As her eyes adjusted, however, she thought she saw something move.

Kate blinked, not believing that anyone would be

out in such weather. She kept looking, waiting for
another sign of motion. She stared for a few minutes,
and was about to turn away and go back to bed, when
she saw it again. Something—or someone—was
steadily, deliberately making its way across the lawn,
heading toward the conservatory.

She was suddenly and illogically gripped by fear.
She'd all but put Andrew Hilton and the incident in the
carriage from her mind recently, convinced that the two
were unconnected. Now, however, her concerns came
rushing back.

Suddenly, the figure began to run, bolting, in fact,
across the lawn and emitting the most horrible grunt, so
loud that Kate could hear it from her room. She squinted
hard to see what the figure was running toward and saw
that there was a small, gray object several feet in front
of it. That object turned now and screeched. The two
figures collided, barking, hissing, and sounding like the
very devil.

A dog. She had nearly fainted in fright, and all
because old Topper, the Bannisters' ancient mastiff, was
chasing a cat.

Oh, God—a cat! Kate quickly recollected that the
Bannisters didn't keep any cats, and that it could only
be Myrna Peters's Persian, a miserable ball of fur and
an almost permanent fixture at the woman's side.

Another screech came echoing up from the lawn,
and she was moved to action. She couldn't very well
leave the thing down there to get eaten—Myrna would
suffer an apoplexy, and once recovered would call on
unplumbed reserves of wrath to avenge poor Kitty. It

was the last thing the Bannisters needed to worry about with the wedding in just a few days.

Kate threw on a robe, not worrying that she'd chance upon any other guests in the storm. She opened her door, wincing at the awful creak it made, and raced down the hall. She hadn't bothered with her slippers, and her bare feet made little sound as they hit the floor.

Once downstairs, she crept through the kitchen to the back door, not stopping once to stare at the scullery maid, asleep in a drunken stupor beneath the table. The second she reached the door, she was out it, grabbing a broom to shoo with on the way and lifting her robe to her knees to run unhindered. The darkness didn't slow her down one bit—Kitty was making more than enough racket to guide her.

When she reached Topper and Kitty, broom raised above her head and curses on her lips, the combatants stopped, gawking wide-eyed at her as if she were a banshee. Banded together in fear, they yelped in unison and headed for the conservatory posthaste.

"Topper!" she called, forcing a good-humored ring to her voice as she followed the animals across the lawn. "Topper! I have a treat for you!"

The conservatory door was open—Kate didn't pause long enough to wonder why—and she entered, dropping the broom and feeling her way blindly through the darkness. The air was hot and damp, forming beads of moisture on her skin. The steady patter of rain hitting the roof mixed with the quiet bubbling of the fountain, and she crept along, scared but determined, until the soft sound of breathing told her she wasn't alone.

"Who's there?" Kate spun around in the darkness, ready to scream, ready to run, but not knowing which direction to go. An arm reached out, wrapping around her and covering her mouth before she could yell.

"Quiet," Ben whispered, his mouth so close to her ear that she could feel his breath. "We're not alone. I want you to stay right next to me, okay? Hold my hand and follow me out."

He uncovered her mouth and grabbed hold of her hand, pulling her behind him. She didn't know where he was taking her, but followed him so closely she almost stepped on his heels.

They crept along blindly for a few moments, Ben feeling his way just as Kate had done. She felt him stop, bumped into his back, actually, and heard him turn a doorknob. Suddenly, light spilled into the conservatory, and Ben yanked her through the door and back into the house, closing the door quickly behind them. Blinking, she looked around. They had entered into the study, and in the dim glow of a single lamp, she noted a half-finished glass of brandy and the faint scent of tobacco.

"I take it you didn't enter the conservatory through this room?" Ben asked, running his hand through his hair and scanning the room with his eyes as if searching for something or someone.

"No. I entered from outside."

He nodded, then just stood there staring at her for a moment as if debating what to do next. But he quickly recovered, grabbing her hand again and pulling her briskly across the room. Kate had to run to keep up.

"What's happening?"

"Quickly, we need to go somewhere secure. Then I'll tell you what's going on." He pulled her through the door, into the hall and up a short flight of stairs, stopping only to open yet another door and thrust her inside it.

His bedroom. Without being told, Kate knew that was where they were.

He noticed her shocked look and snorted. "Oh, don't go and act maidenly on me now, please. I didn't bring you here to seduce you."

"Oh."

"Why don't you start by telling me why you were wandering around outside at this time of night?"

His bitter tone made her flinch.

"I was trying to save Myrna Peters's cat from Topper."

"In nothing but a robe?" Ben asked, reaching out and lifting the flimsy fabric of her sleeve.

His sarcasm hurt, and she could only add weakly, "And my nightgown."

"I want you to tell me the truth, Kate. Were you meeting someone? Philip Bannister, maybe?"

"No!" She couldn't believe he would ask her that question, didn't know how to react to the harshness of his tone. Ben was looking at her in disgust, and suddenly she burst into tears.

He just stared at her, groping for words but not finding any. He felt like a cad for deliberately making her cry, and he wanted more than anything to comfort her, to take back his words. But he fought the urge. He was too angry and too confused. Only a fool would have gone out into that storm to save a bloody cat, and she was no fool. He didn't believe her, but he also didn't know why he should care. So what if she was meeting a lover? What concern was that of his?

He took a deep breath and tried again. "I was in the study having a drink when I heard a noise in the conservatory. I went out to investigate, thinking that a plant had fallen or a window was open. There was somebody in there, Kate. I couldn't make out any details, but I know someone was there." Ben paused to search her expression, trying to gauge her reaction. "They saw me too—jumped back into the shadows once they knew they weren't alone. But then I heard you enter. Quite a coincidence, don't you think?"

Kate wiped her eyes slowly. Her face ashen, she asked, "You have no idea who this person was?"

"Not if you don't."

That was more than she could take. "Not if I don't! How dare you imply that…that…" Her lip trembled and she trailed off, unable to verbalize his insinuation. "Look, I told you why I was there—it's you who is choosing not to believe me. You're hardly one to speak, anyway. Can I ask what *you* were doing, wandering around at this time of night?"

"Storms make me restless."

"And I'm supposed to believe you? Maybe it was Sarah Thomas lurking in the conservatory, just waiting for you to come and find her!"

The second these words left her lips, Kate wished she could take them back. He was truly angry now. His eyes darkened, and his lips thinned into a hard, cruel line. He'd been annoyed before, but now he was furious.

"Jealous? Maybe you'd like me to come find *you*."

Ben took a step forward as he asked this question, smiling humorlessly.

The wise course of action would have been to shut up and run, but instead she retorted, "I hear you like variety."

"I reckon you've heard a lot," he said, moving even closer, "but there's only one way to find out what I like."

Kate had backed up to the bookshelf, was edging sideways toward the door as he approached. She tried to make a run for it, but as she dashed to the door he reached out, catching her robe, spinning her around, and pulling her hard against his chest.

It was like hitting a wall: solid, muscular and unmoving. Kate looked up, knowing that to meet his eyes would mean there was no going back.

Chapter Ten

The instant she looked into Ben's eyes, seeing his anger replaced by passion, Kate gave in. It was one of the easiest things she had ever done. He ran his hands up her arms, stopping at her shoulders so he could push her back a step and take a fuller look. She blushed as he did so, thinking of her messy hair and wet robe, but what Ben saw was white silk, made translucent by the rain, covering pale skin that was silkier by far. He took a deep breath and exhaled slowly, watching her nipples pucker under his gaze.

Without speaking—this was no time for words—he tugged on the ties of her robe, then pushed it off her shoulders and let it fall. Kate looked down, watching it pool at her feet, but Ben reached out, running his finger along her jaw, lifting her head so he could see her face. He ran his finger along her cheekbone and over her lips, blazing a trail down her neck to her collarbone. Here he paused to toy with a heavy lock of hair, lifting it in his hand to feel its softness and see it shine in the warm light of the fire. He laid it down, then pushed her masses of copper-colored hair over her shoulders, letting it fall down along her back. Ben returned his attention to Kate's face, his eyes lingering on her stubborn chin, her luscious lips, her pert nose…when his amber eyes returned to hers, she felt her knees go liquid and her stomach drop. His gaze never faltered, and without so much as a blink, Ben brought his fingers back to her face, tracing a line along her cheek and reaching his hand behind her head. With his hand in her hair, Ben drew her toward him, moving in for the kiss that would seal the bargain.

Ben had barely even touched her at this point, had used only his fingertips and his eyes to arouse her desire. But the time for moving slowly had come to an end. Where his touch had awakened, teasing her with its subtlety, his kiss was a revelation. Kate felt her resolve crumble beneath his expertise, her body moving closer despite her will, molding itself against his unyielding form. She reached her hand into his hair, matching him in urgency, opening her mouth without thinking, and inviting him to delve further.

He obliged with a groan, wrapping his thick arms around her. His hands trailed down her neck, her back, and he cupped her buttocks, pulling her against his hardness, lifting her up, in fact, as if she weighed no more than a feather. Ben carried her across the room, lowering her at the foot of his bed and savoring the feel of her as she slid down his body. He shrugged off his jacket, watching her pupils dilate as he did so.

"Ben?"

"Hmm?" Ben was unbuttoning his shirt, wanting to rip the bloody thing off but forcing himself to go slowly. He didn't want to talk. Talking would interject reality. She was his best friend's sister and he knew he should stop. But he wanted her more than he'd wanted a woman before, and he couldn't have stopped if his life depended on it.

"Are you going to make love to me?"

He didn't answer right away, just shrugged off his shirt, looking at her the whole time, watching her face.

"I am," he finally answered with deliberate slowness. As he spoke, he reached out to grasp one of her hands, placing it on his chest, sensing her nervousness and guiding her through it.

Kate stared at her slender hand, momentarily frozen. He was all muscle, and she was fascinated by his hardness, his golden skin, and his penetrating heat, all so far beyond her experience. She was nervous, but curiosity and desire made her bold. Fingers splayed, she began to move her hand, trailing it with excruciating slowness over his nipples, then down the hard ridge of his belly, lower…her mouth suddenly felt very dry, and she licked her lower lip unconsciously.

Ben had been watching her lips intently, and when he saw her pink tongue peek out, he groaned. It was such a provocative gesture, and yet done so innocently…his groan was out of desire, yes, but also out of frustration. God, he felt green. His whole body was throbbing intensely, and he wanted more than anything to rip her clothes off, throw her down on the bed, open his trousers and thrust inside her full-force, unmindful of her pleasure. Perhaps she wasn't a total innocent—he didn't think so after recent events—but she definitely wasn't that experienced either. He had to slow down.

Ben grabbed her hand, needing to reclaim control. He took a steadying breath and a step back.

"Take your gown off," he said, watching Kate blink and knowing that her nervousness had returned. He didn't offer to help her, positive that if he touched her just then he would ravage her on the spot. But he also knew that she would do as he said without his help, wanting it as much as he did.

Kate hesitated just a moment before lifting her night-gown over her head. She blushed as she did so, feeling more vulnerable than she had ever felt in her life. But before her nerves could get the better of her, Ben stepped close, gently laying her down on the bed and kissing her once more.

This time the kiss didn't end at her lips, but traveled across her cheek, down her neck, her chest…she gasped and shot up from bed as his hot tongue brushed her nipple.

"Stop!" she cried, alarmed at the new sensation that flared through her body. "You can't do that…it's…it's not proper."

Ben looked up, his mouth a sensuous curve. "Not proper? I should hope not." Then he resumed, just the barest touch at first, but then slower, circling the peak of her breast, licking, softly nipping. While his mouth worked at one breast, his hand worked at the other, plumping, teasing and driving her wild with the most exquisite torture.

Kate forgot her protest, was too mindless with the

pleasure that he was giving her. His tongue traveled farther down her body, across her belly, stopping at her navel to tease some more while his hand moved lower, opening, unfolding, gently teasing her soft flesh. She spread her legs to accommodate him, first one finger, and then two, and suddenly, unconsciously, she was thrusting against his hand, meeting him stroke for stroke, moving faster, slower, faster again, without reserve, without anything but passion. Her vision became blurred, and her lips softened and parted to cry out. Oh, God! Kate felt pleasure like she'd never felt before, washing over her with a suddenness and a force that made her cry out.

Then with a moan of his own, unable to wait any longer, Ben was inside her, thrusting home, pausing only slightly at the tug of her maidenhead. Kate felt no pain, only the slightest discomfort at the breach, but then the sweetest sensation as he began to move. She had no idea what was going on inside of her, only knew that it intensified with every thrust, that she could hardly bear it, that she never wanted it to stop. Then, in a thousand lights of pleasure, the feeling exploded, sending shock waves pulsing down to the tips of her toes. She called out his name, and he met her cry with a kiss, driving hard, harder, until he climaxed with a pleasure so strong it made him shake.

Neither of them moved for several minutes, too shaken to do more than lie very still, hearts pounding. But eventually Ben dragged himself off her, propping himself up on his elbows to look at her face.

"How do you feel?"

Kate considered this question for a moment. She felt incredible, every sense alert, her body alive. She wanted to touch him, to explore his body some more, taking her time without the cloud of passion that had enveloped her. But she also felt vulnerable beneath his perceptive gaze. She had just undergone the most momentous experience of her life, and she wasn't sure that the feeling was mutual.

"Fine."

He leaned over and gently kissed her on the lips. At her blush, he laughed, rolling over onto his back and bringing her with him so that she lay across his chest.

"Just fine? I'll have to try harder next time."

"No! I mean, I feel wonderful," she protested, afraid that he'd make her lose control again. He only chuckled.

"Umm…how do you feel?" Kate nearly cringed as she asked this question, but she couldn't help herself. She had to know the answer.

"Fine," Ben answered solemnly, then gave a mock grunt when she hit him playfully in the chest. "I'm sorry. I meant I feel wonderful, too."

He didn't add that he'd felt pleasure like he'd never felt before, that he was already thinking about making love to her again, that if he'd known she'd been a virgin he would have tried a lot harder to resist her…as if he could have. He'd always stayed clear of virgins, far too wary of the complications they presented. In fact, he hadn't made love to a virgin since he, too, had been an inexperienced lad of sixteen. He wasn't quite sure what to think of Kate's innocence, other than that he'd been surprised as hell by it, given her twenty-four years, the circumstances of the evening and her passionate response. He'd also felt a wave of possessiveness, satisfaction and relief unlike any he'd ever known, but he tried not to examine these feelings too closely.

Thinking about her virginity made reality rush back to his brain, superseding his post-lovemaking euphoria. Ben felt like a bounder, and for good reason. He'd not only made love to an innocent, but to the innocent younger sister of his best friend. Sure, he'd done his part to avoid her by leaving London, but even as he tried to justify his behavior, he knew he was only making excuses. He'd spent nearly five months in the country waiting for Rob's wedding to arrive just so he could see Kate again, and from the moment he'd seen her he'd thought about her almost nonstop.

Ben was truly angry with himself for getting into this predicament, and his anger suddenly and irrationally included Kate. He knew that she was all but engaged to Philip Bannister—it was common knowledge. He'd seen the proprietary way Bannister had looked at her over dinner, not to mention that she had as much as told him so herself. Could she have forgotten it so quickly? Ben couldn't forget it for a minute.

And yet here she was, in bed with him.

It shouldn't have bothered him that she was being disloyal; in fact, Ben had always rather disliked Philip and couldn't care less if Kate made a cuckold of him. But her infidelity did bother him, whether she was formally engaged or not. For whatever reason, he expected more from her than he did from other women.

He looked at her hard, immediately suspicious. He

knew she was looking for a husband, and he'd be damned if she'd turn her machinations on him.

"You've surprised me, you know…so passionate. How is it possible that you aren't already married, with a child on the way?" He was being deliberately cruel again and knew it.

Kate blinked, stunned at the sudden change that had come over him. "What?"

"That's your plan, isn't it? You told me so yourself. Whatever will your husband think when he finds out that his wife just couldn't wait for the marriage bed?"

Kate was stunned. Her emotions were still jumbled from making love, and her brain too foggy to make sense out of what was happening. How could he could say this to her after what they had just shared? She wanted to hit him, or throw something or scream, but for once she refrained; she was too painfully aware that what he said was true, and her dread overpowered her fury.

"I will tell him…before we are wed," she said, carefully picking her words and fighting back tears.

"You think he'll still want you?" Ben asked with studied casualness as he climbed out of bed and pulled on his trousers. He hated himself as he said these cruel words, but for some reason he could not stop.

Kate did not know what to say. She quickly began yanking on her clothes, few as they were. She bit her lip to keep from crying, but hot, hurt tears trailed down her cheeks nonetheless. Blinded by anger, she shoved past Ben, pulled open the door and slammed it shut behind her, oblivious to the risk she ran by making such a loud noise in the crowded, sleeping house. So overcome by rage and embarrassment, she didn't hear the sound of him cursing at his stupidity behind the closed door.

She raced down the hall, tears streaming down her face, not knowing what to do. She'd never been so intentionally hurt before, had never felt like such a fool. How could she have let her defenses down? How had she been stupid enough to trust him? She'd been kidding herself, pretending that he felt differently about her, that he wasn't using her, that he actually cared.

She paused at the top of the stairs, not remembering which direction would take her to her room. Peshley was huge, and Ben's room seemed to be in a wing opposite of hers.

"Kate."

She swung around, not having heard Ben walk up behind her.

"Kate—just wait a moment so I can explain…"

She wasn't waiting for an explanation, was too angry to listen to anything he had to say. She bolted down the steps, not caring if she was headed in the right direction, only caring that she put as much space between them as possible. He waited a moment, debating whether to follow, then cursed, heading down the stairs in her wake.

At the bottom of the steps, she turned a quick left and opened the first door she came to, hoping to elude Ben. It was the study, and she entered without pause, almost smiling at her good fortune. The study let out into the conservatory, and from there she could cross the lawn to her wing of the house.

"Kate!"

She didn't bother to look behind her to see how far Ben followed. Instead, she slammed the study door, dashed across the room and through the next door into the dark conservatory. Blindly, she edged down the path, brushing past unseen plants, knocking over a pot and hearing it shatter.

"Kate!" he called after her, entering the conservatory to follow.

She pressed on, taking a path that twisted sharply to the right, feeling with her hands, listening for the sound of Ben's footsteps behind her. Blind in the darkness, her other senses grew more acute: she heard the rustle of branches being pushed apart, the shuffle of feet on the ground, the sound of breathing, close, much closer than it should have been. Kate stopped dead in her tracks, visionless but suddenly certain that she was not alone. Her mind clouded by recent events, she had thought only to run away from Ben. It hadn't occurred to her that someone else might be out there, and that she was running to them. Until now.

"Ben?"

There was no answer, only the quick motion of an arm reaching out from behind her. She had barely enough time to call out, briefly and sharply, before a fist struck her in the face, just above her left eye. She stumbled back, feeling total blackness threaten. Kate didn't lose consciousness, but her body felt limp and numb, and she closed her eyes, trying to fight the bolts of searing pain that throbbed in her head. She turned to try to escape, but she was unfamiliar with the conservatory and could barely see anyway. Her attacker grabbed her by the hair and she had just enough time to cry out once more before he stuffed a rag in her mouth and tied it behind her head to stifle her. Then he picked her up, hefting her over his shoulder and making his way stealthily toward the door. She kicked and hit, but he was far larger than she was and her efforts were completely ineffective. Tears welled in her eyes, and she swallowed hard, feeling vomit rise. She was so afraid she couldn't think and, hanging upside down from the man's shoulder, she was in no position to do much anyway. Where was Ben?

"Kate!" Ben had heard her cry, was desperately shoving his way through the low-hanging trees, trying to locate her in the darkness. Her attacker began to run, clumsily and noisily in his haste and she began to struggle again, desperate to slow him down. Ben heard him and changed his track, ignoring the path and leaping through a small grove of trees. He stepped through the fountain, soaking his shoes, his trousers, almost falling in the slippery wetness. But he raced on, his shortcut bringing him up right on their heels.

Kate still couldn't see, but felt the man turn his head to look behind them, knew that Ben was close and that the man was scared. The conservatory door was already open, and her attacker ran faster, hastening outside and jostling her, making her stomach heave. Ben ran faster still, out the door and nearly abreast with them in the cool, dark night—but then he fell back abruptly, calling out in surprise. Kate lifted her head to look just in time to see a second man leap out from behind the conservatory door, throwing himself at Ben and making him stumble and fall to the ground with a thud. She tried to scream, but her voice was muted by the gag. The second man landed on top of him, and in an instant they were rolling on the ground, punches flying.

Kate's captor stopped, swinging around to watch the two men fighting on the lawn. She could see very little, draped over the man's back as she was, but she craned her neck as much as possible, trying to get a clear look at the men, needing to know the faces of her enemies. She could see nothing of the man who held her, but she could tell that he was quite tall, and could feel that he was almost skeletally thin from the sharp shoulder that poked her in the ribs. But she did have a better view of the second man. He was quite heavyset, but muscular and stocky. She shivered, looking at his face, seeing his square jowls and heavy brows, a menacing sneer on his lips. Although Ben was taller and stronger, the other man had the element of surprise in his favor. Ben struggled to throw him off, nearly managed to once, but the heavy man had too great an advantage. Kate gasped as he rose above Ben, his hands at his throat, choking him. Then with sickening fear, she saw the cold glint of metal in the man's hand. A knife.

But he never even used it. The tall, thin man walked over, carrying Kate with him like a heavy sack.

"We don't want any blood, mate," he said, shoving the large man off Ben with his booted foot.

The large man rose, his breathing heavy and his eyes still bright with exertion. He paused, standing over Ben and looking down at him as if contemplating his next move.

"This won't make 'im bleed," he said, and kicked

Ben, swiftly, ruthlessly, in the ribs. He jerked to the side at the impact, then didn't move. Kate felt fear like she'd never felt before. The kick had been so loud she'd heard it, had heard the solid thud of boot meeting flesh. What if…oh, God.

She began fighting with all of her might, kicking her captor, thrashing her body in his arms. She tried screaming, but the rag muffled her yells and she only managed a muted, hoarse wail. Her captor threw her on the ground, stunning her with the impact.

He bent down and slapped her across the face. "Ye'd better watch it, gel. I'll only 'urt ye if I 'ave to." He glared at her for a moment, then he hefted her over his shoulder once more.

"Get the gent as well," he said, turning to his partner. "We'd better take 'im with us."

"D'ye think 'e saw me face?" the heavyset man asked, brushing the dirt from his coat.

"Dunno. Can't take any chances, though. We'll let Billy figure out what to do wit' 'im. Pick 'im up, will ye?"

"Why the bloody 'ell do I get to lug this one, when you get that pretty piece o' baggage? That don't seem fair."

The thin man smiled. "Ain't fair, George. But I got 'er first."

George grunted, lifting Ben over his shoulder. The men started walking, each with a limp body swaying from over his shoulder.

Kate wouldn't try to escape again—not yet anyway. Even if she was successful, she couldn't leave Ben behind. Unconscious, he was unable to defend himself. Instead, she started recording facts in her mind. George.

Billy. George was the heavy one. She didn't know where Billy was. And then there was the tall one, the one who held her. That made three.

They moved through the shadows next to the conservatory, slowly, stealthily. Once past the conservatory, however, the cover of the shadows disappeared. They picked up the pace, running across the open lawn toward the shelter of the woods.

Kate, facing backwards, watched the house recede into the distance. It was early morning and a few dim lights shone from the windows. The servants had roused and were beginning to start the day. Soon all the guests would awake, and over breakfast they might start to wonder where she was, where Ben was, too.

The rain had stopped.

Chapter Eleven

Several small dirt roads ran through the woods, mainly to connect Peshley to town and to their nearby hunting lodge. After about ten minutes of walking down one of these roads, the two men reached their destination. A coach awaited their arrival, a very small man perched in the driver's seat.

"Took ye bloody long enough," he said impatiently. "And what the 'ell do ye 'ave there, George? No one said nothin' 'bout any bloke."

"Ask John. 'E'll tell ya."

John. The man who held her must be John, Kate thought as she peered covertly at the little man. And he must be Billy. He was barely any larger than she was— was, in fact, probably an inch or two shorter. Billy jumped down from his seat nervously, moving quickly like a sparrow.

John opened the carriage door and threw Kate unceremoniously inside. "Easy, there, Billy. We didn't 'ave no choice but bring 'im. 'E was pokin' round, lookin' for trouble, and 'e saw us do it. 'E'll tell, and before we know it, we'll all 'ang."

George followed suit, dumping Ben inside the coach and landing him on the seat next to Kate. "Should we tie 'em up, Billy? The bloke took a pretty good blow, but 'e might come to sooner or later."

"Don' bother—it's day, now, and we ain't got time. The coach'll be locked. 'E can't go nowhere."

George nodded and slammed the carriage door, locking it from the outside. Kate heard the three men climb into their seats above, heard the click of a tongue and the snap of a whip. With a jolt, the horses were in motion.

She opened an eye, wondering if Ben was still unconscious, but he didn't move. She leaned forward in her seat, examining his face for any sign of serious injury, at the moment unmindful of her own bruises, of her own gagged mouth. She feared that the real reason he hadn't been tied up was that the men knew he'd been too injured to cause any harm. She leaned her face very close to his, hoping to feel his breath.

She got much more than she bargained for. Suddenly, Ben opened his eyes and swiftly reached over, untying the knot behind her head and yanking the gag from her mouth. In the brief instant before she could speak, he grabbed her and replaced the gag with his hand, covering her mouth lest she call out. Kate could see that he was most alert.

And then she got angry. This was the second bloody time that he had muffled her in such a fashion that evening, on top of everything else. She'd had enough, and she kicked him in the shin.

He removed his hand to rub his leg, glaring at her.

"I'm not stupid, you know. I know when I need to be quiet. I don't need you to make me shut up—"

"Kate?"

"Yes?"

"Do be quiet."

She sat back in her seat, deflated but not defeated. She also wasn't done.

"Ben?"

"What?" he all but snapped.

She ignored his tone and continued. "Do you have any ideas? Because if you do, now would be the time to share them...." Her voice trailed off as she realized that he wasn't listening and was, in fact, quite angry.

Several minutes passed before he spoke. "I reckon you have more ideas than I do, Kate."

"*What* do you mean by that?"

"I'll explain later. Right now we need a plan."

"I might have one."

He raised a supercilious brow.

"Well, part of a plan, anyway," she explained. "Perhaps you can add to it. You see, there are only three of them—"

"Noted."

Kate bit her tongue at that arrogant tone and continued. "—and that's just one more than you and me—"

"Do you propose to challenge them yourself, Kate?"

She closed her eyes and counted to ten this time. "No, I don't. But we do have several advantages."

"Such as?"

"In the first place, we're smarter than they are—I

mean, can you believe that they would leave us alone in here together? In the second place, you're stronger than any one of them…why, I believe you could polish off *two* of them with no trouble."

"Are you trying to flatter me?"

"Flattery is the last thing you need. And third," she barreled on, knowing that he would protest her third argument, "I am distracting."

"Irritatingly so, but what is your point?" he asked suspiciously.

She flushed. "I am, as you noted yourself, in a state of partial *dishabille.*"

Ben's eyes raked down her scantily clad form, wishing that she wasn't right. No man could think straight looking at her like that. There seemed to be no help for it—the only way he'd manage to beat all three of them was if she did some serious distracting.

"They don't know that I'm conscious," he offered.

Kate nodded, silently thankful that he hadn't fought her plan.

He continued. "I want you to rap on the roof—beg them to stop. Say you have ample money to pay them."

"But I don't…and what if they won't stop?"

Ben was worried about this possibility as well but ignored his fears. "It's the best we can do, unless we want to wait for them to stop of their own accord. Personally, I think we'd better risk it. There's a good chance that they'll stop for you anyway. They're sloppy, and as you noticed they're not very bright. Besides, they'll also want to hear you beg—that type gets pleasure out of defeating those who are weaker than they are. When they stop and open the door…" He paused, looking critically over her body. "Come here."

Kate rose and sat next to him on his seat. She sucked in her breath as he swiftly yanked the tie from her robe, and sat numbly as he started to tear the hem of her gown, ripping it until it reached midthigh. Ben put the end of the fabric in his teeth and tore it off. He put the tie and the long strip of fabric in his pocket.

"I might need these," he explained, and then sat back, examining her all over again. "Much better."

She was too shocked to respond.

He squeezed her hand. "We'll be fine. Just stay calm. When they open the door, look as enticing as possible. If you get the opportunity, I want you to get out of the carriage. Pretend that you're trying to escape, if you have to—anything that will draw their attention away from me. I won't let them hurt you. All right?"

Kate took a deep breath and nodded. "I'm ready."

"Go ahead and give the roof a good rap. And put your gag back in, or they'll wonder how you got it out."

"But they didn't tie my hands. I could've taken it off myself. I didn't really need *you* to remove it."

"Oh, never mind. Do what you like," Ben grumbled, then lay back down on the seat, assuming the position that George had deposited him in.

She reached up and rapped on the roof. The carriage didn't stop, didn't slow. There was no response. She rapped again, harder this time, and then began pounding on the roof with all her strength. She *had* to make them listen to her.

Her effort got results. The carriage slowed and came to a halt.

"What's the bleedin' racket for?" Billy shouted from up front.

Kate faltered for a moment, but Ben squeezed her hand again. Reassured, she continued. "I want to speak to you. I have something to offer you."

"I'm sure ye 'ave plenty to offer!" Billy answered with a lecherous cackle. "But it ain't my place to accept it."

"I will pay you! Money is what you want, isn't it?" she shouted, bluffing in panic as she felt the carriage lurch into motion. But those were the magic words. The carriage halted.

There was the sound of a brief consultation above, followed by the sound of several footsteps—one pair? two pairs? three?—climbing down. The carriage door was yanked open. All three men—luckily or not, Kate wasn't sure—stood waiting...and gaping.

She felt her face heat, and looked down at herself self-consciously. Dear heavens. With nothing to tie it closed, her robe parted, revealing her thin, silk gown that stopped in tattered fringes above her dirty knees.

Look enticing, she reminded herself, wondering how that was possible, and not realizing that she wouldn't even have to try.

She smiled. "Thank you, gentlemen, for stopping. I only wanted the chance to speak a moment...you see, I have a proposition to make you. I hope you don't mind that I took the liberty of removing my gag." She threw that last sentence in for Ben's benefit.

John, George and Billy simply stared, slack-jawed and tongue-tied.

She continued. "You see, I am quite wealthy—surely you know that, or I can't imagine why you'd go to these lengths. I will pay you to let me go."

Scrawny, nervous Billy was the first to speak. "Why, that's mighty gen'rous of ye, m'lady, but we're already gettin' paid fer this." Billy glanced into the carriage where Ben feigned unconsciousness. "'Sides, both ye seen our faces…prob'ly even know our names. Can't take any chances, now, can we? But maybe ye want to step outside an' try an' convince us?"

That was about the last thing that Kate wanted to do, but she still eagerly complied, thankful that they were making her job easy. She silently prayed that Ben's plan, whatever it was, worked.

She stepped from the carriage, but didn't get very far before Billy grabbed her tightly around her wrist. "Not so fast, there, gel. George, ye stay 'ere an' keep an eye on the bloke. Me an' John are gonna go 'ave a discussion wi' th' lass."

"Why th' bloody 'ell do I have to stay 'ere? Make John stay," George said angrily. "It ain't bloody fair—"

"'Cause yer the only one who can take care o' 'im if 'e wakes up," John answered, glaring at the possibility that he would be the one to stay behind. Then without further ado, he scooped up Kate one more time. "Lead th' way, Billy."

She immediately began to struggle. There was no way in hell that they were dragging her into the woods to do God only knew what with her person. She punched

John in the back, and in the neck. She grabbed hold of one of his ears and pulled without mercy.

He screamed, loud and high-pitched like a woman, and chaos ensued. All eyes turned to Kate and the commotion she was causing, and as Ben burst out of the carriage, George didn't even see him coming. Ben struck the large man in the face, sending him reeling. John dropped Kate flat on her bottom, and she quickly scuttled across the ground, trying to get out of the way. Ben simply stepped over her, grabbing John by the neck and squeezing until he fell to his knees. Ben grabbed John by the hair, and in one swift motion connected his knee to the tall man's face.

Billy had already begun a hasty retreat to the woods, and Ben started after him. Before he left, however, he tossed something down into Kate's lap.

"Tie them up before they regain consciousness," was all he said before vanishing into the woods.

She looked down into her lap and recognized the sash to her robe and the missing half of her nightgown. She wasted no time picking them up and getting to work, wanting to have both men taken care of before they became dangerous again.

Ben returned as she was fastening John's ankles; George was already trussed up and propped against a tree. Kate saw no sign of Billy, but noticed that Ben carried a small bundle with him.

"Ready to go, then?" he asked calmly, helping her up from the ground.

She nodded. "Did Billy get away?"

"No. I left him in the woods. I sacrificed my cravat

to tie him to a tree. Don't want him running off before he's found." Ben touched his throat as she said this, and Kate noticed that, indeed, his cravat was missing. "We'll have to notify the authorities once we reach safety."

Kate nodded. Notifying the authorities would mean making explanations that she wasn't quite ready for, but she couldn't worry about that now. "What is the bundle?"

"It's for you, m'dear. Billy kindly offered to lend you a few articles of clothing, seeing as it's his fault that you're currently without. Generous of him, don't you think?"

"You left him—" Kate paused here to lower her voice "—unclothed?" The mental image produced by such a prospect pleased her tremendously.

Ben noted the devilish gleam in her eye and grinned. "Your mind is in the gutter yet again, love. Billy wasn't *that* generous. He requested I leave him his drawers, and as I suspected you wouldn't want them anyway, I agreed."

"That's charitable of you," Kate said, taking the clothes from Ben and quickly donning them behind the carriage. When she returned, he was already in the driver's seat, waiting to go.

"I'm ready," she said, looking up at Ben and shielding her eyes from the bright morning sun. She was surprised when he held down his hand, but took it. He pulled her up onto the front of the carriage, onto the seat next to him.

"I'd rather not let you out of my sight for a while, if you don't mind," he explained. "And I have a few questions for you as well."

She had been expecting at least a few questions, so she didn't worry overmuch. Instead, she settled back against the seat as they started off, relieved to be safe for the moment. Her tiredness, which she'd ignored through the entire ordeal, hit her now, full-force.

With a relieved sigh, she said, "Back to Peshley at last. If we're quick about it, no one will even notice we were missing!"

"We're not going back to Peshley, Kate."

Chapter Twelve

Kate hadn't been expecting that response. "What do you mean we're not going back to Peshley? Where are we going?"

"I have a house out this way…it's my father's house, actually—remember when I told you about it?"

She shook her head, still confused.

He carried on. "I don't think it would be safe to head back to the Bannisters'. It might mean putting you in danger again, and perhaps Charlotte's family as well. I don't know who those men were, Kate, but they won't think to look for you at my father's. The house isn't far from here, and I'll send your brother a note as soon as we reach it, letting him know where we are."

"But it will take hours for a note to reach him! Everyone will be so worried. Rob and Charlotte hardly need this sort of disruption now."

"There's no choice, Kate. Perhaps you'll be able to return later this evening, but not just yet. We should at least try and locate some more respectable clothes for you before you return—showing up looking like a cutpurse won't help matters a'tall. I'm sure I can find you something slightly more appropriate at my house. I've a sister about your size."

She looked down at her clothes and nodded in reluctant agreement, knowing that her brother would have a fit when he realized that both she and Ben were missing. But at the same time she was strangely relieved by the thought of going to Ben's house rather than returning to Peshley. She didn't have time to dwell on this odd realization, however, before the interrogation began.

"It seems rather odd, Kate, that in the short time that I've known you, you've been abducted twice. Please don't try to tell me that it's a coincidence."

"My life isn't *always* this exciting…you just have a talent for showing up at all the right times—"

"Kate—remember what I said in the carriage? About how I thought you had more ideas about what was going on than I did?"

She swallowed hard, knowing that she could stall no longer. When Ben was determined there wasn't much she could do to prevent him from getting an answer.

"Yes…"

"Clearly there is something going on here that you're not being honest about. Don't insult my intelligence—just tell me the truth."

"I will, though you may have a hard time believing it."

"Proceed."

Kate took a steadying breath. The truth was that she

didn't really know for sure *what* the truth was. All she had were suspicions.

"Well…my family, as you know, owns a shipyard."

Ben nodded. "Alfred and Sons. My shipping firm recently purchased several of the company's ships. Whoever is in charge of design has a rare talent."

"Yes, well, my grandfather founded the company, and my father followed right along in his footsteps."

"Robert had told me all this. I've never understood, though, where the name comes from. Who was Alfred?"

"He was my grandfather's Pekinese."

Ben blinked. "What?"

"You see, he didn't want our name to be sullied by any connections to trade—he was the first Sutcliff to have a title and we were as poor as church mice when he started. That's the reason he took on the business in the first place. And why is that so funny?" she asked, noting the faint tics at the corners of his mouth with annoyance.

"I'm sorry," he apologized, still smiling. "But if 'Alfred' was the dog, 'Sons' isn't accurate either, is it? Especially since Robbie has little to do with the company."

"Funny thing, isn't it? My grandfather was a bit of an eccentric."

"It does sound rather arbitrary."

"Oh, no…I didn't mean that he was eccentric in that way. You see, 'sons' refers to me."

"I know for a fact that you are *not* 'sons.'"

Kate smiled with forced patience. "Not literally, no. My father was 'sons' before me. He taught me everything he knew about the business, and when he became ill, I ran it for him."

"You?"

His disbelief annoyed her. "Shocking, isn't it? And it's because of precisely that reaction that I have concealed my involvement. During my father's illness, and since his death, our clerk, Andrew Hilton, has presided over all meetings, signed all papers, given every *appearance* of running the business, although I have been the one with the final say in all decisions."

"I trust your brother knows about this arrangement?"

"Of course. It's stated in my father's will. I own the company and am the sole beneficiary of its profits."

"I see. And how, exactly, does this relate to last evening's events, or to when you were abducted the first time?"

Kate paused for a moment to deliberate, and then spoke. "I'm not even certain that it does. But soon after my father's death, Andrew Hilton began to, well…court me, I suppose. Except I didn't want him to—"

"Didn't want him to? What do you mean?"

"I mean I didn't want to marry him, but he kept trying to persuade me…I tried to ignore him at first, but he only became more and more insistent. And then he began to threaten that he'd expose me if I didn't agree. I…I feel so stupid. We should have known that he was dishonorable, but he concealed it so well until my father died."

"So you think he wants to gain control of the company by marrying you."

"Yes. If I were exposed, my company would be ruined and as for my family name…don't you see?"

"And presumably he followed you to London and has been behind these attacks."

"I'm almost certain. It's the only possible answer, even though it doesn't entirely make sense."

"Why?"

"Even though Hilton has been a scoundrel, I've known him for most of my life. I don't really think he'd actually try to hurt me, no matter how much he wanted the company."

"Well, he never did hurt you. You may have been scared but no one ever harmed you physically. Maybe that was his plan."

She looked Ben straight in the eye. "I suppose. I'm sure you can understand now why I had to do something about it."

He nodded tentatively, but then asked, "When you say that you decided to do something, *what* exactly do you have planned?"

Kate huffed, as if there were only one rational course *to* take. "I wouldn't have this problem if I were married, would I? That is why I came to London, remember?"

"You intend to escape these threats through marriage? A husband will protect you?"

"Bother that. I don't want a husband for protection. I want a husband so I can protect my company. It's the only way. Don't you see?"

Ben nodded again, pretending to see when he actually didn't see at all. It made no sense. What husband would let her carry on such business? Would she really marry someone without love? Even as these thoughts began moving about his brain, he snuffed them. Nearly everyone married without love—most were lucky to marry with a modicum of affection. It was the way of the world, and there were more pressing concerns than whether she married for love or not.

In truth, he was quite astounded by Kate's admission. Alfred and Sons was one of the largest and most successful ship designing firms in England, and it was run by…her? He was having a difficult time taking it all seriously. Not that he doubted her intelligence—she was one of the most intelligent people he knew. It was just that he'd been in so many laughably bizarre situations with her…instantly Ben was visited by the image of Kate seated behind a desk, sporting a man's suit and cravat and smoking a cheroot. The image was absurd, and he felt a smirk itching uncooperatively about his lips. He tried his damnedest to suppress it but failed.

Her eyes glowed with fury. "So you think it's funny, do you? You only prove my point…the thought that a mere woman might be able to run a business is laughable. I daresay you wouldn't have done business with Alfred and Sons if you'd known it was run by a woman."

He didn't answer right away, mulling over the question. "I'm not sure if I would or not…but knowing now that it's run by a woman—even a hothead like you—wouldn't deter me in the future. It's a fine company, Kate. I'm impressed."

"I hope someday you sink," she grumbled, averting her eyes. Ben seemed sincere, and she wasn't sure how to take his compliment gracefully. She felt thrilled to her toes that he would praise her—she'd dreaded telling him the truth, afraid he would despise her for being involved in such unfeminine pursuits. But she couldn't help but feel like he was mocking her slightly, treating her as a novelty.

She decided to turn the questioning around. "You have me at a disadvantage. You know all about me, and I know next to nothing about you. Surely you have a few skeletons of your own."

"I am an open book. Ask me anything you like."

"Hmm…" She had many questions but was too embarrassed to ask most of them. She picked an innocuous subject. "Tell me about your family."

"No secrets there. I spent most of my youth at Sudley, the house we're headed to now. Lived there with my father and mother, and my three sisters."

"Three sisters? Goodness."

"That's how I often feel myself. Fortunately, I am bigger and older than they are, so they don't give me too much trouble." He paused, smiling as if at some long-forgotten memory, and continued. "After me, there's Beatrice. She's twenty-four and only recently married. We thought we'd never see the day."

"*I* am twenty-four and unmarried."

"I won't hold that against you."

She could see that he was trying hard not to laugh. Damn him. He'd made the remark about his sister's age just to get a rise out of her. She chose to ignore it.

"Who comes after Beatrice?"

"After Beatrice is Eleanor, who'll turn eighteen next week. She'll have her coming out next summer. Helen is the baby of the family—she's fourteen now."

"That's quite a lot to remember. But I can see that you care for them a great deal."

Ben nodded. "Tremendously. I don't see them as much as I'd like…only when I make it down to Sudley to visit. Get to see Beatrice even less because she's moved to Kent with her husband, although she was at Sudley for a visit during my recent stay. She might still be there and you can meet her. I'm certain you'll get along."

"And why—if you don't mind my asking—did you nearly give up on Beatrice marrying?" Kate asked curiously. "Twenty-four seems a perfectly sensible age for a woman to marry."

Ben smiled, and behind that smile Kate thought she could detect a trace of unholy glee. "I don't mind your asking at all, and she was actually twenty-three when she wed. But I should *love* it if you ask her the same question—"

"Is it a touchy subject?"

"Well, no…it's just that Bea had a string of rather unfortunate seasons. My sister is a little too fastidious for her own good, and after a few seasons out she garnered the reputation of ice princess. I assure you that title is *somewhat* undeserved—it's just that our parents had an exceptionally happy marriage, and Beazie wouldn't settle for anything less. But then her lout of a husband came along and they've lived happily ever after."

Kate suspected that she and Beatrice would get along famously. She also suspected that Ben liked his sister's husband despite calling him names. But she didn't pursue the subject any further. "You said your father lives at Sudley—will your mother be there as well?"

"No. She died just after Helen was born. I was fifteen."

"I'm sorry." Kate really meant it, feeling the greatest

sympathy for anyone who lost a parent at a young age. "My mother died when I was a baby."

He turned his head, the traces of a sad smile on his face. He reached out and tucked a stray strand of hair behind her ear.

"I should warn you before we arrive that Sudley is a bit of a madhouse. My two younger sisters are usually in the midst of some prank or another, and they won't make any exceptions because you're a guest—be on your toes. And my father is the Master of the Hounds for our local hunt, a title he takes very seriously."

Kate frowned slightly, not quite understanding. "Surely that's not so unusual. Everyone needs a hobby."

"Kate, it is not a hobby. Trust me—you will see. I presume you ride well?"

"Yes, very well."

"Then you shall be all right."

They drove along in companionable silence for quite a while. Strangely, Kate couldn't remember a recent time in which she'd felt more at ease. The sun had risen fully, casting a warm, silver light on the dew-covered woods along the road, and the countryside was as beautiful as any she had ever seen. She inhaled deeply, leaning back in her seat and closing her eyes.

She was in the midst of a pleasant dream. She was seven years old, standing on the seashore by her home on the coast of Dorset. Her brother was racing up and down the beach, whooping and swinging his piratical wooden sword about to send the seagulls soaring. Her father stood by her side, seeming impossibly tall. Her hair whipped about in the ocean breeze, and her father had pulled her close, opening his heavy wool coat and wrapping it around her. Oh, how she had loved that coat!

"Kate?"

She looked up at her father, and he began to fade.

"Kate?" The voice came again, more insistent this time. Someone was calling out her name…

"Hmm?" She opened her eyes, blinking in the light.

"Time to wake up. We'll arrive in a few minutes."

Kate sat bolt upright. The sun was high overhead, and she estimated it to be midmorning. If so, she had been asleep for over an hour.

"What will you tell your family, Ben? They'll want to know why you have arrived with a strange woman dressed in men's clothing."

"I believe you're right."

"Please don't tell them all I've told you…it's important that I keep the details of my company secret. You may tell them what happened, but please not my suspicions."

"I'll tell them the truth."

"But what truth?" Kate asked, pleading with her eyes.

"That we're getting married."

Chapter Thirteen

Ben could not have been more pleased. For once Kate was at a loss for words, and as they approached his house he knew that she wouldn't have time to recover before his family and twenty dogs descended upon them.

"The stables are just over the rise to your right," he told her, nodding in the appropriate direction. "You can just see the boathouse in the distance...our lake is perfect for rowing. Perhaps we can take a boat out on the morrow."

"Ben?"

"Ah! And here is the house." He pulled the carriage to a stop, scanning the facade of his home. He'd always taken his family's wealth for granted, but for the first time ever he found himself looking at his house with the critical eye of an outsider, anxious that there was nothing to find fault with.

"It was built in the fifteenth century, although the

family has refurbished it here and there over the years. The main facade, though, dates from the Restoration…."

Kate had no idea what he was talking about. She just sat there stupidly, watching him climb gracefully from the carriage and waiting for him to tell her that he was only jesting. Marriage?

He held out his hand to help her down. She didn't move. "Come now. This is no time to get shy. Give me your hand."

Kate still didn't budge, and Ben could see that she wasn't about to. So he took matters into his own hands—literally—by grasping her lightly around the waist and lifting her from the carriage as if she weighed nothing. He didn't put her down right away, but let her down slowly, sliding her down the front of his body until her feet touched the ground.

"Everything will be fine, Kate," he said, still holding her as he spoke. She had absolutely no response. She'd been flustered to begin with, and now…oh, God, he was so close. She couldn't think at all.

He kissed her. Not a hot, passionate kiss like the ones he'd given her before, but a kiss meant to reassure: warm, safe, comforting. Kate felt her reason return.

"I need to speak to you, Ben."

"We'll speak, but later. Right now I need to make introductions."

"Hmm?" she asked, spinning around in alarm. Facing her were three girls—one about her age, two younger— and they were staring. His sisters, she assumed, noting that they looked just as dismayed as she felt.

"Ben! We've only just got rid of you! Why are you

back so soon?" Beatrice, the oldest of the three girls, asked this question with a teasing sparkle in her eyes, while the other two girls edged behind her as if hiding.

How peculiar, thought Kate.

Ben grinned, walking forward to embrace his sisters. "I'm happy to see you, too!"

Kate just stood there, forgotten for the moment while she observed the happy scene in front of her. The family resemblance between Ben and his sisters was uncanny. With the exception of Eleanor, who was petite and dark haired, all were tall and blessed with rich, honey-blond hair. And, like Ben, they were all remarkably attractive.

Even fourteen-year-old Helen, with mud on her face, stains on her dress and grass in her hair was beautiful….

Goodness, she was dirty. In fact, Helen was soaking wet. Kate hadn't noticed it at first, so blinded was she by the striking good looks of the family, but all three sisters were filthy and dripping, looking as if they'd just come from jumping in a swamp.

Slowly, this dawned on Ben as well. He pulled away from Eleanor, looking down in bemusement at the muddy, wet impression she had left on the front of his jacket.

"What in the name of God have you three been doing? You smell bloody awful."

"It's only one of Eleanor's plays, Ben," Helen piped in. "She just read…what was it, Eleanor?"

"Hamlet," Eleanor mumbled, clearly embarrassed.

"Hamlet, Ben, and she wanted us to act it out. I wanted to be Ophelia, but Eleanor said I'd be no good, so we had to…"

"Audition?" Ben supplied helpfully.

"Yes. To see who could float downstream the best."

"And who was the best?"

"Eleanor was the only one who floated at all," Helen said, before turning on her sister with a vengeance, "because she's a *witch!*"

With that, she threw open the front door and flounced inside, slamming it behind her.

Eleanor merely rolled her eyes.

"Looks like I caught you red-handed," Ben said, clearly amused by his sisters' escapade.

But Beatrice wasn't about to let him gloat. "You shouldn't talk, brother," she said, casting a sly glance toward Kate. "And just *what* is going on here?"

He turned around, seeming to have forgotten the reason that he was there in the first place. Kate smiled at him tightly, never having felt more out of place in her life.

"Oh. Beatrice, Eleanor, I'd like you to meet Kate Sutcliff. She is my friend Robert's younger sister— you've met Robert, right?"

His sisters nodded in unison and continued to look at Kate curiously. Ben continued. "Well, she has most generously agreed to marry me."

Beatrice and Eleanor looked momentarily shocked, then burst into merry peals of laughter.

"My," Eleanor said, using her handkerchief to wipe her eyes, "that *is* generous."

"I'm not in jest," Ben responded, his firm tone telling them clearly that he was indeed serious.

Beatrice was the first to collect herself, a look of horror slowly dawning on her face. "You mean it, don't you, Ben? Oh, goodness, how rude of us. You're *really* not having us on?" At his nod, both sisters began apologizing and congratulating at once.

Beatrice stepped forward to introduce herself. "I'm pleased to meet you, Miss Sutcliff. I'm Beatrice, and this is Eleanor. The one inside is Helen. I assure you we're not normally so impolite, or so…unkempt."

Kate smiled, liking Ben's sisters right away. "A pleasure to meet you as well—call me Kate, please. I must assure you that I, too, am not usually so…unkempt."

"That's quite an outfit," Eleanor remarked, warming up to the novel situation. "I'm sure there's a fascinating story behind it…?" She leaned forward and grinned hopefully as she asked this question, her eyes aglow with keen interest.

"It will have to wait for later," Ben cut in. "Perhaps the two of you can scrounge up something for Kate to wear? In the meantime, I need to have a word with her, and to locate Father as well."

"He's in the stables!" Eleanor called out as Beatrice grabbed her hand and dragged her, giggling, into the house. The heavy front door slammed shut a second time.

In the silence that followed his sisters' exit, Ben said, "I suppose you feel as if you've been run over. My family can have that effect on the uninitiated."

"I'm a bit shaken, but it's not because of them." She was actually a bit annoyed, not to mention hurt and confused. She hadn't agreed to marry him at all. So why had he said that she had? "Ben, this is all very new…how can you introduce me to your family as your fiancée when we haven't even properly discussed marriage?"

"Kate, there is no discussion. We have to marry. If I don't marry you, no one else will. Your reputation has been thoroughly compromised."

"Yes, but—"

"Let me continue. You need to marry, and I'm about your only prospect at this point. Plus, Robert will have my head if I don't marry you—hell, he might have my head anyway. Surely you don't dislike me enough to want that to happen, do you?"

He smiled winningly as he asked this question, but Kate was not about to be put off. "I don't want your head on my conscience, no, but the fact remains that you don't want to marry me. Not really, anyway."

"Who says so?"

"Well, everybody says so. You're a confirmed bachelor. I…I don't think I would be happy if…you felt forced by the circumstances."

Ben was silent for a moment as he considered her words. "I don't know, Kate. I think we could get on well enough."

"I wasn't sure that you even liked me."

"Where would you get that idea?"

"Well, I've had several very strong indicators, foremost being that you were avoiding me. You already compromised me—several months ago, remember? I know it wasn't your fault, Ben, but it happened all the same. Only you disappeared while I had to suffer the scandal out alone."

"I disappeared because I promised not to touch you again."

"What does that have to do with—"

Ben cut her off with a kiss. "I stayed away because by the time I happened upon you in the park I had realized that I wouldn't be able to help myself, Kate."

"Oh."

"Are you satisfied?" He hoped to God she was. He hadn't planned on suggesting they marry. The idea had simply occurred to him, and the second the thought came to his mind, he'd spoken. Yet he didn't regret his impulse…oddly enough, he found himself trying to talk *her* into it.

He certainly wouldn't accept a refusal.

"You might ask me," Kate said tentatively.

Ben looked at her, filthy and clad in Billy's ridiculous woolen trousers. He thought she was the most beautiful woman he'd ever seen.

"Will you marry me, Kate?"

It sounded so strange, that question coming from him. She thought it over for a minute. There was nothing she'd like better, if only she could be confident that he meant what he said. Could she really say yes?

"Yes." There. She'd said it. She hoped she wouldn't regret it.

He kissed her once more, long and slow, not caring that they were still standing in the driveway where anyone could see them. They were oblivious to the world, knowing only the taste of each other, their feel.

Until the world downright intruded.

"Watch out, Kate. Out of the way, quickly," Ben said, yanking Kate to the side as his father rounded the corner of the house to descend upon them. The ninth Viscount Sinclair galloped up at full speed and leaped from his horse before even bothering to slow down, much less to stop. In one swift motion, he'd engulfed his son in a hearty bear hug.

"Congratulations, my boy! The girls raced to the stable to tell me the news! I never thought I'd see the day—where is she?" He pounded Ben on the back and scanned the area as he asked this question, his eyes passing over Kate without pause.

"Has she gone inside already? Here, your groom can take my horse and we'll go inside to find her." The viscount handed Kate his reins, still without looking at her. He put his arm around Ben's shoulders and began to head toward the door. Ben didn't move.

"Um, Father?"

He stopped to turn inquiringly toward his son.

"Father, you seem to have overlooked her. She's right here—I'd like you to meet Kate Sutcliff. Kate, this is my father."

When the viscount turned to look at her, a blank expression of disbelief on his face, Kate wasn't there, not really. Her feet may have been firmly rooted to the ground, but her mind and spirit wished her far away. To keep from crying, she began to make a mental list of things that were worse than her present situation.

Like being mauled by a tiger in India.

Or being stranded on a desert island and forced to marry its cannibal king.

Hell, at least she wasn't naked.

As Kate smiled weakly and offered her hand, she consoled herself with the knowledge that it could be worse, although not by much.

* * *

The Sinclairs' butler, Henley, had shown Kate to her room, a sun-filled chamber at the far end of the west wing of the house, allowing for windows on three of the walls. From these windows she could see one of the Sinclairs' immaculate gardens. Ben's father had informed her that they had over one hundred acres devoted to gardens alone, including a kitchen garden, a rose garden, an orchard and a formal knot garden that dated back to the seventeenth century. Part of her wanted very much to explore the grounds, but another part of her was reluctant to do so. It hardly seemed real that this immense and beautiful estate would soon be her new home; she didn't want to get too attached to the notion, lest she suddenly awake and find she was dreaming.

The supper hour was approaching, and Kate knew that she was expected downstairs very soon. But she just couldn't bring herself to open the door. She didn't want to face Ben's family again…not that they weren't all very nice. Ben's father, once over the initial shock of his son's sudden decision to marry *and* Kate's rakish appearance, had gone out of his way to charm her—an easy enough feat given his lopsided grin and tawny hair, almost untouched by gray. His resemblance to his son was uncanny, and Kate could tell from him that Ben would age well.

Indeed, it was the very pleasantness of Ben's entire family that made her dread seeing them again. She didn't want them to like her, and she didn't want to like them in return. Kate had hated seeing the viscount's happiness, had nearly cringed when she'd seen him hug his son with such exuberance. She'd felt even worse when he'd hugged her. There was really nothing to celebrate, and she felt guilty for deceiving them.

Despite Ben's assurances, Kate had serious concerns about marrying him in the first place. Certainly she *would* marry him. There was absolutely no alternative. But she almost wondered if her fate would be that much worse if she didn't marry at all, and simply let her reputation and her company go to the dogs. She was just too vulnerable where he was concerned, and all her systematic methods and dispassionate objectives were completely forgotten when he so much as looked at her. She lost control and feared that she could easily lose her heart. Ben would be easy to fall in love with, but Kate knew that her love would never be returned. She wasn't a believer in reformation. Once a rake, always a rake; her brother was an exception to this rule. Just because Ben had accepted the fact that they had to marry didn't mean that he'd agreed to change his ways, and she couldn't afford to have her heart broken.

In that moment, Kate decided that he would put off their inevitable conversation no longer. She would speak to him that very night, and they would discuss expectations for their marriage. She needed to set boundaries, to regain her perspective, to regain her control….

There was a knock at the door. She tensed, knowing that Ben was on the other side.

"Kate?" he called quietly, slowly opening the door and peeking his head around it. "Supper will be served in an hour. D'you want to come down and have a drink in the drawing room beforehand? Everyone is there."

Kate shook her head. "I'm not feeling quite the thing. But perhaps we could talk for a moment?"

Ben entered her room and closed the door behind him. It was a dreadfully improper thing to do, but she'd already realized that propriety didn't apply to him, especially in his own home. He leaned back against the door, his expression masked as he waited for her to begin.

"Well," she began nervously, "I just wanted to talk about this marriage…I have decided to accept your proposal."

Kate was staring at the floor as she said these words, so she didn't notice Ben exhale, visibly relaxing. He didn't point out that she'd already accepted, having sensed that she'd been debating the wisdom of that decision all day. He merely crossed the room and sat down in an armchair.

"I'm glad that you've seen reason at last," he said, trying to lighten her obvious discomfort. Why did she look so reluctant?

"Yes, well…there are still many things we have to discuss."

"Such as?"

"Well, for one, there is a paper you must sign. It regards my company."

"What sort of paper?"

Kate began to wring her hands nervously without noticing it. "Well, it's something I had my solicitor draw up when I realized how problematic marriage really could be. It just states that, once married, my husband…um, you…will in no way hinder my involvement in Alfred and Sons and will in no way attempt to control the company. It will remain solely my property."

"I see," Ben said blandly, giving no indication of his emotion.

"I, ah, only thought to create this document when I realized that although marriage would protect me from Andrew Hilton, it could also lead to a new set of problems if my husband should prove…less agreeable than might be hoped."

"I am not a fortune hunter, Kate."

"I know—that's another good thing about this marriage. You have ample funds of your own, so I can be certain you're not marrying me for my money."

"Why, thank you, Kate, for your generous estimation of my character."

She looked up at Ben, trying to gauge from his expression whether he was being sarcastic or not. She was certain that he was, but his face gave nothing away. He had every right to be angry with her, had every right to tell her that she could forget about her bloody marriage. She was making a total muck of it, yet carried on, wanting to get all of her conditions out on the table.

"There's just one more thing."

"Only one more? Is that all?"

"Yes," Kate said, lifting her chin slightly. "When— if—we marry, I will continue to live in Dorset."

"Dorset."

"Yes, Little Brookings. You visited my brother there many years ago. Robert actually owns the house but he hasn't lived there since he went to school."

"Please, Kate, remind me why we're getting married? I seem to have forgotten."

She lost her temper. Why did he have to make this

more difficult than it had to be? "We're getting married because we have no other choice! *You* asked me to marry you, not the other way around. If I live at my own house, then you can carry on your life pretty much as you always do, and I can do the same. Neither of us wants to marry, and I just want to make the best of a bad situation. Besides, I need to live in Dorset just in order to run my company—that's the whole point of this exercise, isn't it?"

The second Kate said these words, she wished she could take them back. She sounded like a total shrew, and she knew that she didn't really mean what she said. Truthfully, there wasn't anything that she'd like better than to marry Benjamin Sinclair and live happily ever after, to let herself fall in love...but that would never happen, and she knew it. Living in Dorset meant less time spent together; it would lower the risk of having her heart broken. She had to protect herself.

"Send the necessary papers to my secretary. I'll have a look at them."

"You will?" She couldn't believe that he'd still want to marry her.

Ben didn't bother to answer. He just nodded curtly and left her room, without a smile, a word or a backward glance.

Kate sank into her bed shakily, hating herself for being such a fool. Oh, God. She'd just thrown away any chance she'd ever had of being happy with him. Since she had met Ben, he had saved her neck twice and had, if she cared to be honest with herself, been the most exciting thing to have ever happened to her. Granted, he'd also been extremely improper, but never mind! She wanted desperately to believe that he was a total reprobate, a scoundrel…but she had come to realize that Ben was much more complicated than that. She liked him very much. Hell, she was infatuated with him, and if that combination didn't mean she loved him already then she didn't know what love was.

The last thing she wanted was for him to despise her, but there was no help for it. Better he hate her than hurt her. She sighed and rose, steeling herself for the trip downstairs and a most uncomfortable supper.

Ben felt like a fool, and he was furious. He'd bloody well never proposed to anyone before, had never wanted to, and wasn't sure why he'd changed his mind now. He didn't *have* to do it—he'd be a dishonorable cad if he didn't, but that had never bothered him before.

He sighed, looking across the dining room table at Kate. His father was talking to her about his new racehorse. Thankfully, she seemed to know a thing or two about racing, so his father was quite pleased. In fact, he was beaming at her as if she were some saintly creature capable of any miracle; given Ben's previous attitude to matrimony, this probably didn't seem like too much of an exaggeration. She seemed to be enjoying the conversation, too, and every time she laughed at something his father said Ben felt himself growing more and more annoyed.

Obviously she wasn't too upset.

His whole family had actually been rather awestruck when Kate had first entered the dining room, so surprised were they by her transformation. Her grubby trousers had been exchanged for a simple, pale blue gown borrowed from Beatrice. There was nothing particularly outstanding about the gown itself, yet she looked utterly radiant in it. The blue of her dress made her indigo eyes sparkle and her fair skin glow with health. She was an utter vision, and despite himself Ben's breath caught in his throat as he marveled at her beauty.

To his chagrin, he also noticed that the gown fit just a little too snugly in the bodice. He'd always known that she had lovely breasts, but seeing them so prominently displayed was almost more than he could bear.

If he were by himself, he would have buried his head in his hands. Instead, he drank his wine hastily and called for another glass.

He would have liked to have been able to tell himself that Kate's beauty was all that had compelled him to ask her to marry him, but his feelings were more complicated than that. She'd fascinated him from the first time he'd laid eyes on her, and he actually liked the idea of waking up with her in the morning, of having someone to talk to about even the most mundane things....

Bother that. Clearly she hadn't allowed herself to wander into the same sort of romantic delusions, and he swore that he wouldn't do it again. Theirs would be a marriage of necessity, nothing more. He'd marry her, and she could bloody well live in whatever godforsaken region of England that she pleased. And if he put his mind to it, Ben prayed, he'd be able to resume his life where he'd left off.

Truth was, however, he wasn't sure that he *could* go back to his normal life. Kate was simply the only woman he wanted. At first, he'd tried his damnedest to alter that fact; he'd visited two of his former mistresses, not to mention Madame Dupont's. But each and every time, he just couldn't go through with it and had left unsatisfied. In fact, since he'd met Kate over six months ago, she'd been the only woman he'd made love to, and that had been just the previous night.

Six months of abstinence. It was laughable.

Hell, it was a personal record.

Unfortunately, it was also a personal record that Ben could feel in his loins even now, despite the fact that he was furious at Kate *and* surrounded by his family. Now that he knew how sweet she tasted, he didn't know if he could forgo the pleasure again, injured pride be damned. He began to plot, wondering if there was some way to patch things up enough to make love to her again, that very night….

At that moment, Henley entered the dining room, distractedly wringing his hands and muttering to himself. One glossy section of his hair, usually so neatly and uniformly fixed to his head, had escaped from its pomade and now stuck out at a jaunty angle from his crown. Something was clearly amiss.

He approached Ben, cleared his throat, and announced in a near whisper, "Lord Gordon is here to see you, Lord Sinclair."

The viscount looked up from his plate. "What's that you say?"

"Lord Gordon, my lord."

"In the middle of supper? Unannounced? It's preposterous. He'll simply have to wait."

Ben groaned. He hadn't had time to inform his father of their impromptu and scandalous departure from Peshley. He glanced over at Kate to see how she was taking this news. She looked pale and ill, but other than that gave away no emotions.

Henley was looking even more upset. "I attempted to ask him to wait, my lord, but he, uh, rather forcefully stated that his business was quite urgent."

From beyond the dining room door came Robert's furious voice, bellowing, "Sinclair, you have ten seconds to get your worthless hide out here and start explaining!"

Kate scraped back her chair and rose shakily. "Oh, Ben—do you think he got the note?"

Ben didn't answer her question. He simply rose from his seat and walked out of the dining room, looking calm and collected. Not waiting for an invitation, Kate followed him, closing the dining room door quietly behind her.

In the silence that remained after they'd left, Beatrice remarked, "I reckon we can hear better over yonder, by the door, than we can sitting here at the table."

In an instant, all three sisters, followed closely by their father, leaped from their seats and dashed to the door, to which they unabashedly applied their ears.

In the hall, the scene was not so comical. Robert was angry—angrier than either Ben or Kate had ever seen him before. His shirt was untucked, his boots were caked in mud and his complexion was florid with fury.

For a moment, Kate, Ben and Robert just stood there, staring.

Kate was the first to venture into the silence.

"Robbie—you look as if you've ridden the whole way. Will you have supper?"

He turned and stared at her as if she'd gone daft. "I have been looking for you since seven o'clock in the morning. What I'd like is an explanation—what the hell is going on here?"

"Didn't you get Ben's note?"

He turned a suspicious glare at Ben. "What bloody note? And what the hell could a note do to correct this situation? Every damn soul at Charlotte's house is gossiping about it—how the two of you have gone off…disappeared without a trace. How the bloody hell do you expect to get out of this scrape, eh? You can survive it, Ben, but how about you, Kate? Doesn't matter if you're completely innocent, which—" he paused meaningfully and she felt her blush rise, "I assume you are."

Ben opened his mouth to speak, but before a single word could leave his mouth, Kate interjected. "We're getting married."

Robert stared at her in stunned silence, but as the implications of her words began to sink in, he turned to Ben, his eyes cold and steady. "And why *exactly* are you getting married? Because I know it's not your bloody honor that's making you do it."

Ben took a menacing step forward, his body rigid and fists clenched. "Watch your mouth, Sutcliff, or you might say something you'll regret."

"Answer my question, *Sinclair,* or—"

"Stop!" Kate shouted, stepping in front of Ben to face her brother. "There's no option but marriage! You know that, Robbie. I can assure you it's about the last thing we want to do, but our wishes don't matter anymore. We did nothing—I was taken from the house last night, and Ben risked his own neck trying to save—"

"Taken from the house?"

"Let me continue. Ben was just a victim of circumstances again, but this time the circumstances are too damning. He offered to marry me thinking only of my reputation."

Robert raked his hand through his hair, trying to gain control of his temper. He looked at his sister, searching her face for any sign of injury. Satisfied that she had not come to any physical harm, he let his question drop for the moment. "I see. Kate, you don't have to do this, you know. Whatever happened—and I expect you to tell me exactly what happened—it wasn't your fault. Yes, it'll cause a huge scandal, but eventually that will pass. If you marry just because of circumstance, you'll regret it for the rest of your life."

She nodded in agreement. "I realize that. I tried to convince him, but he wouldn't listen." She turned to Ben, her eyes beseeching him to change his mind. She felt wretched and embarrassed for her shrewish behavior, not to mention that Ben had done nothing to deserve it. She was certain that all that kept him from pitching her on the spot was some misplaced sense of duty, and she desperately wanted to give him an opportunity to bow out gracefully. She could withstand the scandal, but she didn't want to be responsible for ruining his life. He'd only grow to resent her for it. "Ben, you know I don't want you to feel obligated to do this. I…I'm very grateful, but I'm sure we can think of something more…agreeable to us both. Maybe we can just forget about this—I plan to go back to Dorset anyway. The gossip won't be nearly as bad there."

Ben had been listening quietly but intently to the exchange between brother and sister, but as Kate turned her pleading eyes toward him his expression remained masked.

She couldn't read his thoughts at all, but she certainly was not prepared for what he said next. "Unless you're with child, Kate. Then, perhaps, you might want to reconsider."

She gasped in shock. She hadn't even had time to consider this possibility and couldn't believe that he would mention it so offhandedly in front of her brother.

Robert didn't mince words, and the temper that he'd been trying so hard to keep in check let loose. With a growl, he cocked back his arm and punched Ben in the face with all of his force. Ben didn't even try to avoid it, but stood there unflinching as if he welcomed the blow. Robert rained blow after blow upon him, but he did nothing. He could hear Kate's voice pleading with her brother to stop, but it seemed very far away. She tried to pull him off but it was useless. Blackness took over, and he fell to the ground.

Ben was vaguely aware of his family rushing in, followed by several servants. Someone pulled Robert off him—his father, probably. Loud, angry questions and explanations were exchanged, none of which Ben asked or answered. Their echoed shouting bounced back and forth inside his head, but not a murmur passed through his lips. He'd said enough for one evening.

In all this vagueness, he knew only one thing: Kate did not want to marry him. She would, of course—he'd done everything in his power to see to that. Some primitive instinct deep inside of him would not let her go. But he knew that if she could have refused him, she would have: she would rather forfeit her good reputation completely and take the risk of returning to Dorset unwed and possibly pregnant than marry him.

He didn't know if he could accept that fact.

Chapter Fourteen

Ben was looking in a gilt-gesso mirror, examining the progress of his black eye. It wasn't actually black, nor was it deep purple, as it had been the day after Robert had hit him. No, nearly two weeks had passed since that memorable occasion, and the skin around his eye had turned a sickly yellow hue instead. Perhaps by the end of next week, he mused, it would disappear completely. If only the consequences of that night would disappear along with it. He must have been temporarily insane.

With a resigned sigh he turned and looked around the cluttered study. Every available surface was covered by papers, some arranged neatly into stacks but most simply spread out into messy piles. He had a hell of a lot of business to attend to—important business—but it was damn difficult to think straight in such a cluttered space. He'd have to see that a maid was sent in to restore some semblance of order or he'd really go mad.

He walked over to the desk, picked up one small

stack of papers and rifled through it briefly without much purpose. Slowly, as if in the haze of sleep, he sat down behind the desk. He needed to concentrate but just couldn't focus on the task at hand. He couldn't stop thinking about Kate.

His wife.

She'd been his wife for over a week, in fact. The date had been set while he was lying in a semiconscious heap on the floor of his father's hall. There apparently had been some discussion over whether it was advisable to have a leisurely engagement, and thus try to dispel any rumors of a forced marriage, or to wed quickly and hope to put the whole wretched scandal in the past as soon as possible. Ben was glad the latter option had been decided upon. They'd been married a mere three days later—he hadn't even realized it was possible to wed with such short notice outside of Scotland. Money, however, could buy just about anything, including special permits for precipitous weddings. Their ceremony had immediately followed Robert and Charlotte's more celebratory event. It was a private affair with only Ben's father and sisters and Charlotte and Robert in attendance; the latter had glowered darkly the whole way through. They'd even borrowed the priest, who'd been extremely nonplussed by the peculiar events but was too tactful to voice any objection.

Their wedding night was similarly unconventional. Indeed, they hadn't actually had one. Within a few hours of the ceremony Kate had packed what items she'd brought to Peshley and had returned to London to collect the remainder of her belongings. From there she planned to travel on to Little Brookings, where she would stay indefinitely. Ben had learned this information from Charlotte, since Kate hadn't bothered to discuss her plans with him. She hadn't even bothered to bid him farewell. She'd just left. When he saw her again—and it would be sooner than she'd either want or expect—he'd certainly have something to say about it. He never would have permitted it, and her actions infuriated him. It wasn't that long ago that Andrew Hilton had set his hired thugs on her, and he might not yet know of her changed status. She still wasn't safe on her own, even if she seemed to be oblivious of that fact. Ben had always admired her intelligence, but at the moment it was not in evidence.

Of course, *his* behavior had been far from exemplary, and she was perfectly justified in not wanting to speak to him. Announcing to her brother that she could be with child, for one, was pretty unforgivable. He also could have followed her to London as a peace offering; there was no way their sudden marriage would go unobserved by the *ton,* and her return to London was undoubtedly a difficult and embarrassing ordeal complete with whispers and cold shoulders. She wouldn't have expected to see him there since he'd informed her—as they were walking down the aisle, no less—that he'd be staying at his father's for a while and would then sail to the West Indies when the weather was favorable. He'd wanted to give her the impression that he didn't care one whit about being with her. He wanted her to believe that he cared as little about her as she, apparently, did about him.

It must have worked.

The fact was, though, he'd never planned on remaining with his father. In the first place his entire family was furious with him and it would just be too uncomfortable to remain at Sudley, especially to do so without his new bride. He'd been in plenty of scrapes in the course of his life, but his recent behavior surpassed everything that had come before. His father did nothing but sigh at him in disgust. His sisters, on the other hand, just kept asking too many annoying and highly personal questions that he felt, as younger sisters, they really had no right to ask.

He could handle his family, however. His main reason for not wanting to stay at his father's was much more pressing: business. Specifically, business which required his presence elsewhere. He'd been too distracted to face it all morning, but he knew he could avoid it no longer. Determined to focus, he returned his attention to the papers in his hand.

Within a minute, his lips tightened to a thin line. Where the hell should he begin? If his bloody wife were there with him, at least she'd be able to answer that question for him.

His dark expression must have looked unusually foreboding, because at that moment a rather timid voice interrupted his dark musings. "Lord Sinclair?"

It was Tilly, the plump and red-cheeked housekeeper, hovering in the doorway. Ben softened his expression guiltily. Frankly, he was relieved by the disruption. "Yes, Tilly?"

She relaxed visibly. "Shall I serve your tea in here, my lord? Lord Gordon used to dine in here when he was busy, may God rest his soul. Miss Sutcliff…that is, Lady Sinclair, used to as well. It faces west, so you'll get the afternoon sun."

"Yes, thank you, Tilly. That will be all."

No, Ben mused as she left the room, staying at Sudley had been out of the question given the circumstances. He'd gone straight to Little Brookings, of course. Kate's staff had welcomed him with open arms, and why not? He was her husband.

She would probably be arriving within the next few days. He reckoned she'd be less pleased by his presence.

That thought almost made him smile. Much as he might dislike her at the moment, he couldn't wait to see her reaction. Buoyed by that thought, he looked once more at the papers in his lap.

Right. Pay attention. Andrew Hilton was still out there and he had to find him.

The papers Ben had spent so long poring over had been compiled by Josiah Thatcher, a man his secretary had located in London's East End the day after Robert had hit him in the face. Josiah was an ex-soldier who now made his living performing a variety of tasks for the right money: keeping tabs on unfaithful husbands and wives, threatening those in need of it and twisting arms generally. Ben suspected his résumé got even more colorful but thought it better not to ask.

For Ben's purposes, Josiah was a spy, a function for which he apparently held a formidable underworld reputation. Andrew Hilton was still a danger and Ben knew that the sooner he was gotten rid of, the better. So, the day after his marriage had been settled, he'd hired Josiah and sent him on ahead to Little Brookings to garner what he could by asking a few discreet questions around the town. From Josiah's groundwork Ben learned that Hilton hadn't left Little Brookings for over a year, a fact that caused him to pause and wonder how he'd planned the attacks on Kate from such a distance. He also learned that although Andrew Hilton could be found at the boatyard most days, he hadn't been seen there since the day after Ben arrived. Ben's sudden presence in town had caused a minor, local sensation and news of it had undoubtedly found its way to Hilton. Obviously he'd thought it would be best to make himself scarce—pretty much an admission of guilt as Ben saw it.

Since arriving, Ben had kept Josiah on under the pretense of valet. Although he no longer needed his sleuthing skills, he figured it wouldn't be a bad thing to have an extra pair of eyes around to look after Kate once she arrived. As it turned out, however, Josiah's services weren't really needed: Hilton was remarkably easy to locate. Ben actually just stumbled upon him. He'd gone for a walk into town to familiarize himself with his surroundings and to ask a few subtle questions of his own. It was a charming town filled with people who smiled and nodded at him without provocation—strange, but, the more he became accustomed to it, rather nice. He even found himself smiling back on a few occasions, something that the future tenth Viscount Sinclair would never do in London.

On his way home from this walk, he'd stopped at

what was, in his opinion, Little Brookings's principal attraction: the Seven Bells, its homely, sixteenth-century public house. The first time he'd entered this pub—and he was ashamed now to admit it—his lip had actually curled in snobbish distaste. He would never frequent such a modest establishment in London. Nor had he felt an immediate rapport with the townsfolk gathered inside: farmers, mostly, who spoke about their pigs in funny West Country accents. But Ben had had a frustrating day: he couldn't stop thinking about his wife, and he hadn't had a soul to talk to but the servants and Josiah since his arrival. Damn it, he was thirsty, and Mr. Palmer, the garrulous and compassionate publican, had sensed this. He'd begun pouring generous glasses of whisky while Mrs. Palmer brought him a steaming plate of steak and kidney pie and buttery, boiled potatoes followed with pudding. It was probably the most decadent meal they'd served in years, even if most London clubs and restaurants would have considered it far too humble for their menus. To Ben, it was heaven, and he'd visited the pub several times thereafter…probably several times more than was proper.

As he entered the low-ceilinged main room on this occasion, however, he immediately noticed a difference. Sitting in the chair that he had come to regard as his own was a man he'd never seen before.

"Ah, Mr. Hilton," Mr. Palmer was saying, "will that be all for you today?"

Mrs. Palmer sniffed loudly, causing the other customers to snicker. "Can a whole bottle all to himself be enough, Mr. Palmer? Surely he can't have finished *yet*—

he certainly hasn't paid yet." She followed this tart statement with a meaningful glance.

The man just rose on shaky legs and slurred, "Tomorrow, Martha, tomorrow. I promise." He then kissed Mrs. Palmer on the hand with a flourish and swayed right past Ben and out the door.

Ben didn't move for a moment, too startled was he by his good fortune. He recovered shortly, however, and turned and followed.

Outside, the man hadn't gone that far. He had merely walked around to the side of the building and seemed, from the satisfied noises Ben heard, to be relieving himself. Ben sighed in impatient disgust. He'd really been hoping to get this over with quickly.

The man reappeared after a minute. He didn't seem to notice Ben and continued down the street.

Ben reached out and put a hand on his shoulder. "Andrew Hilton?" he asked, wanting to be certain that this was the right man before he planted his fist in his face. Mr. Palmer had referred to him only as "Mr. Hilton" and it was possible there was more than one person of such name, even in such a small village.

The man stopped suddenly and turned, obviously startled at being addressed so suddenly and at Ben's cut-glass accent.

"I'm Andrew Hilton," he replied in a surprisingly friendly voice accompanied by a slight bow. "And who's asking?"

Ben didn't answer, but took a menacing step forward. Hilton backed up speedily. "If you have a problem with me, can we not talk about it like reasonable—"

Ben didn't let him finish. All the tension and frustration and anger that had been stewing in him since he'd asked Kate to marry him burst out. He grabbed Hilton by the front of his shirt and lifted him clear off the ground. Hilton was quite a bit smaller than Ben and dangled uselessly, eyes wide.

Ben lowered him to the ground. He wanted to hit him, but instead he took a deep breath and counted to five slowly. He needed answers before he knocked the man senseless.

Hilton looked warily up and down the street, but didn't run off. He knew that he wasn't a match for Ben and thought it best, for the moment, not to resist.

"You don't know me," Ben began, "but you know my wife."

Hilton paled and began stuttering. " I...I know her...but not in the b-biblical sense you may suspect. I've winked at her, maybe, once or twice, when I've seen her on the green, but...it's just flirtation."

Ben longed to hit him again just for his stupidity. He seemed to think Ben was some jealous husband, a completely unlikely scenario. As if anyone would choose Hilton over him. He quickly clarified his statement. "Katherine Sutcliff, my wife, now Lady Sinclair. Now is everything beginning to make sense?"

Hilton said nothing, but he appeared to be sobering quickly.

"You will stay away from her."

Hilton shook his head in slight confusion. "I haven't seen her in months, my lord. She left Dorset and hasn't been back. I...I'd only just heard she'd married."

"I'm surprised you didn't think it unwise to stay in town. Did you not think I'd find you and see that you paid for your harassment of her?"

Hilton took a small step back at the words "see that you paid." Still he looked perplexed. "I...I've had my differences with her, my lord...but no lasting problems. I've been taking care of the company while she's away...quite well, I thought."

"Your service to Alfred and Sons is terminated."

"You cannot do that. She owns that company, even if she doesn't deserve it. Her father saw to that."

"No, Hilton, I now own the company and I don't like you."

Hilton's eyes grew wide in shock. "She would never let you own it."

Ben raised an arrogant eyebrow. "She didn't let me do anything. I am her husband and I make the decisions. You planned to be in a similar position, did you not?"

"I'm sorry, my lord?"

"You tried to coerce her into marrying you. You must remember."

A deep flush stained Hilton's face. He was completely sober now and for the first time he seemed to understand the cause of Ben's aggression completely. "I only tried once, really, my lord—"

"Not according to my wife. You threatened her."

"No! I only tried to convince her...she cannot be running that company on her own, but she wouldn't listen to reason. I wanted her to sell it to me, but she refused."

"So you tried to force her to marry you instead?"

"No! Not to force her to marry me...I mean, that's

how I put it, but only because I knew she didn't want to marry me…nor I her, my lord. I was just trying to convince her to sell the company to me as a…more pleasing option."

"And kidnapping her?"

Hilton's expression remained completely blank. He stared for a moment, not seeming to understand yet again. "I don't know what you're talking about."

"Twice, Hilton. Surely you remember. You're not that thick, are you?"

"I've been in Little Brookings for the past year at least. You can ask anyone. I don't understand."

Hilton's astonishment seemed so sincere that a tiny speck of doubt entered Ben's mind. He squashed it and took another step forward, this time grabbing Hilton by the lapels of his coat and dragging him forward. "What exactly don't you understand?"

Hilton was shaking his head in desperation. "I don't know what you're talking about, my lord. I never tried to kidnap her. I'd never do anything to hurt her. I just wanted control over the company. I worked for that family for my entire adult life, but I never planned on working for an inexperienced girl. I knew that with her in control we'd lose all business eventually. I'd lose my job as a result. I was owed more than that. I was. But I would never hurt her."

Ben released Hilton abruptly, and in the suddenness of the motion he stumbled to the ground. Ben wanted to kick him, to hit him. He was the cause of every problem in his life. He'd threatened Kate, made her panic, made her need to marry, made her marry *him* even though she hadn't wanted to. Because of Andrew Hilton, Ben was married to a woman who mistrusted and despised him. He wasn't too far from despising her either, these days, although deep down he was afraid he'd fallen completely in love with her and would never be able to change that fact. That was what hurt the most.

But somehow he controlled himself.

"You've lost your job anyway, Hilton. You know that, and you have one more chance to tell me the truth."

Hilton rose unsteadily. "I am telling you the truth! I would never harm her. I…I admit I tried to intimidate her, but never more than that. Never."

Ben looked at him hard, and Hilton looked back, meeting his eyes.

Ben knew in that moment that he was telling the truth. He'd already begun to suspect it, but now he knew it without a doubt. Andrew Hilton was guilty of threatening Kate, and for that he'd lost his position at the company forever. But he'd had nothing to do with the attacks on Kate in London and at Peshley: that had been someone else.

Ben stepped away and nodded at Hilton. Hilton tipped his hat and walked off down the street quickly. When he'd gone about fifty feet he began to run.

Ben watched him go, filled with dread.

Chapter Fifteen

Kate was at once pleased to be returning home and dreading the consequences that return would bring. News of her marriage would already have reached her servants and, although they were too discreet to ask any personal questions, they would obviously wonder why she had come back to Dorset without her husband. They certainly would gossip about it when she was out of hearing. It wasn't natural for a wife to leave her husband so soon after marrying…and Kate had left him, not the other way around. She'd pushed him away before even giving things a chance. She'd left him within a few hours of marrying him and hadn't even told him she was leaving. She'd meant to inform him, she really had…only he was in the study talking to his father and she hadn't wanted to disturb him.

Oh, hell. She hadn't wanted to face him. She couldn't. She was too much of a coward.

Her heart accelerated as her carriage slowed to a halt

in front of the house. Mary had been talking for most
of the long journey, but Kate had barely paid attention.
She was just too worried. What on earth would she tell
everyone? How would she explain her situation? Little
Brookings was quite small and gossip always spread
quickly there. She could say that Ben had been detained
in London, but what would she say when he didn't turn
up in a few days? In a few weeks? And how would she
explain it when she never went to visit him? Eventually
she'd have to come up with something.

As her driver helped her from her carriage, her
family's longtime housekeeper, Tilly, opened the front
door of the house, her wide form and broad smile wel-
coming her home. She greeted Kate with the familiarity
born of so many years, her manner as warm and open as
if Kate had only been gone a few minutes, rather than
several months. Kate felt, though, as if she'd been gone
for ages. Nothing seemed quite the same anymore.
Although she'd hoped to marry and then simply go on
about her business, clearly that was going to take a bit of
effort. Forgetting her husband would not be easy at all.

She forced a smile in return as she walked to the front
door. "Good day, Tilly."

"Lady Sinclair, we're pleased you're home. It has
been a long time…and such a big change!"

Kate didn't want to talk about the big change. She
also wasn't used to being called Lady Sinclair, particularly by Tilly. It actually made her feel rather ill. "I'm
glad to see you, too, Tilly. You've no idea how glad. I've
missed everyone here dreadfully."

Tilly grinned mischievously and leaned in toward

Kate conspiratorially. "It cannot have been that awful, m'lady, with a man like Lord Sinclair courting you."

Mary snorted derisively as she entered the house and marched straight upstairs.

Kate was simply stunned. "I'm sorry?" She didn't quite know how her housekeeper would know what sort of man her husband was. He *did* have a bit of a reputation…perhaps Tilly remembered him from his long ago visit to her brother? "Have you heard of Lord Sinclair?"

Tilly giggled. "Heard of him? You jest, my lady. He's here, as you well know…in the study, having his tea. I've never known a man to take so much sugar! Who'd have thought a man like that would have such a sweet tooth? It will come as no surprise to you, of course."

Kate raised her eyebrows. She hardly knew her husband at all, and she certainly didn't know a thing about any sweet tooth. Nor did she know why he was purportedly indulging it in her study. He was not supposed to be there. He was supposed to be at his father's house, or, at best, in the middle of the Atlantic Ocean. If she'd had any say in the matter, he'd be at the bottom of it. Not here. Anywhere but *here*.

Something was going on. She had obviously entered some sort of a trap. "Of course," she answered Tilly cautiously, hoping her housekeeper would reveal more.

Tilly was hardly paying attention and didn't seem to notice Kate's rather stiff reaction. "I'll serve you your tea in there as well—you must have some catching up to do with Lord Sinclair. Not like most newlyweds, separated before they've been married a week. But I understand completely. He told me everything."

"Oh, please tell me he didn't," Kate pleaded. Dear God. Was he trying to destroy her? Turn her servants against her?

Tilly burst into merry laughter once more, still oblivious to Kate's very real distress. "Indeed he did, and why not, my lady? You had the orphans to attend to, of course. They would miss you terribly, and you needed to return to London to say a proper goodbye, or they'd be abandoned *yet again,* and you simply couldn't let that happen, could you?"

"The orphans?"

"Yes, the poor, sick dears. He told me about how kind you were, sacrificing your time like that, during those long days spent south of the river—the boy with one leg, and sweet, blind Mary. When I heard that I thought to myself, *How very like my mistress that sounds. Absolutely selfless.* He said that was why he fell in love with you—your kindness and charity to one and all. 'Like an angel,' he said, 'especially to me.'"

"He said that?"

"He did. I know it might be impertinent, my lady, but I declare, when you said you were going to London to get married, I never supposed you'd find someone like Lord Sinclair. No, indeed. *So* handsome."

Kate nodded distractedly. He was a handsome scoundrel, and now a handsome liar, too. How he must have enjoyed making that remark: *angel.* Ha. He would have to leave—and if he refused she'd simply have to poison his tea. There was no other choice. He'd charmed her servants. They were now firmly on his side and would have little sympathy for her. He did not own this house, though.

It belonged to her brother, and Ben had quickly plummeted from being Robert's best friend to being his worst enemy. He could make Ben leave if he wanted to. She would write to him immediately. He would advise her.

Kate walked determinedly through the front door and turned to Tilly. "Lord Sinclair is in the study, you say?"

"Yes, my lady. Um…"

"Yes?"

Tilly blushed. "I put Lord Sinclair into the master bedroom, and I began moving your belongings in there as well. I know you didn't want to sleep there after your father died, but now it's different."

Kate had thought things couldn't get much worse, but she hadn't figured this into the equation. Any resolve she'd felt was sapped from her suddenly and completely. She felt sick. Really, really sick.

"I'll go find him," she said weakly, wishing she could sound more decisive. She walked down the hallway toward the study. When she reached the door, she swallowed hard and knocked.

There was no answer.

Kate steeled herself for the worst and opened the door.

He was inside, seated in a worn, brown leather chair. He looked up from the book he was reading but didn't seem at all surprised by her presence. He'd obviously been waiting for her.

"Close the door, Kate," he said coolly.

Any nervousness she'd felt was now replaced by anger. How could he appear so blasé? He'd behaved just as badly as she had. *He* was the one who was trespassing. She wasn't going to follow his orders. Without closing the door as he'd requested, she said in a tone to match his own, "My lord. What a pleasant surprise."

He just lifted one infuriating brow at her sardonic tone. "Close the door, Kate."

"No."

He rose, and for just an instant she caught a glint in his eye that told her he wasn't so unaffected after all. He crossed the room and stood right in front of her. He reached his arm around her and she stiffened. But he only closed the door behind her.

He was so close now, Kate stopped breathing. He looked her straight in the eye. "Now you will sit down, Kate."

"Why?"

"Because I'm longing to talk to you. I've missed you so much."

Kate swallowed hard and almost choked, but there was no alternative. Feeling as if she were walking to her doom, she crossed the study and sat in a chair opposite from Ben's. He reclaimed his seat and simply looked at her without speaking.

Kate began to fidget nervously but stopped herself. She wanted desperately to look away from him but couldn't give in. "Tilly will be in soon with more tea," she said weakly after a moment, needing to break the silence. "This might not be the best place to talk."

"I never said I meant to keep you for long."

She bristled slightly. It was her bloody house, wasn't it? Who was he to tell her where to sit and what to do? And what exactly did he mean by "keep you"? Did he mean he wouldn't detain her for long or was it a veiled reference to what he really wanted: an annulment? Why else would he have come all this way? Why else would he want to speak to her? But could he get an annulment after they'd…consummated their relationship? Would he divorce her? It wouldn't surprise her if he did.

With an edge to her voice, she said, "This isn't your house, you know, and you've no right to be here. My brother owns it and he's not at all pleased with you at the moment."

"So I should be on my best behavior? I'm not too pleased with him either. Nor with you…angel."

She blushed deeply but still refused to look away. She sat up straighter, wrapping her hauteur around herself like a prickly coat. Her tone was sharp when she asked, "Well? What would you like to speak about? Did you need something?"

Ben had no answer for that, and for a moment he just stared back at her flushed and angry face. He didn't know how the hell to begin the conversation he wanted to have with her, but antagonizing her was clearly not the way. He just couldn't seem to help himself sometimes. Maybe he should have left the country after all. Better than sitting in bloody Little Brookings, doing nothing but staring at his beautiful wife who hated him. His beautiful wife who someone was trying to hurt.

That was why he was there.

She began glaring at him and thrumming her fingers on the arm of the chair, impatient for an answer.

That brought him back to reality. She sensed his hesitation and was beginning to gloat. Clearly she was trying to make this as unpleasant as possible. "No, I do not need anything. But if you weren't such an irrational twit you'd have realized by now that you do."

Kate looked patently unimpressed. "Is that so? And do you think you can help me?"

He raised his voice slightly. "Do you not think it idiotic to come back here when someone has been trying to harm you?"

"You refer to Andrew Hilton?"

"Perhaps."

"No, I do not think it's idiotic. I am married now and he no longer has anything to gain. That's *why* I got married, if you don't remember."

Ben snorted. "I have the misfortune to remember very well."

"Then you can leave—"

"Let's not discuss this now, Kate," Ben interrupted. He felt himself beginning to get very angry and desperately needed to regain his composure. "That's not why I'm here, and quite frankly I don't even care anymore. I came here to meet with Hilton because you seem to be completely negligent of your personal safety. He will no longer be a threat to you."

"Oh. Well, that's a relief."

"You're welcome."

Kate blushed. She knew she should have said thank you, but she didn't correct herself. She was dying to ask him about this meeting but didn't want to seem too interested…or too grateful for his intervention.

"He also won't be working for you either."

Kate bristled again. "I had planned on informing him

of that myself. I don't appreciate your stepping in. I am not helpless."

"You're hopeless enough. Maybe I got the two confused."

"I can take care of myself."

"I've been watching you take care of yourself since the day I met you, Kate, and you aren't doing such a splendid job. What did you intend to do after letting him go? Hire someone else?"

Kate didn't have an answer for that question. She'd thought of that problem herself, many, many times, as a matter of fact. She couldn't run the business without Hilton because no one would ever do business with her. And hiring someone else was out of the question. Hilton had had the advantage of working for her family for many years. He'd been there when her father had been there to protect her, and still he'd turned out disloyal. How could she find someone to take his place? No, Kate didn't know what to say to that. She'd vowed to worry about that bridge when she crossed it, although now that it was time, she'd been doing her best to ignore it.

Only Ben wouldn't let her.

He was still waiting for her answer, so she finally caved in. "I don't know. I realize that will be a problem. But I am certain that I'll find a solution in time."

"There's an even bigger problem than that, dear wife."

"Oh? You know, I can enumerate my problems perfectly well on my own, thank you. I don't need your assistance," Kate said, rising. She simply couldn't listen to it anymore. She needed to leave.

"Don't go, Kate," Ben said, rising to follow her.

"Why?" she asked as she walked briskly to the door.

"Hilton is not behind the attacks on you."

She paused with her hand on the doorknob. "But how can you know that? What do you mean?"

"I mean someone else has been trying to harm you all this time."

Chapter Sixteen

It took half an hour to explain his conversation with Hilton, and still Kate didn't believe him, not entirely. She was sitting, looking dejected, in her chair.

"We need to discuss this predicament, Kate."

She looked at him, her expression at once forlorn and defiant. "I'm afraid I have many predicaments at the moment. To which one do you refer?"

Ben paused in his pacing about the room to take a deep breath and count slowly to five. "Who else could be behind these attacks, Kate? You cannot simply ignore that question as you've ignored everything else."

That was exactly what she'd planned to do. "What would you like me to do instead?"

"I thought it might be helpful if, perhaps, we put together a list of possible suspects. That way I can at least know who all of the players are…and the process of doing so might help you to think of people you might not naturally suspect."

"I've done that already in my mind, ten times over while we've been sitting here. There's not a single person I can think of who would want to harm me. I focused on Andrew Hilton before because he's the only person who could logically have had something to gain."

Ben sighed in frustration. "Well, let's try anyway. Sometimes a second opinion…here, I have paper…" He trailed off when she made no move to take it from his outstretched hand. She wasn't making this process easy. He dropped the paper in her lap.

She just stared at it. "What am I supposed to do with this?"

He walked over to the desk and retrieved a pen. "I think we should go through a list of suspects, and take note of what they have going for and against them."

"I'm sorry, but I can't think of one person, not to mention an entire list of people, who'd want to injure me."

"Someone who might know of your involvement in Alfred and Sons who would use it against you, perhaps?" Ben asked, putting the pen in her hand. "What about the men your father dealt with professionally?"

"They would only know me as my father's daughter, not as a…a competitor, or even a possible means of acquiring our company."

"Can you be sure of that?" When she shook her head he pressed her again. "Names, Kate. There must be someone."

She sighed. She'd tried this before. Although Andrew Hilton had certainly tried to intimidate her, she'd never had any real proof that he'd been responsible for her attempted abductions. There'd always been some doubt.

But she simply couldn't think of anyone else and didn't think this exercise would turn up anything new.

Ben was staring at her, however, so she took a stab. "Well, there's Richard Hastings, for one. He was the third son of Squire Hastings and didn't gain anything by inheritance. He dabbled in shipping for a short while...but has never been able to make a profit. He's a neighbor of ours and came to dinner on occasion."

"Did you trust him?"

"He always seemed fairly honorable. He drank too much, though...that's part of the reason why he was never successful."

"So he might know that you were the company's heir and, if so, seems to have as much motive as anyone."

"If he knows—and I doubt that very much—he'd never do anything about it. He would have been aware that I spent an unusual amount of time at my father's boatyard...everyone around here knows that and most find me a bit peculiar for it."

Ben grunted in agreement.

Kate scowled at him. "Hastings doesn't completely approve of me, but he's really very nice. If you're here for any amount of time you're certain to meet him."

"Might he have wanted to marry you himself?"

She blushed deeply. "He...once, perhaps, he expressed some interest in me. I never put much store by it, though. He's a tremendous flirt. He's also married already."

"Write his name down."

"No."

Ben just stared at her for a moment, not saying anything. He shook his head slightly and took the pen and paper from her. He began writing something down on the piece of paper, muttering under his breath as he did so. She couldn't quite make out what he said, but she assumed it was unflattering nonetheless.

"What are you writing?"

He ignored her and carried on. "Aside from Andrew Hilton, who else worked with the company closely?"

"Well…no one else at that level. I suppose any number of men who've worked for us for long enough might suspect something, but no one else could possibly be certain. My ownership of the company was, as you know, a secret. Unless, that is, Hilton spoke about it."

"He might have done so."

"Yes…although he'd have nothing to gain by exposing me. He'd risk his own position by damaging the company's reputation."

"What about your solicitor? He must know about your inheritance, right?"

"Gregory Sithwell? Of course he knows—he helped draw up my father's will."

Ben wrote his name down. "So he's a suspect. And if not, who knows? Perhaps he inadvertently told someone of your inheritance."

Kate shrugged. She couldn't rule out that possibility, but she was certain that her solicitor was completely benign. "Mr. Sithwell cannot have done it. He's at least seventy, Ben, and one of the gentlest men I've ever met. I trust him completely."

"Can you think of no one else? Anyone who might be jealous of your position?"

She thought very hard. "Hardly. There's Edward

Manning…um, you might know his company—
Manning Ships?"

At Ben's slight nod Kate continued. "Well, he's the
closest thing we have to a competitor, although his ships
are of an inferior quality. He sells them for a cheaper
price, though, and manages to make a tidy profit. My
father's company is the only thing keeping him from
dominating the entire industry."

"Would he have any way of knowing who you
really are?"

"Not remotely. He lives in London, I think…I'm not
even sure. I've tried and tried to think of a way that he
could have found out, but short of espionage it's just
not possible."

"Well," Ben said, writing down his name, "it does
happen from time to time if enough money is at stake."

"I'd hardly recognize him if I saw him, Ben. It's
completely improbable."

He nodded, and after a moment of silence asked,
"How well do you pay your employees?"

"How dare you."

Ben closed his eyes briefly, his patience aggravated.
"I'm just looking for a motive, Kate. You don't need to
get so damned offended. Make a list of all your employees," he ordered, handing the pen and paper back to her,
"especially the ones who worked at the company before
your father's death."

Kate dutifully wrote, thinking all the while that this
was the most absurd procedure she had ever gone
through. There were at least forty men working at the
boatyard alone.

It took her several minutes, and when she was finished she handed the list back to Ben for perusal. He read it carefully. "This is everyone?"

"I think so…we've had, of course, the odd man who's worked for us for a few weeks and then left. I will add to that list if I remember anyone else."

"What about servants?"

She didn't like where he was going with this line of inquiry. "We've had most of our servants since before I was even born—none of them would ever wish me harm, not to mention that, being in my employ, they'd have nothing to gain by ruining me. And besides, none of them know the details of the company."

"Servants know everything, Kate. Make a list of them. Start with house servants."

She almost lost her temper but managed, just in time, to restrain it. "Well, there's Tilly, Mr. Randall, Flossie, Kenneth, Graham—"

"What about your lady's maid?"

"Mary? Call her 'companion' or you'll invoke her wrath. She knows about my involvement, yes, of course. She knows everything about me…she's been with us for so long, I don't think I could hide anything from her if I tried."

"Does she have any reason to wish you ill?"

"Absolutely not. She wishes *you* ill, though. Can you squeeze a motive from that?"

Ben chose to ignore that jab. "You said '*most*,' Kate—which servants are newer to your family's employ?"

"Well, there is Owens the coachman—"

"Put him down."

"Why? Owens is extremely loyal!"

"Because he was driving the coach the first time you were abducted, and he was at Peshley when you were abducted the second time."

"I hate to inform you, Ben, but you were conveniently present on all of those occasions as well. Perhaps I should put you on this list."

He made no response. He just looked at her disgustedly, shook his head and took the pen and paper back before she could write anything. He placed Owens's name at the bottom of the growing list.

"And his motive?" she challenged, watching him write.

"Next?" he inquired, ignoring her question.

Kate harrumphed. "You're the only one who's gained anything out of this mess. Maybe I *should* suspect you."

"I beg to differ, madam. I have gained nothing at all."

Kate harrumphed once more. "You're being deliberately rude."

"And you're 'harrumphing' again."

"What?"

"I had a nurse once who habitually harrumphed, and it is not a characteristic I would look for in a wife. Where have you learned this habit? Was it from this Mary? This companion of yours?"

Kate couldn't help it. She began to giggle. The stress of the situation had finally gotten to her, and laughing was the only way to relieve it. She wanted to remain angry with Ben forever—he deserved it—but for just that tiny window of a moment she found it was impossible. "Do not speak ill of Mary, Ben. She will have her revenge, I warn you."

"She won't know unless you tell her."

"I told you, Ben," Kate said as she rose, "she knows everything."

With that, she left the room, trying very hard to suppress a small smile.

Kate was upstairs in her former bedroom, dressing for dinner as slowly as possible. She didn't want to return downstairs and face her husband again, and she stalled by pulling her gloves onto each finger with deliberation, by changing her shoes three times. He was so smug, and she hated him for it. Of course, he had every reason to hate her, too. She'd been a complete shrew to him and had never apologized. But at least she hadn't completely humiliated him in front of his family. That embarrassing treat had been hers alone.

She hated him and she intended to keep it that way.

But then he had to go and be charming—it was damn hard hating him when he acted like that. She'd been furious, yet with little effort he'd made her smile…he'd practically made her want to forgive him on the spot for everything he'd done. How would she possibly stay sane under these circumstances? How would she stay firm?

She turned around in her seat at her dressing table to face Mary, who bustled about quietly in the background. Mary hadn't liked Ben one bit since she'd learned about what he'd said in front of her brother, and she could be counted on to stoke Kate's animosity toward her husband. "I swear, Mary, he's being completely absurd."

"Is he, dear?" she replied without really seeming to listen. Kate had been ranting, more or less, about Ben since the day of their engagement and it was becoming a less compelling topic.

Kate gave her a grumpy look. "He won't listen to me, Mary. I told him that there is no reason to worry, that he has no need to be here and can return to London or do whatever her likes. He *insists* on staying."

"Well, in all fairness, perhaps he should. We don't know that you're safe yet."

"He made me compile a list of suspects. Stood over me and watched me do it."

"Is that so, dear?" Mary's attention still remained elsewhere.

Kate frowned grumpily. "Do you know who's at the very top of that list?"

Mary just shrugged and began laying out pairs of silk stocking on the bed.

"You are, Mary."

That caused her to snap to attention. "The beast!"

Kate sat back, satisfied by that response. So what if Mary wasn't *really* at the top of the list. It was just a little white lie. "I know. I think *he's* a suspect. I told him."

"You cannot be serious, my lady." Mary looked truly alarmed.

Kate rolled her eyes. "Of course I'm not serious—I mean, that is what I told him, but I didn't really mean it."

"But why would you even suggest such a thing? Do you never want peace with that man? I'm hardly an advocate for Lord Sinclair, but I long for the days when our conversations did not revolve solely around his faults."

"Oh, I don't care if he hates me. And anyway, I was just being cheeky. It is rather odd, though. On *every* occasion I've been abducted or otherwise interfered with he's magically appeared. A rather strange coincidence, do you not think?"

"I don't know…perhaps he's your guardian angel?" Mary asked with a mischievous smile.

"Not very likely," Kate said with a grumble. Ben was definitely far better at getting her into trouble than keeping her out of it. "But he does have a strange way of turning up unexpectedly. Banging on my brother's door in the middle of the night—"

"What's this?"

Kate realized she'd never told Mary about her first, scandalous encounter with Benjamin Sinclair. Better not tell her now. She barreled on. "He was on hand to rescue me from my carriage after my brother's engagement party—odd, wouldn't you say? And he was snooping in the conservatory during that storm when I was abducted again. He was even at the lake at St. James's Park when we went there with Charlotte."

Mary cocked her head to the side. "The lake?"

Kate realized that she'd also concealed this meeting from Mary, and from Charlotte as well. "Oh…you remember, Mary—we had a picnic in St. James's Park and Charlotte took you with her when she went to speak with Lady…oh, whomever she was? Would you believe Ben appeared the moment you'd left? It was as if he'd planned it. I was convinced at the time that Charlotte had somehow arranged the whole thing—she simply can't help matchmaking."

"You didn't tell me about this."

She sighed. "Well…since I thought—and still think,

a bit—that Charlotte had somehow planned the whole thing…both she and you were acting rather suspiciously that day…anyway, I didn't want to give her the satisfaction of knowing that her plan had worked. I also didn't want her to try anything like that again because, well, he hardly needed encouragement."

Mary was looking rather pale. "Charlotte told me nothing about having planned a meeting with Lord Sinclair."

Kate gave her a funny look. Mary seemed unduly alarmed. "He denies it, too, so it must simply have been another coincidence."

Mary didn't seem wholly satisfied with that answer. "He did rather have something to gain by marrying you, I suppose."

Kate turned around and looked at her reflection in the mirror, wondering if she should rub some ashes from the fire beneath her eyes to make herself look exhausted. Perhaps she might pull her hair back more severely. Anything to dissuade him from trying to kiss her…her will to resist just wasn't strong enough when he got close. "Oh, don't be ridiculous, Mary. I think we're both aware of how little he wanted to marry me."

"When he asked you, did he know about your inheritance?"

Kate looked at Mary's face reflected in the mirror. "I'd only just told him…no, no, it's impossible. If he didn't know about my inheritance, then why on earth would he have organized my abduction…twice? He's my brother's best friend, for goodness' sake."

"He used to be, anyway."

"Mary, it's absurd. Now, how do I look? Ready for battle?"

Mary nodded distractedly. "Beautiful, Lady Kate, as usual."

As Kate walked from the room, her shoulders back as if she was, indeed, making her way into a war, Mary began slowly and silently to panic.

She left the room and walked down the hallway to the servants' wing. If anyone had seen her they would have known that something was seriously troubling her.

Something very sinister was going on, and the evidence was pointing in the wrong direction.

Chapter Seventeen

Monsieur Richard, the cook, outdid himself for dinner that evening. As Kate sat at the opposite end of the table from her husband, separated by several feet of uncomfortable silence punctuated with steaming silver tureens, she supposed that the decadent feast was his way of celebrating their nuptials. Lukewarm soup and hard bread would have suited her just fine, however. It was impossible for her to enjoy anything just then, anyway. They hadn't spoken at all during the meal. Ben had merely nodded when she'd entered and she'd nodded back. That was it. The only noise in the dining room was the occasional clink of forks and knives. It was awful.

She glanced at him covertly, pretending to pay attention to her food alone. He'd finished eating and was absentmindedly swirling his wine around in his glass. He looked, Kate was afraid to admit, as appealing as ever. He wore a dark blue jacket and white cravat and somehow his skin managed to look sun-kissed and his hair streaked with blond, even though it was already October. It was dangerous, the way he looked, and her heartbeat accelerated slightly as the familiar warmth entered her body. As if sensing her eyes on him, he looked up. When his gaze met hers, he merely raised a brow in question.

She lowered her eyes immediately. Why did he always cause this reaction in her? All he had to do was look at her and her stomach rolled over and her palms began to sweat. It couldn't continue like that.

She began cutting her veal with no particular enthusiasm. She hadn't been hungry to begin with and didn't know if she'd even be able to swallow without choking, but she needed to occupy her hands somehow. Poor Richard. He'd think his meal had been a resounding failure when her plate returned to the kitchen toyed with but uneaten. Kate forced down a bite and grimaced. Perhaps she could deposit a few mouthfuls into her napkin to be disposed of later so Richard wouldn't be too offended.

The sound of Ben's chair sliding back on the wooden floor brought her gaze back to his direction in an instant. He had risen, and when he noticed her gaze on him he looked back disinterestedly and, damn it, raised his infuriating brow once more. "Is something amiss, Kate?"

Yes, she wanted to say. A very big something. The moment she'd been dreading had finally arrived and he knew it. The end of the meal meant the end of the evening. It meant heading upstairs and finding her way into bed…only all her belongings had been brought into the master bedroom…right alongside his. Kate was far too discreet to ask for her things to be moved back to her old room. Not just yet, anyway. Her servants seemed to think she'd found herself a true love match and she just couldn't give them reason to worry…or to gossip. She could change rooms eventually. Many wives didn't share bedrooms with their husbands at all, at least after the initial few months. Besides, he couldn't possibly plan on staying with her that long anyway. He'd leave and things would just take care of themselves.

"Um…have you finished?" she asked rather stupidly.

Ben nodded and began to cross the room toward the door.

"Where are you going now?" Kate asked, trying to keep the panic from her voice.

Ben paused to consider her words for a moment. "I was going to go pour a glass of sherry and take it up to bed. Does that seem strange?"

Her voice sounded small and embarrassed when she answered, "No."

"Care to join me?"

"No." She was plenty firm this time.

"Didn't think so," he remarked sardonically before turning to leave once more.

Kate rose quickly before he reached the door. "Ben?"

He paused, turned around and waited for her to speak.

She bit her lip and began to wring her hands. When she noticed what she was doing she stopped. He obviously knew what was worrying her. Why couldn't he just be gallant for once and offer to sleep on the floor? "Well, Tilly told me that she had put my belongings into the master bedroom, and that that is where you have been sleeping as well."

Ben's expression remained masked. "Perfectly natural, Kate. We've been married for less than two weeks. Usually it takes a married couple at least a month to decide they can't stand each other."

"What do we do about it?"

"Would you like to tell her?"

Kate tried to imagine it. Could she tell Tilly? Not without raising the eyebrows of every member of her staff, she couldn't. And most of them had been employed since before she was born, or not long thereafter. It was just too awkward, and she couldn't suffer that embarrassment. But could she share a bed with her husband?

She shook her head. "No. I don't want to tell her."

"You could sleep on the floor," he offered. "In fact, there's quite a nice sofa in that bedroom, at the foot of the bed. I'm sure you could be perfectly comfortable on it."

"I will not sleep on the floor. You were never invited to this house. If anyone sleeps on the floor it shall be you," she replied, her eyes flashing with anger.

Ben shrugged again. "Then I guess no one will be sleeping on the floor tonight…and you'll have the misfortune of sharing the bed with me." With that, he opened the door and left.

Kate stared at the door for a good long while, not moving.

Ben knew there had always been plenty of sound reasons behind his aversion to marriage, but for a brief spell he'd allowed himself to forget them all. He'd let himself think instead—madly—that maybe it wasn't such a bad idea. But since he'd actually gone through with it all the reasons had come rushing back. As he sat on the side of the bed, where he'd been waiting alone for nearly an hour, he rehearsed each one: women were complicated and demanding; a wife interfered with one's self-determination and limited one's freedom. He'd always feared that marrying would mean he'd be held down to one spot forever, and he simply valued the rootlessness of travel too much for that ever to be acceptable. And yet even though he knew better, there he found himself, fixed to that spot on the bed, unmoving except for growing alert every time he heard a noise in the hallway, wondering if it was Kate making her way to bed.

In the end, he'd brought the entire bottle of sherry to the bedroom, rather than just a glass. He hoped to be inebriated and at least semi-somnolent by the time she arrived; that way he'd be immune to her beauty, to the sweet way she blushed and lowered her eyes every time he looked at her. In fact, he'd hardly touched the sherry. He was just too distracted, and he was beginning to wonder if she was going to join him at all. Perhaps he had nothing to worry about. Perhaps she'd gone out of doors and was sleeping in a tree.

Why the hell had he forced the issue of sharing a room? He actually rather wished they weren't, and he could easily have offered to sleep on the sofa. It didn't matter how furious he was at her, he still wanted her every time he so much as looked at her. Sleeping in the same bed with her would be torture. It was sure to test his willpower to the breaking point and he only hoped he wouldn't break. And he could do it; he could remain strong. His reaction to her, Ben told himself, was purely physical, and he hadn't made it that far in life without having control over his base impulses. It'd be difficult, painfully so, but he could do it. He wouldn't touch her, and it would serve her right, too. Resisting the urge to roll over in bed, gather her into his arms and make love to her would be a victory—not just over his own impulses, but over her desire as well. He knew that he affected her, too. He could see it in her eyes, in the way she breathed just a little bit faster when he looked at her.

A quiet knock at the door pulled him out of his reverie. Kate opened the door only slightly, just enough to slip her slender body through. She shut the door behind herself and stood there, trying not to look at him. She looked painfully shy, something Ben had never really seen in her before.

After a moment, she entered the room more fully.

"I think your belongings are in the linen press," he offered.

She nodded and walked over to the tall, mahogany linen press, located a nightgown and a robe in its drawers, and silently crossed the room to enter the dressing room.

Ben shrugged his shoulders, slipped off his robe and eased into bed. He closed his eyes and tried to fall asleep. It didn't work.

It took Kate several minutes to reemerge from the dressing room. From beneath his lids Ben noted that her robe was thick and tightly belted, its sides drawn together at her neck. She paused in the middle of the room for a moment, as if expecting him to do or say something. He lay still, pretending to be asleep. After that moment passed, Kate quietly snuffed out the lamp. In darkness, she climbed into bed, careful not to touch him as she did so. She lay down so her back faced him, and she kept herself so close to the edge of the bed that she was in danger of falling off in the middle of the night. It was a rather difficult position to maintain, too. He was considerably heavier than she was and the bed naturally dipped in his direction. If she let herself fall asleep—not that she was in any danger of doing so anytime soon—gravity was sure to do its work and pull her in his direction.

So instead she just lay there restlessly. Her heart beat quickly and she could think only of the large, warm body beside her. For over an hour, she lay very still, listening to him breathe. Eventually, his breathing became slow and even, so she assumed that he, at least, had managed to fall asleep. With the exception of some slight adjustments, he remained very still. Yes, she told herself, he had to be asleep. She didn't know why it mattered so much, but she knew that she wouldn't be able to sleep herself until she was confident that he was no longer awake. She simply felt too vulnerable.

Several more minutes ticked by and she knew that if she didn't find out for certain she'd go mad.

Very carefully, she sat up in bed. With painstaking slowness, hoping that the bed wouldn't betray her movements and disturb him, she leaned over to see if his eyes were closed.

They were, and his dark golden eyelashes created

peaceful half-moons. She only meant to look quickly for confirmation, but she didn't lie back down immediately. For a moment, she just looked at the man who was, so suddenly, her husband.

She'd never seen him sleep before and it allowed her an entirely new perspective. He was sinfully handsome and Kate knew that, try as she might to maintain her independence, she would never be unaffected when she looked at him. He did something to her, deep inside of her, that made her feel weak and soft and warm.

His chest was bare. She wondered what he was wearing down below, beneath the sheet, but she didn't dare look. She contented herself with just his chest. She'd seen it only once before, but on that occasion she'd been so angry and confused and scared that she hadn't had time or the peace of mind simply to look, to enjoy. But now...she let her gaze wander even lower, to the hard ridge of his abdomen. He had a lot of muscles. She liked that about him, his strength. His body was firm, so unlike her own soft, curved and pliant body. She liked that contrast, too. Liked the way her fair body glowed against his darker tones, liked the way his slightly calloused hands felt on her smooth skin.

She let her gaze travel up again, toward the tiny pulse in his neck that seemed to be beating faster; her gaze roved even farther still, to his face.

His eyes were open, watching her. Her own eyes widened slightly, but she didn't look away. Once his eyes met hers, she couldn't have looked away if she wanted to. And she didn't want to. A hot swirl of desire filled her stomach and she held her breath.

"I don't want to want you," Ben said, his voice rough and quiet.

Kate shook her head. She didn't want to want him either.

But she couldn't help it.

With the frustrated groan of defeat, he pulled her down to meet his lips.

It felt like heaven. His hands were in her hair, her hands cupped his face, and in one swift motion he turned her over on the bed so his body covered hers. He dragged his lips from hers only to trail them roughly down the column of her throat, to her breasts. She still wore her robe, but she reached down to untie it, quickly, urgently, needing to be as close to him as possible. His lips followed, pausing to lick her nipples, to make them swollen, pink, erect. She mewled at the sensations he caused and he eased up, letting his lips travel down her stomach, delving into her navel. She arched her body beneath him, held his head tightly, not wanting to let go. His lips trailed lower still, scandalously low. Kate gasped in shock.

"Ben? What are you—"

"Don't talk," he broke in before she could articulate her nervousness, his voice hoarse, almost pained. For a moment her whole body remained rigid, too self-conscious over this extreme intimacy. She closed her eyes, not knowing whether she liked it or not. It was the most unusual, incredible feeling she'd ever experienced—insistent, intense. But then, oh, God, the sensations that washed over her...she writhed on the bed, unable to keep still, but it went on and on, growing to a crescendo pitch with every second. She cried out, wanting, needing—desperately—something more. Only she was still too inexperienced to know quite what…

With a swift motion, he entered her, answering her need. Kate went very still at the sudden, strange feeling of having him inside of her: a fullness and pressure that urged her on even further. They'd not had a wedding night; this was only the second time they'd made love.

"Ben?" she asked again, raising her head slightly.

"Shh," he said, nibbling on her lips. He began to move slowly, just a rhythmic rocking, in and out, and her worries disappeared instantly. She gripped him close as the feelings deep inside of her built up once more, swelling until she thought they would burst. Her nails left crescents on his shoulders, but she didn't notice. All she could think about was her own pleasure. He moved faster, lifting her body to match his tempo, to meet his thrusts. And then everything exploded inside her, around her. She cried out as pleasure throbbed through her body, pulsating waves that traveled to her fingers and toes and sapped her strength.

His gaze never left her face, watching as the last jolt of pleasure racked through her body. And as she gradually stilled, he allowed himself his own pleasure. It wasn't a matter of effort; he simply let go. With a groan, part pleasure, part defeat, he thrust one last time, feeling, in that fleeting but intoxicating moment, that she truly belonged to him.

Sated, limp and drained, they collapsed into each others' arms.

* * *

Ben was asleep. His breathing was deep and steady; this time Kate was certain of it. But she was still wide-awake, staring at the ceiling, her eyes tracing the paths of tiny cracks. She was terrified.

She'd allowed herself to fall in love. There, she'd admitted it. She hadn't meant to do it, but it had happened anyway. It was a disaster. Falling in love meant abandoning something she'd always clung to and cherished: her independence. And giving up her independence meant she'd gradually become someone only in relation to another, a wife to her husband, or a mother to any children they might have. A large part of her would love to be these things, but she knew that to do either would also mean forfeiting something she held very dear. Katherine Sutcliff, owner of Alfred and Sons, was simply not compatible with Lady Katherine Sinclair, wife.

She didn't actually know what that latter role entailed; the truth was, she didn't have the faintest idea of how to be a proper wife. Ben hadn't wanted a wife to begin with but she was certain that, having one now, he'd probably want her to behave like one. But all she knew how to be was bullheaded. He'd laughed at her—she could remember it vividly—when she'd confessed to him her true role in Alfred and Sons; she took that role very seriously, and yet he'd treated her as an absurdity, a trivial thing playing at a man's business. How would he feel about her when he realized how totally unsuitable she really was? He knew she was unconventional—she'd hardly tried to hide that fact—but did he realize that she couldn't tell a hollyhock from a petunia, that she couldn't draw…or sing…play a musical instrument…or sew? He'd expect his wife to be accomplished in these sorts of things, and Kate knew she'd never be. She didn't even want to try. Eventually she'd become an embarrassment, and she cared too much about his opinion of her to let that happen. She didn't know if she could endure his rejection.

No, she could not allow herself to soften. She might love him already, but surely that was not an irrevocable state. She would need distance, though, if she were to have any hope of making this emotional about-face. He needed to leave, and although she couldn't force him to go, she could make staying there most unpleasant. If he remained, he'd only break her heart.

Chapter Eighteen

November 1817

To an outside observer, the scene in the breakfast room one month later appeared to be one of domestic tranquility. The early morning sun streamed in through parted curtains, skipping across the gilded highlights of porcelain plates and cups and saucers. Ben, still in his dressing gown with his hair rather devastatingly mussed, was pouring himself a cup of coffee while Kate—fully dressed and looking particularly pretty— quietly turned the pages of a book.

Of course, it *was* rather rude to read at the breakfast table. One might even suppose that she was ignoring him....

"I think we will have a party," Ben said, breaking the silence.

Kate looked up over her book with narrowed eyes. Like hell they were having a party. "I think we will not."

He sighed. These were the first words she'd spoken all morning. In fact, she'd spoken to him very little in the past month. He'd thought, after that first night together, that things might change between them, but that had not been the case. It was as if by getting Kate to open up just that much, he'd caused her, somehow in the bright light of day, to close down in other ways instead. In place of their previous bickering, they'd developed a strange sort of peace...with anger and mistrust never far below the surface. She stayed sequestered in the study for most of the day, although Ben hadn't the faintest idea what she did in there since she told him nothing. Without Andrew Hilton her capabilities were extremely limited. She couldn't arrange deals with suppliers or organize any meetings. She couldn't do much, really, although she didn't seem ready to admit that yet. That was why she spent so much time looking busy, he suspected. He would have helped her if only she'd asked him, but she hadn't and he knew she wouldn't. She was too stubborn to ask for help, especially from him, and he wasn't about to offer his services. She probably wouldn't accept them anyway.

During the night, however, it was different. Inside their bedroom he experienced the most passionate love-making of his life. Still, she hardly said a word, but without fail she eased into bed and into his arms, turning to him for comfort or perhaps something more. He didn't know what. During these moments he actually let himself wonder if she didn't have feelings for him, too. On occasion, even during the day, he allowed his mind to wander down this path: sometimes he'd catch her watching him when she thought he wasn't looking and he'd detect something in her eyes, something soft and even vulnerable. When she realized she'd been discovered she'd blush and look away…and when she'd meet his gaze again she'd always reverted to dispassionate form once more. He wished they could just start over. No one had forced him to marry her—he'd actually been daft enough to try his damnedest to convince her. She was the one being so blasted difficult with all of her stipulations. Kate had done her best to push him as far away as possible, and he wasn't always sure if she hadn't succeeded.

His irritation began to show. "I think you have little say in the matter—"

"I have every say—"

She broke off as Mary entered the room, halting any argument that might have erupted between them. It was as if she'd been standing at the door, waiting for raised voices and prepared at any time to come to the aid of her mistress.

"Yes, Mary?" Kate asked, trying to keep the annoyance out of her voice. She wasn't actually in the mood for rescuing. She was prepared to fight.

"Oh…I…was just looking for something, Lady Kate. I won't be a minute."

"Of course," Kate said, moderating her tone slightly. Mary was only trying to be helpful and she should be pleased at the interruption. She didn't believe for one moment that Mary was really looking for anything. It was obviously just some pretense…she'd been extremely solicitous of Kate for the past month, at least where Ben was concerned. Kate wasn't entirely sure why. Mary had heard her complain about him often enough in the past without getting too concerned.

Ben just gave Mary an annoyed glance. He'd seen far too much of her lately and didn't like the suspicious glances she kept sending in his direction. She kept looking at him as if she expected him to attack at any moment. It was bloody impertinent. "That party, Kate?"

"I see no reason why we should. I think we can end the debate there."

He smiled to himself. She'd been cold and stiff since he'd entered the breakfast room and it felt good to annoy her. At least he could get *some* reaction that way. Anything was better than her silence. "Well, wife, it would seem a logical thing to do—celebrate our nuptials with the local populace. They might even be expecting it…would perhaps think it odd if we didn't."

"They already think I'm a bit odd. A party won't change their perception."

"Is that why you're so annoyed that I've come here? You're afraid I'll find out how…odd…you really are?"

It was part of the reason, anyway. She'd caused her fair share of gossip over the course of her life with her rather unfashionable clothes and lack of interest in feminine pursuits, not to mention her frequent appearances at her father's boatyard. The more conservative members of the town, as well as many of the women, thought her most improper.

Ben lowered his voice so Mary wouldn't hear. "It would also give us a chance to invite our suspects."

"Oh, please don't speak like that," she whispered back furiously. "It sounds so…so sinister."

"Well? Isn't it?"

"No, it isn't," she maintained stubbornly. "There is no longer any risk. I am now married and therefore there is nothing for anyone to gain. Whoever it was who was a threat can no longer be a problem."

"Kate, the question is not whether we will hold this party or not. We will. I have decided. The question is whether you'll cooperate."

"No. I told you—everything is fine now."

"Leave us, please, Mary," Ben instructed, noticing that the woman was listening intently.

She hesitated for a moment and then left. He suspected she was eavesdropping by the door.

In an angry whisper, he asked, "Why? Just because nothing has happened yet?"

"Nothing *will* happen. You'll just have to accept that."

He looked at her hard for several seconds, trying to gauge what she was really thinking. Finally, he asked, "Accept that and leave? Is that what you would really like, Kate?"

She didn't mean to be nasty, and she didn't want him to leave. Not really, anyway. She would love for him to stay, to fall in love with her; she would love to allow herself to love him back. But it just wouldn't happen. She'd spent the past few years worrying about her independence, but independence couldn't be compatible with being a wife, could it? Not in his eyes it couldn't be, she was sure of that.

She raised her chin. "Yes. I would like you to leave."

Again, he was quiet. His jaw tightened stubbornly and he rose from his seat.

"We'll invite the entire village, Kate. I'll work on the invitations myself if you won't help."

She arched a brow in challenge. "You, my lord?"

He said nothing, but he slammed the door on his way out the room. That said enough.

Writing invitations was women's work. That was how Ben had always viewed it. He'd never known a single man who'd sat, as he was at that very moment, over piles of gilt-edged paper, carefully writing names in his best hand whilst crossing them off of an accompanying list. It was the province of mothers, sisters and wives. Not the future Viscount Carlisle.

Only his wife refused to do it so there he was. He would have enlisted the help of one of the servants, but that would only lead to questions of why he was doing such a thing rather than Kate.

Bloody-minded woman.

Chapter Nineteen

The party, held two weeks later, seemed to be going well, although Ben wasn't particularly concerned at just that moment if his assembled guests enjoyed themselves or not. Everyone he'd invited had come, and he'd been certain not to be too exclusive. Although he hadn't actually invited the entire town, as he'd threatened, he'd invited most of it.

As he looked around the overheated, crowded drawing room from his position along the wall, he was aware that he'd hardly seen his wife all night—not that that meant a great change from their usual habits. He'd spotted her once or twice, dancing past with local men or chatting quietly with neighbors. He had to admit that she was everything a gracious host should be, a fact that made her almost total lack of graciousness toward him all the more galling. But why should he care? He had only one thing to achieve that evening: finding out who was behind the attacks on Kate. And once he discovered that and made sure she was safe, he'd leave. That was obviously what she wanted him to do. She'd probably be pleased if he left tomorrow, and that's exactly what he would do if only he weren't in love with her. But he just couldn't leave her. Not yet. Not until he knew she was safe.

To date, however, he'd learned nothing. When he'd first traveled to Little Brookings a month and a half ago he'd figured his task would be simple: he'd find Andrew Hilton, threaten him a bit, bloody his nose if need be, and that would be that. But now with Hilton out of the picture and Kate refusing to be at all helpful…still, the list *was* already getting shorter. Owens the coachman had been crossed off almost immediately after Ben had suggested he be put on—he'd only insisted that Kate write him down to be ornery in the first place. Gregory Sithwell, her solicitor, had also been removed from the list. Ben had met with him earlier that week and thought the man seemed far too honest and concerned for Kate's well-being to be any sort of threat. Ben had had no trouble bringing her up as a topic of discussion—as his wife's solicitor, Sithwell now worked for him, too. He'd merely told Sithwell that he was concerned about her involvement in the company, that he wondered if it didn't expose her to a certain amount of danger, both to her person and her reputation. He'd then waited to gauge his reaction, and it was just what Ben would have wanted. Sithwell agreed with him. Nodded, said that Kate's father had perhaps indulged her a bit too much. He'd expressed his hope that, although Ben had signed the contract, he would find some way for Kate to step back a bit and hand the reins over to someone else. It would be difficult, Sithwell had conceded. That company meant everything to her. And she mustn't be forced to step down completely; she was good at what she did and to do so would destroy her. She just needed to…well, *share* her duties a bit better. That was how he'd put it, and Ben agreed. He also, for once, agreed with Kate: Sithwell was honorable, sincere and innocent.

At that moment, Ben noticed a bluff, red-cheeked and rather convivial-looking man standing near him, muttering to himself quietly. Seeing Ben, he halted his muttering with an apologetic blush. "Good evening, my lord," he said, stepping forward slightly and bowing his head. "I haven't had the pleasure yet of being introduced to you."

Ben was slightly taken aback by the man's forwardness, but supposed that things were a bit more relaxed so far from London. "Oh? How do you do—"

"Hastings. Richard Hastings. I live just over yonder," the man explained, pointing in the direction of the hall, "just on the other side of the rectory."

Ben momentarily forgot the man's rudeness. He couldn't believe his luck, especially after the disappointing evening that he'd been having so far. Richard Hastings, one of Kate's prime suspects, introducing himself. It certainly saved Ben a bit of work. "Um…west, that is?" he asked.

The man grinned benignly. "West, indeed."

Ben nodded as if he were mulling this information over. His interpretation of this meeting as luck was beginning to change because, as Kate had warned, the man hardly seemed capable of committing any sort of crime.

Hastings cleared his throat. "Well, Lord Sinclair…I know it's not really my place to say so, but I am relieved that Miss Sutcliff…er, I mean—"

"Lady Sinclair."

"Yes, Lady Sinclair. I'm relieved that she's finally wed. And wed to you, that is, of course. Never thought it would happen. No one had much hope, in fact."

"Is that so?" Ben asked curiously.

Hastings began to shift his weight as if he were frightened of causing offense. "What I mean is, Lady Sinclair is lovely and kind…and much admired by everyone in the village. But no one thought she'd ever…how shall I put it…"

"Condescend to marriage?"

Hastings smiled broadly at Ben's assistance. "Condescend. Yes. That's the word exactly. A stubborn girl who's determined to be in charge of her own life, I'd say. We were all wondering not only if it would happen, but also what sort of man would…well—"

"Take her on?" Ben queried. He knew the answer: only a raving madman, obviously.

Hastings nodded with enthusiasm, rocking back on his heels in pleasure so that his round belly protruded from his coat.

"And who, may I ask, is 'we'?"

"Oh, sorry, Lord Sinclair. I meant my wife and I…also George Smith—now he edits the *Little Brookings Weekly Idler*—and Mrs. Aubrey down the lane, the Misses Powell, Squire Humphries, the vicar…well, the better sort of Little Brookings generally. They're all here tonight if you haven't yet met them. I hope you aren't offended, but it's been the talk of the town since she turned about sixteen. You see, we haven't a surfeit of beautiful, unmarried young ladies in the village so one can't help but speculate."

"I see."

"Might I venture a question, my lord?"

Ben figured the man would anyway, so nodded.

"Well…do you plan to curtail her activities?"

Like devil worship? a perverse voice asked inside his head, although to Hastings he merely asked, "To which activities do you refer?"

"Well, we all rather hoped that, now she's married, she'd perhaps stay at home a bit more…be more domestic, perhaps. I don't mean to be impertinent, of course…"

Ben thought he was definitely being impertinent but sensed Hastings was looking for agreement and would open up more if he got it. "I have been thinking long and hard about this issue, Mr. Hastings," he said reassuringly.

Hastings beamed. "I'm pleased to hear it, my lord. Perhaps I could suggest…well, you see, a group of ladies in town spend several afternoons a week together embroidering church vestments and the like—I think they're working on an altar cloth at the moment—and for this Vicar Sampson is most grateful. Perhaps Lady Sinclair would like to join them one day? It's good company, too, or so m'wife informs me. The ladies talk of their children, gowns, flowers, puppies…men, of course, but I'm sure Lady Sinclair is too much the, er, lady, to indulge in that sort of gossip."

Ben nodded slowly. He very much disliked women who talked only of clothing and children, but played along with Hastings. "I can think of no more proper subject of conversation for a wife than puppies and flowers. I will certainly suggest she joins these ladies someday soon."

Hastings's florid face brightened with pleasure again. "I'm pleased to hear that, my lord. I've often worried about Lady Sinclair. A boatyard is no place for a young lady to go wandering around."

Ben leaned in, keenly interested. "You know about my wife's interest in her father's company?"

Hastings looked mildly taken aback. "Didn't know she was interested in the company, *per se*…thought she just did it to be ornery. Some have suggested," he leaned in and lowered his voice, "that she just enjoys male company."

Ben narrowed his eyes angrily at the man's gall. "But you wouldn't say that, would you, Hastings?"

"Oh, never. Not I. Her father, although too indulgent, was a great man. I would never dream of saying anything to offend him or his family. It's just, well…" he paused, trying carefully to plan his words, "I often feared that it could set a bad example to the rest of the town for a young lady of the aristocracy to be so headstrong. She should be setting an example for her inferiors. Vicar Sampson, in particular, has worried that her behavior will lead to some sort of female rebellion."

"And there will be no one to embroider his altar cloths."

Hastings nodded. "Precisely, Lord Sinclair. You understand so well."

"You have nothing to fear any longer. She will behave herself in the future."

"I'm grateful, my lord, that she's married a man not scared of taking her firmly in hand."

Ben nodded in agreement, thinking as he did so that Hastings really was a fatuous old goat. Disingenuously, he said, "That's been my plan all along, of course. By the by, did you ever do anything to…indicate your feelings of disapproval?"

"I wouldn't presume! I was friendly with her father, as I say, but I don't suppose he would have taken too kindly to my advice. I should have said nothing to you, Lord Sinclair, but I figured…well…since you married the vixen it's only to be expected that you also intend to rein her in."

Ben frowned at Hastings's mixed metaphor but didn't comment. He played, instead, to what he thought Hastings would like to hear. If he had attempted in any way to harm or intimidate Kate, this was one way to find out. "I have already instructed my wife to stay out of the boatyard, you will be pleased to know."

Hastings opened his mouth to answer but closed it abruptly, merely nodding instead. Ben thought he saw him glance nervously around his shoulder. Hastings picked a bit of lint from his jacket and changed the subject. "Cabbage has done well this year."

"Oh?" Ben asked. He was already beginning to lose interest. Hastings was innocuous enough, and quite obviously innocent as well. He didn't want to be impolite, but as the man started to expound on the price of runner beans he had to put an end to the conversation.

"Yes, well, it's been a pleasure, Mr. Hastings, but I really must go find my wife."

He turned to leave and almost walked into her.

Ben wondered how long Kate had been standing behind him. From her dark expression, he reckoned she'd overheard the worst of the conversation. Before she could spit at him, he held out his arm.

"Dance with me, Kate."

She merely stared at him, her mouth ajar in disbelief. *Dance with him?* Was he serious? She didn't move, didn't speak. Her body felt frozen with shock, but inside she boiled with fury.

Ben sensed that she was mere seconds from exploding. Before she could scream, he leaned in toward her, his voice laced with warning. "Look, Kate, just take my hand and dance with me. You can't yell at me here."

Numbly, she took his hand and they moved onto the dance floor. After several moments of angry silence, Ben began to wonder if she would bring the subject up herself, or if he should prod her a bit. The things he'd said had been damning indeed, but he would expect her to know that he had a reason for saying them. She couldn't possibly think he *really* felt that way about her, could she? Maybe he should introduce a completely uncontroversial subject and she'd just forget about it.

"Have you been enjoying yourself?"

"No."

He gave up. "Yes, well, at least you're feeling garrulous tonight. What a pleasant change from your usual manner."

"You seem to be saying enough for both of us."

"Will you let me explain?" he asked, spinning her around so that her back faced the room. If any of their guests saw her expression just then...

"I'm not interested in your explanation."

"You look interested," he retorted, leaning in close.

She couldn't deny that. That bit of conversation she'd overheard had been the most interesting—and enlightening—thing she'd heard in years. Why had she ever dared to hope that he might be different, that he might actually want a wife who had a brain, an opinion and a strong will? "You are not welcome here. I've told you that before. I will not have you telling me what to do."

"You're not listening to me, Kate."

"Not listening? I heard exactly what you said. Richard Hastings, I'll have you know, is one of the biggest gossips in town. Everything you just told him will be common knowledge tomorrow. He's probably spreading the word as we speak."

"I had hoped as much."

"Really?" she snarled. "You want to humiliate me on a grand scale?"

Ben was quickly losing his temper. If she'd only just listen to him for one minute he could explain. He shouldn't even have to explain. She should just trust him. "I want to publicize the fact that things are changing, that I have taken over your father's company. If anyone is still trying to harm you, perhaps that will dissuade him from making another attempt."

"Oh? And do you think that you *have* taken over?"

Her anger, Ben saw, was slowly being replaced with

hurt. He could see it in her wide, fathomless indigo eyes, and he could feel it in his own heart. How he hated being the one to have to tell her the truth. She wasn't oblivious to reality, but she never wanted to acknowledge it. "No, Kate, I don't. But how do you intend to do all this on your own?"

She had no answer for that question, so replied with a question of her own. "Do you really think that anyone here can hate me so much they'd want to harm me? You may not believe it, but I'm quite well-liked. I've been congratulated several times this evening."

"Congratulated for what?"

She blushed. "For marrying."

"And do you know why?"

She knew perfectly. She said nothing.

"Because everyone thinks you're a willful brat," he answered for her. "They think you need controlling."

That was true and she'd been aware of it for a long time. But for him to agree with everyone else…that was just what she'd been afraid of. "That's a lie."

He didn't answer.

"So your plan is to change that, is that right, Ben? You plan to make me behave…to make me act like a proper wife."

He didn't have any plans to change anything. She was a willful brat, but she was his. He'd gotten used to her being that way and suspected it was the reason he liked her in the first place. Ben had no interest in women who agreed with every word he said, and he'd married her precisely because she didn't, because he loved her. But before he had the opportunity to defend himself, she said, "I will never be a good wife to you. I will not embroider altar cloths, if that's what you want."

"Oh, for God's sake, Kate, who ever said that was what I wanted?"

"You did. I heard you. That's exactly what you told Richard Hastings. You told him you were going to change me. You said you would forbid me to go to the boatyard. You said you would do it because you are my husband and you can. Do you deny it?"

He could deny nothing. He'd said all those things. He hadn't meant a single word, though. It had all been for Hastings's benefit. He just couldn't believe that she wouldn't understand that. How could she possibly suspect him of such underhandedness? Was it possible she could have such a low opinion of him? "You'll recall, Kate, that long before I became your husband, I was your brother's best friend. If you won't believe that my intentions to you are honorable, then at least acknowledge that I would do nothing to jeopardize my friendship with him."

"You forfeited his friendship anyway. You had no compunctions about seducing me. How can I believe you? Why did you marry me in the first place?"

"Would you like me to leave, Kate?" he asked rather suddenly, his voice flat, his eyes cold and emotionless.

Her head jerked in surprise and she stopped dancing. She hadn't been prepared for those words. Was he really offering to leave? That was what she'd been asking for, wasn't it? She'd never felt as betrayed as she felt at that moment; when she'd overheard him speaking to Richard Hastings she'd wanted to…well, to die, to cease to exist, to dissolve. She'd been beginning to trust him—she'd been fighting it, but she had all the same. She'd been expecting the worst but praying the whole time that he just might love her for who she was. "I think we'll both agree that I'm pretty safe here," she said slowly. "If you would like to leave then I think you should."

Ben nodded. He felt hollow. His question had been a last resort; he'd been giving her a chance to ask him to stay. He needed desperately to hear those words. He'd wanted his marriage to work, but he'd been a fool, apparently.

Yet could he really leave? She obviously hated having him there. He could go back to London and back to his old life. He could go anywhere: to the Indies, East and West; to Jamaica; Egypt; Greece…he needn't just *stay,* doggedly waiting for her to come round. Strangely, he didn't have the familiar urge to travel, but he could force himself to go; it had always cured him before. She obviously wouldn't allow him to share her life and he didn't think he had much chance of regaining her trust. But would she be safe if he left? Maybe he was just being stubborn by insisting on this futile investigation. Maybe he'd just been using his suspicion as an excuse to stay with her. But it was well-known now that Kate had married; he'd also done his part that evening to advertise that he was in control and that she was no longer an easy target. Besides, as she'd pointed out, who in Little Brookings was capable of harming her anyway?

Perhaps Andrew Hilton had been behind everything after all. During their meeting, Ben had felt certain the man was telling the truth, but maybe he was simply a brilliant actor. At any rate, Ben knew that he had scared him off and that he would never be a threat again. So what was keeping him here?

"Then I'll leave, Kate," he said, hating the finality of those words, wishing he could revoke them the instant they left his lips.

With that, he bowed and walked off. He left the drawing room completely, Kate standing without a partner in the middle of the floor. It was impolite in the extreme, but he didn't care. He would return to London in the morning anyway, and he could figure out there what to do next. Kate could deal with any gossip his sudden departure aroused—she'd brought it on herself anyway.

As he left the drawing room, Kate watched him, feeling desolate, unmindful of the curious stares cast her way. She bit her lip to stop its quivering. This was exactly what she'd asked for, wasn't it? So why did she feel like her life was over?

Chapter Twenty

February 1818

Kate had always rather disparaged women who devoted their lives to the perfection of wifely talents and feminine graces. Of course, if she'd been any good at these things she probably wouldn't have disparaged them quite so freely; she had several friends, in fact, who were both wifely and feminine, and it had never impinged on her good opinion of them. These characteristics were perfectly fine for others…just not for her. And indeed, she'd never felt the lack until now.

"Damn." She looked down at her thumb, a small dot of blood forming in its middle. She was kneeling on a damp patch of earth in the garden, and she scowled at the cause of her injury, the barren rosebush in front of her. Gardening was certainly not her strong suit, and it hadn't helped her self-confidence one whit when her head gardener had stopped by to point out to her that early February was not the time to start learning. He did have a very good point…she'd only figured that one needed to plan a garden in advance, was that not true? By spring, if she kept at it, perhaps she'd be able to coax a few buds out of the hard soil. Besides, as close to England's southern coast as she lived, the temperature rarely dipped below freezing. A few things continued to grow all year long.

She didn't actually care that much about the garden, though. Sure, she enjoyed plants well enough—they smelled nice, they looked nice—but she couldn't imagine herself, come spring, swelling with satisfaction over the botanical changes she'd wrought. No, she was really trying to change herself.

She shivered and pulled her shawl more tightly around her shoulders. What a fool she was to be kneeling in the dirt in the middle of winter. She supposed she'd simply been a bit overeager in her attempts to correct a lifetime of bad and unseemly habits. She didn't think she'd go as far as joining Vicar Sampson's thrice-weekly sewing circle—she wasn't that desperate yet—but she certainly was trying to gain some mastery of the traditionally feminine arts. Gardening was a good, ladylike thing to do, wasn't it? If she was correct it was held in similar esteem with embroidery, and her other thumb was already sporting a small bandage from her recent attempts at that endeavor.

She may not be enjoying herself, but if Ben ever came back it might all be worth it. He'd been gone for over a month and a half, had left, in fact, the very morning after their party; he'd probably begun packing his bags after he'd left her alone on the dance floor. She'd had a lot of time to think since his departure and had come to one startling conclusion: he occupied her mind and heart completely. He meant everything to her. He was more important to her than even Alfred and Sons, and she had made up her mind: if she ever had a second chance to choose between living happily ever after with Ben and maintaining control over her company, she'd choose him. She wasn't at all certain that she'd *ever* live happily ever after if it meant giving up her company, but at least she'd be *happier.* Nor was she certain he'd welcome her back, particularly after the way she'd behaved, but she was willing to compromise more than a little to find out. She was going to become a proper wife, a proper woman, too. She had to. She was about to lose her husband completely, if she hadn't lost him already. She had sacrificed her happiness and his, all because she was too stubborn to let someone else run her business. And why not? What was so terrible about letting someone else help? Why did she have to do everything by herself?

She answered her own question silently and automatically: *because she liked it that way.* Because it was her company, because it had belonged to her, at least in her mind, since she was a small child. Because it had belonged to both her father and her grandfather. But as much as it would hurt her to give it up, it would hurt her even more to lose her husband. She had treated him abominably, and she couldn't blame him for wanting to leave her, but she had to make one more try. If he ever came back—hell, she wasn't even so averse to swallowing her pride and seeking him out—perhaps he'd forgive her if he saw how changed she was; perhaps some sweetness and light would infiltrate her combative character and let her love him, plain and simple.

The only problem was she was only just beginning to realize that mastering the feminine arts was not the easy victory she had thought it would be. With a sigh she sank down fully onto the muddy ground, not caring that her dress got soiled.

"Lady Kate?"

She turned her head slowly but didn't rise. Mary was looking down at her, concern and not a little bit of disapproval in her eyes. She was returning from a walk to the village, and her arms were still weighed down with overflowing parcels. "Is everything all right, dear?"

Kate nodded and rose, brushing debris from her dress. "I suppose, Mary. I've just been thinking."

Mary lowered her parcels to the ground, frowning at the wet earth. "Thinking about what?"

"Oh, I don't know. This and that."

"Must you think of this and that whilst sitting in the mud?" Mary scolded.

Kate evaded that question. "Did I tell you that I got rid of my brown dress?"

Mary opened her eyes wide in mock shock. "Not *the* brown dress?"

She nodded, smiling slightly. "I did, although I could certainly use it now."

Mary let her gaze wander over the soiled—and cream-colored—dress that Kate currently wore with mock censure, clucking for effect. She smiled slightly, but her smile didn't quite reach her eyes. "You know, dear, after all these years complaining about that awful dress, I can't say that I'm too happy it's gone. It hid stains well, anyway. I suppose I didn't mind it that much, after all."

Kate shrugged. "I plan to go shopping later today. I thought I'd replace it with something a bit prettier…but if you prefer I can buy a dress to equal it in drabness."

"Better not, dear. And what's this about shopping? *Voluntarily?* I'm getting worried."

"I know. It does go against the grain, but every once in a while I guess a girl just has to do it. Perhaps I'll get a new bonnet, too. I saw one in the window of Mrs. Fletcher's with netting and tiny pieces of artificial fruit…I think that must be what's fashionable now."

Mary looked unconvinced. "I think you'll need my help. Shall I come with you?"

"If you like," Kate replied. The sky was darkening and she'd need to leave soon or get caught in the downpour. "I don't need a chaperone around here, though, so if you've other things to do please go ahead. Besides, aren't you just returning from the village? Surely you don't want to go back so soon."

"I don't mind. Perhaps we should take Graham as well."

"I hardly think we'll require a footman for this excursion, Mary. I don't plan on buying so much that I can't manage to carry it on my own…there's not that much one *can* buy around here."

Mary nodded slowly. "Perhaps. It's just that I…"

"Is something the matter, Mary?"

She hesitated. "Well, I couldn't say for sure. I just think I saw something a bit odd while I was out."

"Well? What was it?"

Mary paused again as if considering her words, and then rather suddenly she asked, "Didn't Lord Sinclair take his valet back to town with him?"

Kate nodded. "Josiah Thatcher? I believe so. He didn't tell me as much, of course, but Mr. Thatcher left on the same day. I can only imagine that's where he went. Why do you ask?"

"I believe I saw him in town today."

Kate wrinkled her brow slightly. "Could you have been mistaken? I cannot imagine why he'd still be here."

Mary shook her head firmly. "No, I don't think I was mistaken. He's got an unusual face…and a rather menacing scar on his cheek, if you recall. I always thought there was something…well, not quite right about his face. I'm almost certain it was him."

"How peculiar," Kate said. "There was a scar, wasn't there? I always thought he looked an unlikely valet. At any rate, perhaps he didn't travel to London after all. Maybe he found he quite liked it out here and wanted to stay."

"I can ask the other servants if you like, Lady Kate. Perhaps someone knows why he would have stayed behind."

"The other servants? Goodness, I shouldn't think there's any reason to do that. Leave the man in peace, Mary. You're such a meddler." She defused her scold with a smile. "Now, I suppose it's about time I went back to the house and dressed for my trip into town. Will you come?"

Mary nodded and reached down to collect her

parcels. As she rose and took a step to leave, she thought she saw something move in the dense rhododendron bushes that grew to towering heights only twenty or so paces from her. She looked again, long and hard, her heart beating a little bit faster, but this time she saw nothing but leaves. Quickening her pace nervously to catch up with Kate, she, too, headed back to the house…but not without a few cautious glances behind her to make sure she wasn't being followed.

Nearly two months had passed and it was getting easier. Well, that wasn't exactly true. Nothing had actually gotten easier at all, but it soon would. Ben was confident of that. In another few weeks, if he hadn't committed himself to Bedlam by then, perhaps he'd even be able to say that he'd made real progress. "Real progress," given his current state, meant nothing more than thinking about Kate only a few times an hour, rather than almost constantly as was now the case. That was exactly what he was doing at the moment, in fact: sitting in the gloomy library of his London home, trying unsuccessfully to concentrate on his book and thinking about his wife instead. He wasn't even thinking fond, loving, wistful thoughts much of the time: just as often his thoughts revolved around rubbing mud in her face. She seemed to bring out his inner eight-year-old, and—puerile though it may be—he longed to grab hold of a braid of her hair and yank. But no matter how satisfied these thoughts left him, they would have to stop, and if he put his mind to it, they would. They had to. He was a grown man, a lord, and he was supposed to be above such pettiness.

He'd realized, soon after departing from Little Brookings, that leaving her had been something of a tactical error. It certainly hadn't been a solution. In his experience, lengthy separations from Kate only caused him to think about her even more than he already did. This time it was even worse, however, because no matter how often he tried to reassure himself, he just couldn't be completely certain that she was safe. He wasn't as worried as he *might* have been—he'd left Josiah in Little Brookings to keep an eye on her, with instructions to report anything unusual that he might observe. Josiah couldn't continue to stay in the main house, of course, without causing the other servants to question why he hadn't gone back to London with his master. Instead, Ben had installed him in a small cottage on the outskirts of town. Few people outside of the house staff had ever met him anyway, so he was unlikely to be noticed, but still Ben had requested that he keep to himself just in case.

To date, Josiah had reported very little. He complained of long, cold hours spent hiding in the shrubbery, and he also complained of Mary, whose sharp eyesight and suspicious mind were apparently making his job very difficult. Ben could sympathize on at least the last count. Officious old woman. In a way, though, it was her annoying vigilance that reassured him most: if, for any reason, Josiah missed some crucial development, Mary was sure to remain alert and do everything in her power to protect his wife. No doubt Kate was perfectly safe and faring extremely well without him.

The situation couldn't remain like this forever, however. With little to employ him, Josiah would ask to return to London eventually, and Mary, attentive though she may be, would not be able to prevent a grown man from attacking Kate if another attempt was made. Ben couldn't help feeling that she'd only be safe when he returned to Little Brookings to look out for her himself, but he could hardly do that yet. He didn't know if he could ever return. If she didn't feel directly threatened then she'd certainly not welcome his presence—dratted woman wouldn't even pretend to be grateful.

Ben closed his eyes and thought once more about mud.

The library door creaked open and his ancient butler, Rawlings, teetered though it. "Lady Charlotte Gordon to see you, m'lord. Shall I send her in?"

Ben cracked open his eyes. He didn't feel like seeing anyone, much less the well-meaning but meddlesome Charlotte Sutcliff, née Bannister. What was it to be—he'd gone out for the day, was indisposed or just terribly busy? Perhaps he'd gone temporarily mad and was at that moment wandering around the house naked with a fire poker and she'd better leave immediately or else he'd…

That cheered him up. "I'd rather not see her, Rawlings. Please tell her I'm—"

But before he had a chance to make his excuse, Charlotte had stepped bravely out from behind Rawlings and into the room. With characteristic self-assurance, she announced, "I'm in already, thank you."

Ben rose reluctantly from his seat, frowning at the way Charlotte's critical gaze roved around his library, noting the peeling green paint, scattered papers and dusty shelves. He'd actually been expecting this visit since he'd arrived in London and had been starting to wonder what had delayed her from interfering with his marriage for so long. She couldn't mind her own business to save her life and word had obviously spread that he had returned to London without his wife. Robert, no doubt, had forbidden her from trying to make contact. Since she was about as obedient as his own wife, she'd obviously ignored his instructions.

"Charlotte," he greeted her rather coolly.

"Lord Sinclair," she replied stiffly, bowing her head.

He lost his patience. "Oh for God's sake, Charlotte, you needn't 'lord' me. A simple 'Ben' will do."

She nodded and seated herself gingerly on the settee, not failing to notice its worn upholstery. She folded her hands in her lap and waited for him to begin.

He sighed. Her hauteur was ridiculous. *She* was the one invading his private space and time, not the other way around. "Well, how have you been, Charlotte? Haven't seen much of you lately."

"No."

"Nor your charming husband. And how is he?"

"He'd be much happier if you had proved him wrong."

Ben sat down wearily. "Ah. If I proved him wrong in what way?"

"I had hoped," Charlotte said, leaning forward, "that things might have improved between you and Kate. When I heard that you'd followed her to Dorset, I thought that you might even apologize to her for your misconduct. But now you are back. Alone. Have you left her?"

Ben would have loved to correct her and tell her that

his misconduct wasn't even half of it, but he refrained. "That is none of your business."

"Have you?"

"Yes, Charlotte, I have, but only because she asked me to go. I was merely doing as she wished. That is the end of it."

"I see." She didn't seem to believe him.

"Now, does your husband know you're here?"

"No. He would not have allowed me to come."

"Right. So you're not supposed to be here and, judging from your behavior, you'd prefer to be just about anywhere else. Why have you come, Charlotte? Did you think I might be bored?"

She hesitated before answering and appeared to be deep in thought. "I know you'll just think that I can't mind my own business, but, well, it's just that I received some rather peculiar news today. From Kate's lady's maid."

"The omnipresent Mary. That woman hates me I'll have you know, so you might treat whatever she's told you with a modicum of skepticism."

Charlotte leaned back with a sigh, dropping her guard for the first time. "I would, Ben, I really would, but I just don't know what to make of it. I was hoping you could shed some light."

"Well? What is it? Nothing you can say to me will make my life any more difficult than it already is."

"She wrote me from Little Brookings asking me to watch you closely. She is suspicious of you."

"Yes, she looks at me as if I'm plotting to murder my wife in the night with an axe. Although I must admit that

I've entertained the thought on occasion, I can guarantee you I'll never act upon it. So you may rest easy, Charlotte. Dear God, you haven't *really* been watching me closely, have you?"

He was pleased to see that he could at least embarrass her. She blushed. "No…and I only got the letter today, anyway. I would not even have come here over such an absurd suggestion, my lord, if the evidence did not point in your direction."

Ben's eyes flashed with anger. "Evidence? What evidence?"

"Well—"

"Look, if you think I married Kate for her money you're as daft as she is. And if you think I would try to intimidate her into marriage then you're confused."

"Then how do you explain the note?"

"What note? I wrote no note."

"You certainly did," she insisted stubbornly.

"Explain yourself, Charlotte."

She rose and began pacing. Ben also rose, too much the gentleman to remain seated although very much inclined toward rudeness at the moment. What the hell was she accusing him of? Charlotte turned to him. "After the night of her first abduction…the night of the…the…"

He sensed she was struggling with a socially acceptable word to describe Madame Dupont's, so he nodded for her to carry on.

She looked relieved. "Yes, well, the following morning Kate received flowers from an admirer. There was an unsigned card attached, although she never saw it. It requested she meet this admirer in St. James's Park at a specified date. I hadn't the faintest idea who might have sent them at first, but…"

Ben walked over to the window. "If the card was unsigned and Kate never read it, then how do you know about all this?"

"Mary read it—"

"That's hardly surprising," he cut in with a snort.

"—and she knew that Kate would just think it absurd and throw it out if she were to see it. But she also knew how much getting married meant to her. Well, she wrote to me to inform me of this note and I persuaded Kate to come to the park on that day…I left her alone for a short while, hoping that this admirer would make himself known. I was fairly certain it was my brother, Philip, at the time."

"Was it?"

"No. Funny thing, it was you, Ben. Kate told me at the time that no one had appeared, but I'm now informed that, in fact, you were there."

"I haven't the faintest idea what you're talking about. Am I not allowed to walk in the park?" He could hardly remember this incident.

"Certainly…but it seems an unlikely coincidence."

He turned to her angrily. "It sounds to me that you are the only one who has any idea about what's going on here. I certainly do not. You simply cannot mind your own business, Charlotte."

She was unused to being addressed so discourteously and her eyes brightened with anger of her own. "Perhaps. And perhaps I wouldn't have done a thing about this letter if I didn't know how desperate she was to get married. You certainly weren't helping her."

"And you think that you were? Did you reply to this note under her name?"

She blushed again. "I did…just once, to say that I—Kate, that is—would attend this meeting in the park. The sender requested that I leave my response under that large stone urn on Robert's front steps."

He shook his head with a mixture of disgust and disbelief. "Did it not occur to you that you were risking Kate's reputation and safety by doing such a thing, Charlotte?"

She had the grace to look sheepish. "I wouldn't have done it," she admitted guiltily, "but, you see, Mary didn't think her handwriting looked educated enough."

He said nothing for a moment, trying to take all of this in. "It's neither here nor there who wrote the note, Charlotte…you're both guilty of this deception. Tell me bluntly, just what exactly did you hope to achieve by coming here today?"

She resumed her seat. "Mary thinks you were behind the abductions. I know, I know, it's madness…but it's also quite logical, you see, since your shipping interests would make her a particularly tempting package. Perhaps, Mary has speculated, you learned of her unusual inheritance through my husband. She thinks you married Kate for her money, and she thinks that you went out of your way to compromise her irreparably and that you succeeded."

Ben was stunned. "You can't possibly believe that."

"I don't believe a word of it, Ben, but the evidence is damning. Can you not explain yourself in some way?"

"I don't have to explain anything. Ask my wife to explain it. She was bloody well there, too."

"I suppose," Charlotte said without conviction.

An awful thought occurred to him. Was this why Kate so distrusted him? "Mary hasn't been feeding her this rubbish, has she? Kate's prepared to believe just about anything about me at the moment and she doesn't need that harridan's encouragement."

"I don't think Mary has said a thing. She doesn't know what the truth is—"

Ben snorted.

"—and she doesn't want to say anything incorrect. She's just being cautious."

He didn't want to hear any more. It was bloody well insulting. "Good day, Charlotte."

She blinked, a bit stunned at being asked to leave so suddenly. But seeing that he meant it, that she'd seriously crossed the line and had tested his temper well beyond breaking point, she rose and walked to the door without saying anything. With a nod of goodbye, she left.

Ben returned to his chair and sank into it slowly, a headache coming on. He couldn't believe it. What bloody nerve. He, accused of being a fortune hunter. It was simply preposterous…he had a fortune of his own and, well, what a sordid accusation it was to begin with. He could hardly even remember that day in the park…well, that wasn't entirely true. He could remember very well how he'd felt when he'd seen her, now that he thought about it. He'd been longing to see her, in fact, and been wondering if he could visit her at her brother's house without sending Robert into a rage.

He had thought at the time that it was a blasted good stroke of luck to find her alone like that....

Of course, she hadn't been alone.

He went very still as he remembered that fact. There *had* been someone else there, a man. He could recall him only very vaguely—a man who'd vanished the moment he'd appeared. A man he'd never seen before, but whom she'd thought she recognized.

So who was he? He must have written the note. Was he just some lovelorn chap who'd seen Kate at a ball and written to her out of pure besottedness...or had something more sinister been going on? A deep feeling of fear settled over him. What would have happened if he hadn't come along that day? It was, as Charlotte had pointed out, quite a coincidence—had nothing but simple luck saved her from harm? It was a chilling thought, and he couldn't depend on luck to save her again. She was still in danger; he felt this as truth and believed it completely.

He rose and walked to the door. It would take him several days to reach her, and he would leave immediately. He wouldn't stop worrying until he knew she was safe.

Chapter Twenty-One

Kate had had an unsettled feeling all morning, although try as she might she couldn't explain it. Perhaps it was merely the weather. The sun hadn't broken through the clouds in several days, and the dull clink of slanting rain hitting her bedroom window had caused her to wake up early that morning, in total darkness. At first she hadn't known where she was; she'd been having a series of nightmares all week. But after a minute her head had cleared, and she'd decided she might as well rise and get on with her day. She'd done enough moping about recently to last the rest of her life.

It wasn't that she had a lot to occupy herself with these days, however. In fact, she had almost nothing to do other than entertain herself with mundane and insignificant tasks around the house. Alfred and Sons had been pretty dormant since Andrew Hilton had left, and that had been…well, about six months ago, hadn't it?

Oh, dear. It was horribly depressing to think how long it was. There were still enough back orders to keep her workers busy and satisfied enough not to ask questions—she was thankful for that—but as for starting any new projects…it simply hadn't been possible.

She certainly hadn't figured her life out in all that time, and she hadn't heard a word from her husband, either—not that she'd been expecting him to communicate. Where did it all leave her? With no company *and* no husband, that was where. That certainly wasn't how it was intended to work: the latter was supposed to make the former possible. If *only* she'd just been sensible and let her brother sell the company in the first place. If only she hadn't insisted that Ben leave; if he'd stayed, then at least he'd be able to help her. Why did she have to be so proud? Why, oh why, did she always have to make her life more difficult than it needed to be?

Kate looked rather forlornly around the breakfast room, where she'd been for over an hour. The dark day provided the room with little sunlight, making her feel even duller. She'd been trying her hand at watercolors, and the rather murky seascape she'd been working on lay temporarily neglected on the table in front of her. Painting was a skill any young lady worth her salt had supposedly mastered by the age of ten. Charlotte, for example, was always producing pretty landscapes with sheep and children and rustic cottages. Kate's ten thumbs weren't taking to it naturally, but at least she could console herself with the fact that she was making some progress in other areas. She'd managed to embroider—adequately if not beautifully—a new set of linen napkins for the house. The maids had all professed great pleasure at the results, although Kate suspected their praise was generous rather than wholly sincere. Still, it was satisfying to know that they appreciated the Herculean effort it had required. Effort was important.

The window just behind her rattled, making her start and turn around quickly in her chair. She rose and crossed the short distance to the window, strangely alarmed. She parted the curtains but saw nothing but endless gray sky, rustling shrubbery and lanky, bowing trees. The noise was nothing but the wind—why was she so jumpy? If only she could relax.

Perhaps it was Mary's fault her day had started on such an uneasy note. When she'd entered Kate's bedroom that morning to open the curtains, she'd looked extremely preoccupied. It was only after several minutes of potent silence that she'd finally spoken. She hadn't said "good morning" as a rational person would have done; instead, she'd turned to Kate and all but blurted out, "My lady, there's something I must tell you. Something that's been troubling me for many weeks now."

Good God that sounds dire, Kate had thought to herself. She was still drowsy and in no mood to discuss anything troubling. She'd had a good idea what it was about, but asked anyway. "Is it about my husband?"

"It is, I'm afraid," Mary replied, sitting down at the foot of her bed, still looking anxious.

"Then I don't want to hear it," Kate replied with finality, tempering her words with a rather wan smile. She thought about him most of the day, and she didn't want to start talking about him, too. "You look lovely today, Mary. I do hope you'll be taking the morning off?" She really *did* hope she would. Kate had had about enough of her well-meaning concern. Perhaps even Mary was beginning to go daft through inactivity.

Mary blushed. "I thought I'd walk into town, actually. It's a rather nice day."

Kate frowned. It was a nice day for ducks, perhaps, and Mary hated taking exercise. Very suspicious indeed. "A walk?"

"Yes…well, actually, I thought I might have a look once more for that Thatcher chap. I just don't like the way he's still here."

Kate rolled her eyes. "Oh, Mary, don't be silly. I'm certain you never even saw him."

The window rattled again, bringing Kate back to the present. No wonder she was feeling so off when even sensible Mary was acting barmy. She returned her attention to the watercolors. The paints had begun to bleed together and the calm day at sea she'd been hoping for was officially beginning to take on hurricane conditions. She frowned.

She corrected her expression when she noticed that Tilly had entered the room and was clearing her throat discreetly at the door, waiting expectantly for her attention. Kate smiled in greeting and tried to shield her painting from view with her arm. How embarrassing. It looked like the work of a child. "Did you want something, Tilly?"

"There's a man to see you, Lady Sinclair. A Mr. Wilson. He first asked to see Lord Sinclair, actually, but I told him that he was still in town. He agreed to see you instead."

"Oh? Mr. Wilson, you say?" This was rather peculiar. She didn't think she knew anyone by the name of Wilson. "Did he say what his business was about?"

"Yes…he says he has news from London."

Kate rose, feeling worry begin to swell in her chest. Oh, God. What if something had happened to Ben? They'd parted under such difficult circumstances. Could this be the reason she'd felt so uneasy all day?

Tilly seemed to sense her concern and added, "It is family news, so he says, but by that I guess he must mean your brother or Lady Charlotte…not, I should think, Lord Sinclair, since he requested to see him here. I would have asked but didn't think it really my place. Oh, I do hope everything is all right."

Kate shrugged, trying to look calm. "I'm sure everything is fine, Tilly. Where is he?"

"The sitting room, my lady. He seems anxious and in a hurry. I can't imagine what news would have caused him to come all this way."

Kate really wished Tilly would conceal her anxiety a bit better—it certainly wasn't helping her own nerves. "Well, I'd better hurry, then." She rose and left the room, trying to move at a measured pace but wanting to run.

The hall was silent and empty; it actually felt a bit eerie, although Kate could attribute her discomfort to the threat of bad news that lurked inside the sitting room. She took a deep breath, smoothed the wrinkles out of her dress, and crossed the hall and opened the door.

The sitting room appeared, at first, to be empty.

"Hello?" she called out, but no one answered. How odd. Perhaps Tilly had meant to say drawing room instead, although generally only the most important guests were shown in there. She turned to leave the room, but the sound of footsteps made her spin around quickly.

She didn't see Mr. Wilson. She didn't think she did, anyway. The only person she saw was Josiah Thatcher, standing uneasily by the window, just in front of the long blue damask curtains.

"Mr. Thatcher?" she asked uncertainly. Perhaps Mary had seen him in town. She must have. But why would he…?

"Why are you here?" she asked, keeping her back to the door.

"I'm so sorry," he answered, a good deal of fear in his eyes.

She walked forward, drawn by the awful thoughts that immediately filled her head. Why was he apologizing? What on earth was wrong? It could only be that something was wrong with her husband. "Sorry? But whatever for? Please, you must tell me—is everything all right?"

He didn't answer. He couldn't have answered if he'd wanted to. Before he had the chance another man stepped out from behind the curtain. He pressed a pistol into Josiah's back and regarded her indifferently. There was something remote and inexpressive about his eyes.

Kate stopped walking, stopped breathing. This new man looked familiar, but at first she just couldn't place him. He appeared to be about fifty years old, had light brown, graying hair, and was about the same height as she was. There was nothing remarkable about him physically—there was, in fact, something bland and unmemorable about his face. Yet she was certain that she'd seen him before, that she'd even met him.…

Yes. She certainly had: twice. The first time had been several years ago, when he'd come to her home to have a meeting with her father. The other time had been far more recent. Just last spring, in the park, only she hadn't remembered him at that time. But now she did.

"Mr. Manning?" she asked hesitantly, her gaze nervously flickering to the gun in his hand. Edward Manning was a London shipbuilder, and a successful one, although his company was not as profitable as hers. She hadn't really thought of him in years; she *had* suggested him as a potential suspect to Ben, but even then she hadn't been serious. What on earth was going on?

He smiled, but his smile was every bit as unemotional as his eyes. It made her shiver. "I wouldn't have thought you'd remember me."

"What…um, what are you doing here?"

"Thought I'd congratulate you on your marriage," he said, beginning to walk forward slowly. Josiah edged along with him, having no other choice but to follow.

Instinctively, Kate took a step back, but she wasn't fast enough. Before she could gain any real distance he'd grabbed her by the arm and jerked her forward. She tried to scream, but he quickly snaked his arm up around her head and clapped it over her mouth. She turned her head to the side and looked desperately at Josiah, but Manning caught the direction of her gaze. With a swift movement, he hit Josiah on the head with the butt of his pistol. He slumped to the floor, unconscious.

"Now," Manning said, his breath hot in her ear. "Would you like the real answer to your question?"

"Know about what? Your marriage?"

That wasn't what she'd meant, but she suspected he was aware of that. She waited silently; she certainly wasn't going to admit it to him.

Manning shrugged. "Ah. You mean how did I learn that you were such a wealthy young woman…and in such an enviable position. At the head of a company—not many people are awarded such lucrative positions without having to earn it first. Certainly not too many girls."

She raised her chin, trying to look defiant even if she didn't exactly feel that way. Was it money he wanted?

He smiled, seeming to enjoy patronizing her. "I found out about your good fortune by lucky accident, my dear. One of my employees worked for your father many years ago, you see…and one day at the boatyard I overheard him complaining about the way your father allowed you to run free around here."

"Yes, but that tells you nothing—"

"And when I heard that your father died, I wondered who would take over his company. I'd known your father had a son and heir living in London, but he was never announced as successor. When no one was announced after a few months I started to become suspicious…so I sent my man back to investigate. He figured out what had happened and he told me."

She desperately tried to remember who this man could have been but came up with no answer. It was entirely conceivable that some man *had* worked there for just a short while and left suddenly without anyone paying much heed. Such an action would be hardly noteworthy; like any other business their employees

Chapter Twenty-Two

Kate already knew the answer to her question, and congratulations had nothing to do with it. She shook her head.

"Then shall we sit? I wouldn't recommend screaming," Edward Manning advised, pressing the pistol into her side.

She nodded, wanting to cry but knowing she needed to appear strong and brave. He pushed her onto the striped sofa and seated himself in the armchair opposite, pulling it close. He crossed his legs and laid the gun nonchalantly but menacingly across his thigh, insurance that she wouldn't call out for help or try to escape.

She took a deep breath. She needed to think, to remain calm. It wasn't entirely obvious why he was there: she was married and therefore well-protected from any attempts he might make against her finances. But clearly he knew about her inheritance, and still thought he had something to achieve.

Bluntly, she asked, "How do you know?"

sometimes came and went. What an awful thought, though, to think of someone spying on her…even worse, she'd been paying him to do it.

A quiet knock came at the door and Tilly entered unobtrusively. "Shall I serve you tea in here, my lady?" she asked.

Kate looked desperately around the room, her heart thumping. Josiah's unconscious body had fallen to the floor on the other side of the sofa and was thus concealed from Tilly's curious gaze. Manning had slid his pistol beneath his coat when she entered, and he looked, at that moment, like any other visitor. Tilly was her only obvious chance of rescue, but there was nothing really to alert her that anything was amiss. Kate wanted to scream, to tell Tilly to run and get help, but she could think only of the gun concealed in Manning's coat.

"No thank you, Tilly. Mr., um…"

"Wilson," he supplied with a harmless, polite smile.

"Yes, Mr. Wilson won't be staying for long. We won't require tea."

Tilly cocked her head to the side inquisitively, a bit surprised by that answer. But given no further instructions she merely nodded and closed the door behind her as she left.

Kate turned her attention back to Manning, her eyes flashing with anger. How dare he do this to her? How dare he destroy her life out of avarice? "So you decided to marry me, is that it?" she asked. "You thought that was a way to obtain my business?"

Manning nodded, that frightening, detached calm returning to his eyes. "Well, that would be one way. I was quite pleased by the thought, especially when I heard my man describe you…not only rich, but comely, too. That's all a man really needs in a wife, after all. But then it occurred to me that you'd never accept my proposal, that you would think you were above me."

His greed was sickening and Kate was losing patience. She should have been scared, but she was so angry at that moment that she just couldn't be. It was preposterous; why was he doing this to her? "As you know, Mr. Manning, this is all irrelevant. I am now married and you have nothing left to gain. I cannot imagine why you bothered to come here and tell me all this. Surely *your* man could have told you that you were wasting your time."

Manning sighed with theatrical disappointment. "It *is* unfortunate that you had to complicate things by getting married—blasted inconsiderate, in fact. How can I get you to give me what I want now?"

"What *do* you want?"

He leaned forward, suddenly no longer playing at being nice. "Your business gets in my way. You take profits that would otherwise be mine. It's quite simple. Without you, think of how rich I'd be. So what I want is to have what you have, and I can only get that by getting rid of you. But how can I do that?"

There were any number of ways, that was the awful part. But she certainly wasn't going to supply him with any suggestions, so she said nothing. She wasn't at all safe from him, and any bravado she'd formerly demonstrated was quickly fading.

He smiled tightly and stretched out in the chair,

noting her distress. "Well, I have a few ideas for how I can get you out of my way. There's your brother and his charming wife, for instance. I do, you'll probably recall, know their town house rather intimately…the coach house, in particular."

She sat forward tensely, remembering the night of her abduction in London and how terrified she'd been. If only she'd known at the time that she wasn't the only one at risk, if she'd known he would try to harm her family, too…she would have told her brother of her suspicions. She should have. He would hurt them and it would be her fault. "What would you do to them?"

Manning steepled his fingers, pretending to mull over the possibilities. "Hmm…I wouldn't want to go up against your brother so 'them' might be a tad difficult. But his wife would be easy. From simply watching the house these past few weeks I've learned her movements and habits. I know when she walks in the park, goes shopping, goes for visits. She's quite predictable."

"You will not do a thing," Kate insisted, trying to make her voice sound firm. "I will notify my brother and if anything happens the authorities will know exactly where to look."

Manning smiled. "Perhaps I have a man waiting there already and you won't get the chance to notify anyone. You remember Billy, do you not? He managed to escape after you so cruelly left him tied to a tree in the woods, and I'm afraid that night left him with a grudge against you. All I have to do is give him the word, and he'll be happy to oblige."

"You would not be able to tell him in time."

"Would you care to test that theory? I shouldn't think so, Lady Sinclair. But your sister-in-law is innocent, and it would be cruel of me to hurt her. I don't want to be cruel, but I won't have to do a thing if you cooperate."

"You plan to blackmail me," Kate stated bluntly.

"It's a thought…you see, you've provided me with such good material that I can hardly pass up the opportunity. There's your unladylike involvement in your father's business, for one. If the prospect of that fact being made common knowledge doesn't persuade you to do as I say, I can spread the news that you spent the evening in one of London's more disreputable gaming houses…I know about that, of course. Billy also tells me that the night you were kidnapped from the Earl of Tyndale's home you were wandering around with barely a stitch on your back. You've hardly been circumspect."

She sat back and folded her hands in her lap, unwilling to let him cow her and trying to look unimpressed by his threats. "You can say whatever you like, Mr. Manning. Society already knows I was compromised and my husband will refute everything else."

"Will he? And where is your husband now, may I ask? He must be *very* concerned for your safety to leave you here alone like this. He's been in London for what…about two months now? Do you really think he cares about you enough to defend your honor?"

Kate looked away from him, afraid that her face would betray the true state of her emotions. She wasn't in control at all, and she didn't know how much longer she could keep up her brave front. She wanted to cry. Manning meant to upset her, and it was working. She

feared that his words were true: if Ben had ever cared
about her, his feelings must now surely be dead. But
would she ever have the chance to convince him otherwise, to make him believe that marriage to her needn't
be the constant battleground she'd made it? And how
would he feel if she caused more scandal? He'd
probably never return.

"And you don't love him either, do you?"

She looked back sharply. He was just trying to manipu-
late her; she needed to remind herself of that. She loved
her husband deeply, and she did so because he was an
honorable man. "Don't be absurd," she replied defiantly.

He arched an eyebrow doubtfully. "When I wrote to
you in London, you responded. If you were so in love
with him you certainly wouldn't have done so."

"What are you talking about?"

Manning clucked his tongue. "How am I to trust you,
Lady Sinclair, if you keep lying to me?"

"I'm not lying! I received no communication from
you, Mr. Manning. I love my husband and I always
have. Nothing you say will change that."

"I see. Perhaps you do…but if so you won't want to
embarrass him even further than you already have."

He knew exactly what he was doing. She didn't want
to embarrass Ben. She wanted, desperately, to be the
sort of wife he undoubtedly wished to have. A fat tear
slowly ran down her face. She couldn't stop it.

Manning saw it and smiled; he knew that he had
finally won. He leaned forward, sliding his pistol from
under his coat once more. With his hand resting on it,
he said, "You will do what I want, Lady Sinclair, or I'll

tell everyone. What do you think your husband would think of that? Quite a reputation for a new wife."

"If I close down the business you will leave my family alone? You will leave me alone?"

Manning leaned back into his seat, visibly relaxing. He crossed his legs nonchalantly. "Well, now, that's very generous of you, but it occurs to me that I could close your business down myself by simply telling your secret. I won't require your help in that respect. But perhaps that's not the answer after all...you could *give* me the business, how does that sound? I'd simply take it off your hands for you...you're hardly capable of running it anyway. I would have your profits and you wouldn't have to worry anymore. You're a pretty young thing, Lady Sinclair, and I'm sure that there are many other things you'd rather think about than boats and ledgers. We'd both win."

They wouldn't, of course. She had no delusions about it. He'd win and she'd simply retreat, but she no longer had a choice. He'd threatened her family and her marriage, and his silence was worth everything to her. It was time to surrender. She wanted Ben to love her, to forget the conditions and difficulties she'd brought with her to their marriage. She couldn't embarrass him again. She simply cared about him too much. Her eyes pricked with tears and she knew, in that moment, that she'd give Manning whatever he wanted if it would save her marriage. Ben had never been a perfect gentleman—she supposed she wouldn't have fallen in love with him if he had been—but he had done her a tremendous favor by marrying her. He didn't have to do that, and she hadn't even expected him to. But he had, and she loved him. She hadn't even thought that kind of love was possible, and if Manning's silence would keep their marriage together, if it was the only thing that would give their marriage hope, then she would do whatever it took to maintain his silence.

She opened her mouth to acquiesce, but it wasn't her own words that came out.

"You forget, Manning, that I don't give a damn about popular opinion."

She turned her head, and her heart leaped. Ben stood in the doorway, casually leaning against it, hands in his pockets, looking as if nothing were the matter. But Kate knew better. She had seen that look in his eyes before, only it had always been directed at her. He was furious.

Ben walked into the room.

Manning raised his pistol and pointed it at him. "I wouldn't come any nearer."

Kate shot from her seat in fear, forgetting the consequences that such an action might provoke. "Ben, you must stop," she pleaded. Although her husband was bigger and stronger than Manning, he was no match for a gun.

He ignored her, keeping his attention directed solely at Manning. "Will you shoot me?" he asked, walking forward another few steps.

Manning didn't answer, but he, too, rose from his seat, his gun still trained at Ben. Kate stared at his hands, hoping to see them quiver nervously, but his grip on the pistol remained sure and steady.

Ben stopped this time, his gaze never leaving

Manning's face. "I don't think that would be at all wise, Mr....Edward Manning, was it?"

Kate narrowed her eyes. How would Ben know his name? She'd mentioned Manning once before, but how would he make the connection?

"If you shoot me," Ben continued, his voice deliberate, "and if you so much as harm a hair on my wife's head, everyone will know of your guilt. You'll lose your business and I'll see to it that you'll lose your life as well."

Manning shook his head. "No one will know a thing. I've told no one that I'm here, and I gave the servants a false name. I could kill both of you and all anyone would remember was that peculiar Mr. Wilson who came for a visit and mysteriously vanished. I have the upper hand."

Ben raised an eyebrow. "Is that so? Then how do you suppose I learned that you were here? How do I know your name?" Manning paled slightly and Ben took another small step closer to Kate. "I'll tell you right now that I didn't figure it out on my own. Someone else did, and told me. That person also knows you're here, too, and is at this moment bringing the authorities."

"I don't believe you," Manning said, but Kate detected a note of uncertainty in his voice.

"Put the gun down, Manning, and I might be generous with you. Perhaps I'll let you return to London and pretend that nothing happened...as long as I never see you again."

Manning seemed to think this over for a second. He lowered his pistol slightly.

"Come here, Kate," Ben said without looking at her, his gaze still on Manning's gun.

He raised the pistol once more, his grip tightening. This time he directed it at Kate. "She's not going anywhere, nor am I. Not until I get what I want."

"Come here, Kate," Ben repeated firmly, holding his hand out to her this time. She still didn't move, too afraid that Manning would fire.

"You have nothing to bargain with," Manning stated confidently. "I think I'll give the orders."

"Is that so? Turn around."

Manning didn't move at first, but the sound of the window opening behind him made him pivot swiftly. It was true. A man stood at the window, a menacing pistol aimed at Manning's head. Kate recognized him as Graham, her footman. She'd always known him as helpful, affable and shy, but at the moment he was deadly serious. Her eyes widened as she caught sight of Mary, hovering anxiously behind him. It was the most unlikely siege, but it seemed to be working. Manning was trapped.

"Drop your gun," Ben repeated, not a trace of fear in his voice.

For a moment Manning seemed to debate his options. They were few. He could shoot, possibly hurt either Ben or Kate, but he'd lose his own life if he did so.

Or he could do as Ben asked and perhaps be spared.

"Put it down, Manning."

It was over. He lowered his gun and placed it on a table. He stepped away, and Graham climbed agilely through the window to bind his wrists.

Fast, heavy tears flowing down her face, Kate raced across the room and buried herself in her husband's arms. His embrace had never felt so good, so strong, so comforting. She couldn't believe he had come back.

Chapter Twenty-Three

A week had passed, a week in which the house and its inhabitants had slowly returned to normality. Graham became something of a hero in the village, and his brave stunt at the sitting room window was recounted over many beery lunches at the Seven Bells. Josiah, too, was regarded with a new respect, particularly by Mary, who lowered her eyelashes and blushed whenever he walked past. He'd been every bit as brave as Graham. He'd seen Edward Manning in the village, had overheard him asking questions about the house and had followed him there. He'd snuck into the house and entered the sitting room after Manning was shown to it and had planned on accosting him there, but he hadn't counted on the pistol in Manning's coat pocket. The pistol had won in the end, and he was fortunate to have gotten away with only an egg-sized lump on his head and nothing more permanent.

Edward Manning's fate was not so fortunate,

although it might have been worse. As the authorities had removed him from the sitting room, he'd broken down and confessed to everything. He was, it turned out, a desperate man. His company was facing bankruptcy and he was about to lose everything. For this reason Ben had decided to be merciful. Manning was at that moment awaiting transportation to Australia, where sunshine and sweat would, in theory, transform him into a better man. It wasn't exactly the Garden of Eden, but it would be far better than rotting in one of London's dark and damp prisons.

Ben had remained in Little Brookings even though there was no particular reason for him to do so—obviously Kate was now safe and he could return to town with his mind and conscience at ease. But he simply didn't want to leave her, not yet, not ever. She hadn't asked him to either, although he was expecting her to bring the subject up at any time. Nothing fundamental had changed between them and he had no doubt that she still wanted him as far removed from her life as possible.

Ben was alone in the sitting room, a book open on his lap but his mind very far away. He'd never been more frightened than he had been during the drive to Dorset, although he'd tried to reassure himself that the fear twisting inside his gut was nothing but a false alarm. Chances were that Kate would be safe and well—and that she'd be singularly unimpressed by his heroic reappearance. But somehow he'd known that something seriously was wrong, and the very idea that there was someone out there, someone they hadn't even thought of or fully suspected... he'd been furious with himself for leaving her there alone. He'd had a bad feeling all along, and he bloody well should have trusted his instincts. But who was it? He'd spent most of the journey trying over and over again to answer that question but still he'd come up with no answer.

By the time his carriage had pulled into the drive, he'd been in no state of mind to make pleasantries with anyone. When he'd seen the unwelcome sight of Mary, standing perplexedly in the middle of the drive, he'd been sorely tempted to drive on past her, perhaps thumbing his nose and splashing her with mud as he went. It was lucky he'd managed to restrain himself; instead, he'd asked his driver to stop and had reluctantly but politely leaned out his window to greet her. He hadn't realized at the time what a stroke of good fortune it was.

It was she who'd figured nearly everything out. Apparently she'd been following Josiah all that morning and as he'd been following Manning…well, one suspicion had led to another and after an hour passed she'd begun to suspect that her original quarry wasn't the right man at all. She'd trailed both of them back toward the house and had been standing in the middle of the drive for several minutes, letting all the pieces fall into place.

She hadn't returned his greeting. "A man's just gone to the house," she'd said instead. "I think he means to harm Lady Kate."

Ben had responded quickly. "Get help, Mary. I'll find Kate."

For once, she'd merely done as he'd told her, and she'd done brilliantly. Ben didn't know what would have happened if Graham hadn't intervened when he had. With Edward Manning's gun pointed at Kate, he'd had very little leverage. He couldn't bear to think how the situation might have turned out differently.

At least Ben had arrived before Kate had succumbed to Manning's threats; her bravery never failed to impress him. Luckily, he'd also arrived in time to hear her address Edward Manning by his name through the sitting room door. That had been the final piece of the puzzle, and knowing who his enemy was before having to face him was to be his only real advantage.

He'd arrived in time to hear her say something else, too, something even less expected.

She'd said she loved him.

At the time, he hadn't been able to give these words much thought. He'd been far too focused on rescuing her, far too aware of the value of every passing second. But now…well, had she meant it? Was it possible? Or was she just saying that she loved him for Manning's benefit?

The creak of the sitting room door opening drew his attention away from this perplexing question. Kate entered the room, passing through a ray of sunlight that streamed through the window as she did so. His breath caught in his throat. She was lovely, and he wanted to look at her every day for the rest of his life. He didn't want to leave her again.

She smiled a rather diffident greeting and then wandered around for a moment, pausing to rummage through the desk. She stopped in the middle of the room, looking slightly lost.

He returned his gaze, if not his attention, back to his book. Officially, they still weren't on full speaking terms, and he wasn't yet ready to try once more to smooth things over with her. Not if she was just going to reject him again, and he had no doubt that was exactly what she'd do. Yet despite what he assumed her feelings were, she'd been uncharacteristically demure since he'd arrived. In fact, she'd smiled, nodded and agreed with every statement he'd made in the past week—and he'd said some pretty bizarre things just to test her. Who was this docile woman? He couldn't quite figure it out. He *supposed* he could attribute this change to the scare she'd been through, but she'd been through plenty of scares before and had always come away swearing at him. He didn't like this change at all, in fact. She wasn't acting like herself; she was acting like…well, he wasn't sure what, really. She even dressed a bit differently, and she seemed to have developed several strange habits in his absence, like the pianoforte (she didn't seem to realize it was badly out of tune) and knitting. Generally speaking, he didn't approve of women who filled their time with such practices. Speaking specifically, however, he found these habits—and knitting in particular—rather distressing in his wife. If she ever returned to normal she might turn her knitting needles into weapons at whim.

He tilted his head, an interesting thought suddenly occurring to him. Perhaps she was with child. Knitting was an indication of pregnancy, wasn't it? It *was* possible, even if he hadn't really contemplated the prospect before. He looked at her curiously. She didn't seem to be any bigger. Had she been craving any odd foods? He couldn't recollect.

"I can't find my embroidery," she announced, still standing in the middle of the room and speaking to no one in particular.

He sighed. "Pity."

"Have you seen it?" she asked, the barest hint of impatience entering her voice.

"Do you miss it that much?" Ben asked, enjoying the prospect of a fight. As far as he could tell it was the first time he'd managed to rile her since his return. He *did* like to rile her.

"No, but I need it," she replied, giving him a rather sour look.

"That's completely illogical. You don't *need* it. Maybe you lost it on purpose."

"I didn't, Ben." She looked around the room with displeasure. Of course she didn't miss it, but she was still working on it. All in all, she felt that her attempts at becoming more ladylike, serene and composed were working wonderfully. She still felt a certain distance around her husband, but she supposed that it would only take time. He hadn't fled back to London yet, had he? Wasn't that proof enough? And yet why was he being so provoking? It was as if he *liked* it when she argued with him.

She found some knitting in the desk instead and took a seat across from him. She forced a pleasant smile onto her face.

"It is your birthday soon."

Ben didn't realize she even knew when his birthday was. He just lifted a brow and kept his attention on his book. He could see she was getting seriously miffed now, and if he looked up at her she'd see the gleam in his eyes and the grin threatening the corners of his mouth.

She rose from her seat and crossed the room to stand before him. She dropped a lumpy, amorphous woolen object into his lap.

"Am I to understand you made this?" he asked, looking at it quizzically.

"It is a scarf," she explained, trying hard to keep her temper under control.

"I'm glad you told me," he said. "Did I need one?"

Kate could have kicked him. "You could just say thank you, you know. I tried."

Her face was turning red. He loved it. "Well, don't try. Since when have you taken up knitting anyway? It's a bloody ridiculous habit to adopt having avoided it for so long. What's come over you?"

Kate imagined taking a thread and needle and sewing the bed sheets around him one night while he slept. That'd show him trying. *He* was trying, trying both her nerves *and* her patience. "I realize," she said very slowly as if to a simpleton, "that I'm not very good at it—"

"This is true."

"—but I am trying to improve. It is about time I learned…I may need these skills in the future."

"What possible future situation would require this scarf, Kate?"

"Well, we'll have children someday—"

"Will we?"

She blushed and looked away, feeling deeply humiliated. Why did he have to make this so difficult? Couldn't he see how hard it was for her already? "All right, perhaps we won't. But if it *did* happen...well, I really ought to set a proper example, particularly if we have any girls. I ought to be a role model for them, and I ought to be able to teach them this sort of thing so...so they don't turn out like me."

Ben's eyes flashed in annoyance. He laid his book down on his lap and stared at her. "What's wrong with you?"

"Well, nothing, but..." She trailed off. His expression was downright intimidating. "Never mind."

She turned angrily to leave the room, not wanting him to see her lip quiver. Obviously he hadn't been contemplating the possibility of children, and she'd do best not to dwell on it either. But just as she reached the door, his words made her stop.

"I wouldn't mind a'tall if any girls we might have turned out like you, Kate. I wouldn't even mind if our boys did, either. You're braver and more intelligent than just about any man I know. What would make you think such a thing?"

She turned around slowly, saying nothing. She was still battling back tears. He couldn't possibly mean it.

"Come here."

She shook her head. All she wanted to do was hide. She'd never felt the fool to such a degree before. This was what she'd wanted, though, wasn't it? How many times had she told herself that she was willing to suffer any embarrassment if it would bring him back?

"Come here, Kate," he repeated. "Please."

Slowly, she walked back to him. She stopped just in front of his chair, and he reached out to hold her hand. "Kate, I didn't marry an empty-headed woman who's good at sewing and flower arranging and…well, not much else. When you heard me saying those things to Richard Hastings I was only trying to gauge whether or not he was innocent. By making it known that I had you well in control it would also become known that you were no longer vulnerable. But for God's sake, Kate, I have no delusions about controlling you. I know I couldn't do it even if I wanted to, and that's not what I want. My wife is clever and amusing…perhaps a bit bossy and impetuous…and she's honorable and kind. Would you even believe I admire her?" he asked, pausing to watch her cheeks turn delightfully pink. "If you were the type of woman to spend your time knitting and gossiping around the tea table, I'd never have asked you to marry me."

"But you didn't ask me—"

He pulled her gently onto his lap. "Do shut up, you fool. Yes, I did."

She shook her head. "You wouldn't have asked if it hadn't been imperative. You had no choice."

"I would have eventually. I'm afraid it was fate, my dear."

"Oh." For a moment the only sound in the room was the ticking of the mantel clock. She couldn't meet his gaze; she felt at once vulnerable, shy and deeply aware of his body, his heat. She'd imagined him saying these words so many times that they somehow didn't seem real. Instead she looked at her hands, clasped nervously in her lap.

"Do you know something else, Kate?" he asked.

"What?" she asked, looking up, searching for answers in his face.

"I haven't regretted it for a single moment."

She didn't really know what to say to that. She still didn't know if she could believe him, but she wanted to, desperately. Was it possible? "I highly doubt that."

"It's true. There were times, maybe, when I questioned both your sanity and mine—"

She smiled despite herself, and a tear ran down her cheek.

"—but I've never doubted that I love you," he said, brushing it away with his finger.

She was silent for a moment. "What?"

He squeezed her and held her close. "I love you, Kate. I think I've loved you since the moment you opened the door that night...well, nearly a year ago. There I was, exhausted and expecting to see my surly ogre of a best friend, but I saw this gorgeous vision instead. I tried to stay away from you, but I couldn't. I know I haven't always acted as I should have. I've made a muck of things, Kate. All you need to say to make me a happy man forever is that you forgive me."

She'd longed to hear these words. She loved him, with every fiber of her being. Tentatively, she said, "I've made a muck of things, too. I'm so sorry."

"Well...I suppose you've not always been perfect. But I forgive you."

She smiled, her customary cheekiness slowly reinstating itself. He loved her, did he? How marvelous. "Mary once told me she thought you were my guardian angel."

"What a patent falsehood. I don't believe you for a minute."

Her smile grew. "She did. When I first told her about

the way you managed to appear in my life at every moment of crisis."

"This was before she thought I was trying to murder you, I presume," Ben said with a smile of his own. Mary had been exceedingly kind to him since his return and he knew that she'd think the world of him until her dying day.

"It's true, though," Kate insisted. "How on earth do you do it?"

Ben hadn't the faintest idea, but he quite liked the idea of being her guardian angel. No one had ever accused him of being an angel of any description before and it made him feel rather like a new man. He hoped he'd have many chances to rescue her in the future.

"So," he asked slowly, nuzzling the soft skin beneath her ear, "when are we having these children? Shall we start today?"

"I'm sorry?"

He rose from his seat, bringing her with him. "How many did you say? Eight? Nine?"

She squealed in delight. "Where are you taking me?"

"Wife, I think I'd like to take you upstairs with me," he said, carrying her purposefully across the room.

"What—now?" She pretended to look shocked. "It's midmorning. What will the servants think?"

"I am not made of stone, madam."

He opened the sitting room door and headed for the staircase with her cradled in his arms. He paused before mounting it. "By the way, Kate," he asked, looking down at her, "is there nothing you'd like to tell me?"

She gazed up at him, her eyes sparkling with happiness. Of course she loved him. That was no revelation. She'd known she was hopelessly besotted since, well…since she'd thrown a glass of water at him for insulting her at the age of eleven. Goodness, that had been over thirteen years ago and not much had changed. But for the moment she didn't answer his question, reveling in the power her answer held. He loved her and cared deeply that she loved him, too. He loved her just the way she was and didn't want to change her.

"You know how I feel," she said finally.

"Do I?"

"Of course you do."

"Well, would you like to tell me anyway, my dear? If you don't I might accidentally drop you. Then you'd have to walk up all these stairs."

"I love you, Ben."

He leaned down to kiss her hard on the lips and then proceeded to carry her up the staircase.

"My lord?" she asked when they were about halfway up.

He halted to look down at her in question. "My lady?"

"Perhaps tomorrow we might walk to my office together and have a look at a few things? There's a problem I've been trying to work through these past months and I believe I could use your help. I should warn you it's very cluttered in there but I…I might be able to find a bit of room for you at my desk."

"Are you certain, Kate?" he asked, his eyes showing his concern. "I'm more than happy to do whatever I can to help you, but only if you really want it."

"No, no, really, I'm sure. I need the help and you're

as competent as anyone else would be. I'm sure you'll be perfectly good at it."

He raised an eyebrow at her. "Competent? Good? Madam, I have my own business to devote all my attention to if that's your attitude."

"What I meant to say was that you're the most brilliant and perfect husband on earth. And I trust you completely."

"You trust me?" He was more moved by those three short words than he ever would have thought possible.

"Well, of course I do. I love you, don't I? Now, are you going to carry me up these stairs or not?"

"I'd be delighted," he said, and up they went. At the top of the staircase they disappeared down the hallway, and a moment later the sound of their bedroom door closing could be heard throughout the house. It was just the bang of a door—it wasn't that expressive—but for anyone listening it was the conclusive sound of a happy ending.

Epilogue

September 1818

"George?" Kate asked hopefully. She was sitting up in bed, a teacup resting on her very large tummy. Ben sat up at the foot of the bed, facing her.

He looked unconvinced. "Umm…Georgina?"

She shook her head. "No, no…what about Robert? After my brother, of course. He'd like that."

"Roberta."

"No, Ben, I'm *certain* it's a boy. He takes after you already…demanding food at all hours, kicking me in my sleep—"

"This is why I'm certain it's a girl," Ben replied, gently taking hold of one of her feet and placing it in his lap. "She takes after *you* already."

"If it's a girl, surely I wouldn't be this large. I'm practically a…a whale, an elephant…"

"The Royal Pavilion," he supplied.

She frowned at him. "You needn't exaggerate. I'm not that big."

He smiled back roguishly and began tugging at her stocking. "Size is not proof, darling…for example, I hear *you* were a large baby."

"I was always graceful," she claimed, pretending to be offended: she'd been, according to her father, a monumental ten pounds. "But anyway, we must come up with a name quickly. I think he'll arrive any day now. I hope so—I feel like I'm about to pop."

"I have a second cousin called Hercules, if you're so certain it's a boy. Hercules, future Viscount Carlisle…what do you think?"

She rolled her eyes at him. They probably wouldn't decide on a name until the very day their child was born, and even then she wasn't confident they'd be in complete agreement. She changed the subject. "Are you sure you're ready for our arrival later this week?"

"I have told you many times, fatherhood does not worry me. My own father has written me several relevant letters over the past months and I am prepared for anything. Croup…teething…have we found a nurse yet?"

She smiled. "No, no, I didn't mean the baby, Ben. I meant Robert and Charlotte. They'll be here at the end of the week, remember?"

He sighed, tugging one last time at her stocking. He began slipping it off her foot. "I'm ready for that, too, although I'm not sure I welcome the intrusion just yet. I've been very much enjoying having you all to myself."

"Well, they want to be here when the baby arrives, and we've yet to see our new niece. My brother writes that Charlotte's gotten even bossier since Maria was born. She no longer has any patience with him at all…keeps telling him that now they've a real baby in the family he's no longer entitled to act like one. Harsh words, but you know how he is…always losing things and expecting her to find them—"

"His life sounds far too domesticated at present—I'll have to liberate him. Perhaps I'll take him shooting."

Kate snorted. "He doesn't mind being domesticated a'tall. Besides, he'll probably shoot himself in the foot…and speaking of his erratic aim, he won't be shooting at you for any reason, will he?"

Ben began working on her other stocking. "Not unless Charlotte truly has driven him mad since the birth of their child. As I've told you, Kate, Robert's forgiven me completely. He knows how happy I make you…now that you've finally come to your senses, anyway…and besides, he recognizes you're a difficult woman to please."

"I'm not so difficult."

He began kissing her toes. "And I'm tenacious. I can take it…in fact, I very much enjoy the effort it takes to…please you."

Kate leaned back, closing her eyes with a contented sigh.

"We never had a honeymoon, you know," he said between nibbles. "Perhaps when Robert and Charlotte leave we can travel a bit. How would you like that?"

Kate opened her eyes, a slightly worrying thought entering her head. Before marrying her, Ben had spent much of the year traveling around the globe; since their marriage, he'd remained in Dorset, with only the occasional trip to town to check on his own business. It wasn't a very interesting life. Was he beginning to find it tedious? "We'll be returning to London soon," she suggested hopefully.

"Yes, well, I'd hardly call that a honeymoon."

"No, I suppose punishment is more like it," she responded wryly but then, more seriously, "I do hope you're not bored here."

He raised an eyebrow in surprise. "Could I ever be bored when I have you to entertain me?" His fingers began to trail along her now naked calf.

"Yes, but Little Brookings is hardly the center of the world. Surely you'd like to go somewhere else…somewhere remote and exotic, perhaps. Is that what you're hoping for?"

Ben shrugged. That wasn't why he'd brought the subject up at all. Truth was, he'd merely been thinking of the most efficient method of being completely alone with her…unfortunately not something that was often possible with their unusually familiar servants constantly underfoot. But he certainly wasn't bored. Strange, but so it was. "It's no burden being with you, Kate, particularly when you're in bed like you are now."

She pulled her leg away from his wandering hands. "Ben! Be serious."

"I am serious. I never want to be anywhere else when I'm here with you."

"But you must. You've told me many times how important traveling is to you. How can you not miss it?"

He thought for a long moment, trying to stir up the

feelings of wanderlust that used to call to him frequently, feelings that made his everyday surroundings dull beyond belief. He'd *needed* to voyage out in the world, but now…he simply couldn't recall those feelings anymore. He definitely didn't miss a thing. "It was important, Kate…it's the reason I used to think that marriage was so abhorrent. I thought it'd be a prison, that it'd be the end of my freedom…that I'd never be able to go anywhere again."

"I won't stop you, Ben," Kate said, her eyes wide. She was sincere, but also anxious. She didn't think she'd survive if he left her. "You needn't change your life completely because of me. You…you've allowed me to live the life I was accustomed to. You have never demanded I behave differently."

"But perhaps *I* have changed. Had you thought of that? Perhaps I'm happy just as we are, right here and now. And if I ever do long to travel again, I'll only have to think of you instead to cure me."

"But I could come with you."

"Oh? And what about, um…" He nodded at her round stomach.

"He could come, too," she reassured him.

He mulled it over for a minute. Exploring the world, *en famille*…now that *would* be a new experience, and what was life about if not new experiences? It didn't matter where he was, really, as long as she was by his side. Happiness wasn't about a place, after all. They would be the Traveling Sinclairs: it sounded rather like a circus act. What an interesting and eccentric thought. He'd never had much respect for conventions and, thank

God, neither did she. "All right. But if our son is going to take after your family, then *he* really had better be a *she*. I've traveled with your brother several times and he's not much of a sailor."

"Yes, but perhaps he'll take after you. That's what I'm hoping for, anyway."

"You should be so lucky, living with such perfection twice over."

She stuck out her tongue at him.

He reclaimed her foot and resumed his nibbling. "So where would you like to go, Kate? Your wish is my command."

That was a question worth serious consideration. For all her occasional swagger, she'd never really been anywhere, and she'd always longed to see the rest of the world. What an odd pair they made, both thinking that marriage would necessitate the end of their freedom and independence. How wrong they'd been.

She closed her eyes as his nibbles began to move up her leg. "Surprise me."

* * * * *

RUN, ALLY! Don't be fooled by him. He's evil. Don't let him touch you!

But as the forbidding figure came through the mists toward her, Ally knew she couldn't run. His features burned with dark malevolence, and his physical domination of everything around him seemed to hold her like a net.

She'd heard the tales. She knew all about the Wolverton legend and the ghost that haunted The Willows, an elegant old mansion lost by Micha Wolverton nearly a hundred years ago. According to folklore, the estate was stolen from the Wolvertons, and Micha was killed trying to reclaim it. His dying vow was to be reunited with the spirit of his beloved wife, who'd taken her life for reasons no one would speak of, except in whispers. But Ally had never put much stock in the fantasy. She didn't believe in ghosts.

Until now—

She still didn't understand what was happening. The figure had materialized out of the mist that lay thick on the damp cemetery soil. A cool breeze and silvery moonlight had played against the ancient stone of the crypts surrounding her, until they joined the mist, causing his body to thicken and solidify right before her eyes. That was when she realized she'd seen this man before. Or thought she had, at least.

His face was familiar. . . so familiar, yet she couldn't put it together. Not with him looming so near. She stepped back as he approached.

"Don't be afraid," he said. His voice wasn't what she expected. It didn't sound as if it were coming from beyond the grave. It was deep and sensual. Commanding.

"Who are you?" she managed.

"You should know. You summoned me."

"No, I didn't." She had no idea what he was talking about. Two minutes ago, she'd been crouching behind a moss-covered crypt, spying on the mansion that had once been The Willows, but was now Club Casablanca. And then this—

If he was Micah, he might be angry that she was trespassing on his property. "I'll go," she said. "I won't come back. I promise."

"You're not going anywhere."

Words snagged in her throat. "Wh-why not? What do you want?"

"If I wanted something, Ally, I'd take it. This is about need."

His words resonated as he moved within inches of her. She tried to back away, but her feet were useless. "And you need something from me?"

"Good guess." His tone burned with irony. "I need lips, soft and surrendered, a body limp with desire."

"My lips, my bod—?"

"Only yours."

"Why? Why me?" This couldn't be Micha. He didn't want any woman but Rose. He'd died trying to get back to her.

"Because you want that, too," he said.

Wanted what? A ghost of her own? She'd always found the legend impossibly romantic, but how could he have known that? How could he know anything about her? Besides, she'd sworn off inappropriate men, and what could be more inappropriate than a ghost? She shook her head again, still not willing to admit the truth. But her heart wouldn't play along. It clattered inside her chest. The mere thought of his kiss, his touch, terrified her. This wildness, it was fear, wasn't it?

When his fingertips touched her cheek, she flinched, expecting his flesh to be cold, lifeless. It was anything but that. His skin was smooth and hot, gentle, yet demanding. And while his dark brown eyes were filled with mystery and wonder, there was a sensitivity about them that threatened to disarm her if she looked too deeply.

"These lips are mine," he said, as if stating a universal fact that she was helpless to avoid. In truth, it was just that. She couldn't stop him.

And she didn't want to.

* * * * *

Find out how the story unfolds in...
DECADENT
by
New York Times *bestselling author*
Suzanne Forster.
On sale November 2006.

Harlequin Blaze—*Your ultimate destination*
for red-hot reads.
With six titles every month, you'll never guess
what you'll discover under the covers...